I0579182

THE TREBLE WITH MEN

SCORNED WOMEN SOCIETY SERIES BOOK #2

PIPER SHELDON

WWW.SMARTYPANTSROMANCE.COM

DEDICATION

To J.R., always

And to those who secretly wish she chose the Phantom

CHAPTER 1

YOUR VIBRATO IS ATROCIOUS. VIBRATE
THE STRING; DON'T WRING ITS NECK
LIKE IT'S A CHICKEN.

KIM

A man's voice stopped me halfway down the stairs.

"Kim . . ." His rich voice spoke my real name, though the rest of his words were too muffled to make out.

A chill shuddered down my spine. I smoothed the goosebumps from my arms and tiptoed down the plush carpeted stairs. When the doorbell rang a few minutes ago I had assumed it was one of my parents' endless stream of guests. The only reason I had left my practicing was to get a snack. Snacks were typically my main motivation to move.

The guest was talking to my parents about me?

No matter how I tried to fight my innate curiosity, it always won out. The door to the drawing room was left open so I tucked behind it, hiding from the occupants of the room. The familiar shame at being a guest in my parent's home pinkened my cheeks. Because that's how it felt to me being almost thirty and living in my old bedroom. I wasn't still living at home; I was a guest.

"She should be here for this conversation." It was that new voice, deep and rumbling. Gentle, yet forceful.

1

"She's practicing. She takes her schedule very seriously," my dad stated.

That was like saying the Pope was pretty religious. Control over my schedule gave me peace of mind. I pressed my face into the crack between the door. The slice revealed my dad on the couch, his back to me. Across from him, I saw biker boots and worn jeans where I had expected dress pants and loafers.

A familiar thrill shot through my memory: the open air tugging through my hair on the back of the bike and the deep rattling of an engine vibrating through my bones. I clamped down my wayward thoughts.

"We'll postpone this conversation until Kim is available," the man responded.

"Christine," my father corrected.

There was shuffling and then a pause. "What?"

"She goes by Christine Day now. As you know."

The silence in response filled the room more powerfully than anything else could have. Christine Day had been my stage name for over five years now. The change made it easier to distinguish my former self from my present one. Most of Green Valley thought Kim Dae got caught up with Jethro Winston and the Iron Wraiths only to go MIA. It was better to be known as the girl who'd disappeared than the woman who was going nowhere.

This man's voice was so familiar and yet completely out of place here. It was intriguing enough to have me reaching for the door. My hand dropped just as four heavy steps shook the floor so hard the china cabinet across the hall rattled. I pressed myself back against the wall as the door was thrown open. Thankfully, my foot stopped me from getting a bloody nose.

"Forty-eight hours." He paused in the doorway to announce. "Then the offer goes to the next candidate." The scent of sun-warmed leather filled the air around me. Even with the door between us, his lush smell drew me in.

I shivered.

The stranger didn't wait for my parents' response. His heavy work boots thumped down the marbled foyer. My head poked out to find a hulking frame filling out jeans to their maximum capacity across tree-trunk thighs and a sculpted … derrière. He wore a black leather coat, and a dark baseball cap covered thick, onyx hair that fought for freedom and reached almost to his nape. He was absolutely massive. I let out a slow breath.

This was not how grown women behaved. I should have just walked in the room and demanded that they include me in the conversation. And yet I was here. Behind a door. Creeping on a stranger with a racing heart and the urge to flee. I risked another peek.

I half expected him to knock out chunks of dry wall as he brushed through the front door, but when he reached the foyer, he stilled. His head shifted ever so slightly, like a predator sensing prey. In profile, his eyebrows furrowed into a frown—now, that was an expression I knew well. His leather coat squeaked as he slowly turned all the way around. His gaze found mine in an instant. He looked directly at me. No—within me.

I gasped and tucked myself back.

It was only a glimpse, but it was enough to have my heart slamming against my chest and my face heating with embarrassment. A black bandana with a white painted skull covered most of his face, except where two dark eyes peered out at me from under his cap. In just that glance, his gaze burned up the distance between us. My breath was sucked out of my chest.

The Devil of the Symphony. Known simply as Devlin. One name to rule them all.

He was the new conductor who had been stirring things up in a big way at the Symphonic Orchestra of Knoxville, a.k.a. the SOOK. *My* conductor. I hadn't recognized his voice because he rarely spoke, and certainly never gently. He yelled. Or growled. "The woodwinds need to save some of that hot air for their fortissimo and not for mindless chatter!" or "If I wanted to fall asleep, I'd ask for a lullaby—not allegro!" Everybody knew the Devil of the Symphony came to Knoxville after being fired from several of the biggest symphonies around the world. Nobody knew why he chose the SOOK though.

My stomach dropped. He'd said he had an offer.

What would he want with me? I was a nobody in the back. The other cellists probably didn't even know my name. Christine Day kept herself small and unnoticed for a reason. I hardly made it on anybody's radar, let alone the Devil's.

My skin felt weird and hot and tight.

The door swung back and broke me from my internal musings. He gently closed the door, separating me from my parents.

"Christine Day." Devlin stood in front of me and all around me. His head tilted to the side.

"Maestro," I said. "I wasn't eavesdropping."

His eyebrows shot up.

"I mean, not intentionally," I clarified.

"I've already spoken with your parents, but I wanted to ask you directly." He said the words while his eyes bored into me.

His words were clear, not muffled, despite the barrier. The mask only made his focus all the more flustering. There was nowhere else to look. All I could do was stare back into those deep, dark eyes.

My eyes were brown too. Boring brown, like an Ikea side table. They matched my long, brown, stick-straight hair. I was easily forgettable. Tucked away in a corner, most people thought I was a side table. But his eyes were almost black. Where did the pupil end and where did the iris start? And why was I spending so much time thinking about his pupils when he had clearly just said something?

"What?" I smiled. It was a nervous knee-jerk reaction. It usually gave me enough time to disarm somebody until I thought of what I needed to say.

"My showcase. I need a cellist to help me work through some issues with my newest composition, *Smokey Mountain Suite*."

"A cellist?"

"Yes," he said flatly.

I wanted to ask, "What about Carla?" The first chair cellist would love that. I was nobody. I was fourth chair. Literally by rights, I was the fourth most qualified person to help him. But my words got stuck. The longer I stalled, the more the tension built around us. With every second that passed without me answering, the little furrow between his brow deepened.

But what was I supposed to say? Had he even asked me a question?

"I—I … Are you asking me?" That was definitely not what I should have said.

I had meant it sincerely, but he obviously took it as snark. The slice of emotion I could see turned downright thunderous. Suddenly the stories of holes punched in walls and flying music stands were believable.

"Yes," he growled.

This was a big decision. I needed more information. I needed to talk to Mom and Dad. So why couldn't I just say that? I could not decide this right now. Not with him standing there, studying me like that. What did he think my reaction would be to him showing up in my house? I was wearing pink flannel PJ bottoms and a tank top, for crying out loud. I hadn't even messed with a bra today. I hadn't expected to leave my suite of the house.

I crossed my arms over my chest, trying to appear casual, despite feeling anything but.

"Yes or no." Without seeing his mouth, I sensed he was scowling. That more-familiar growl was back in his voice. "Forty-eight hours."

And as though we had both decided the conversation was over, he turned on a heel and left. Only when the rumbles of his bike were no longer audible did I finally breathe easy.

I wasn't sure how long I stood there like a wall-eyed fish out of water. Eventually, my parents came out from the sitting room to find me stupefied in the hallway.

"I'm so confused. What should I do?" I whispered more to myself.

"It's a wonderful opportunity, working with the Maestro every weekend," my mother said, her voice smooth and calm as always.

"But you don't have to do it. If you—" My dad turned to my

mother as if a thought had just occurred to him. "How did he know her real name?"

"Green Valley isn't that big," she said. "Most people know Kim. Gossip probably got up to Knoxville somehow."

That wasn't exactly true. Not many people connected Jethro's ex, Kim Dae, the truant who ruined her chances for Juilliard, with Christine Day, the fourth chair cellist in the SOOK. That was the whole point of the stage name. I had split myself off into a new person.

Of course my friends in the Scorned Women's Society, SWS for short, knew; we all had our own baggage in addition to being Jethro's exes. We took care of each other. *No ex left behind.*

My father argued, "He's got a temper."

"He's an artist," mom countered.

"That excuses it? We're artists. We didn't throw tantrums and break batons."

They stood right in front of me and spoke as though I wasn't there at all.

My mother simply stared at my father, who was absolutely a moody artist, known for locking himself away for weeks at a time until he finished a novel.

"Don't give me that look, Meredith," my dad said.

"I didn't say anything, Lindsay," my mother soothed.

My folks never raised their voices when they fought, they just used names. If ever they get to their full names, it was time to get out.

"You did. With your eyes. And yes, I could be emotional when I had book-brain. But at least I didn't throw paint at the doorman."

"That was one time," my mother retorted calmly. "Artists are fickle. We understand that more than most."

"He couldn't even take off that ridiculous hat and mask in our home," Dad said.

"You know what they say. He's ... different. Maybe he's found his face makes people uncomfortable."

My father harrumphed. "I still don't like it."

"Just think of the one-on-one instruction she'd receive from such a musical genius." Mom, in her silk kimono, shifted her attention back to me. Dad wrapped an arm around her in his own matching kimono—because they were exactly that couple. After forty years of marriage they were morphing into the same eccentrically dressed, gender-neutral person. "What do you think, sweetie?" she asked me.

My toes started to tingle. The room unfocused until only their faces were clear. Distantly, I was aware that my breaths were coming quicker. I was tired of being a passive follower in my life, but I didn't know how to change. It seemed to come so easily for other people: bravery, boldness, and passion. Nobody would describe me with those words. But I did feel those emotions, hidden deep in my bones. What would this opportunity garner? Would I want it? What damage could this decision set into motion?

"I—I don't know." Images flashed through my mind. A cello solo. An icy lake. Wild nights. Bad choices.

Devlin came here to ask me to help him with his composition. He was a hulking, leather-clad biker-composer. He wore a mask with a skull and was quick to temper. Everything about him was designed to scare and push people away. He intimidated me, but he didn't scare me.

What he wanted from me did.

CHAPTER 2

ALWAYS PLAY LIKE YOU'RE FIRST CHAIR, EVEN IN THE BACK ROW.

KIM

He wants me. Devlin wants me.

To play for him. The Devil of the Symphony wanted me to play for him.

"I don't think I can do it," I told Erin.

She was my clarinet homie in the SOOK. In rehearsal, she sat in my direct line of sight and we often passed the hours sending each other looks—as no phones were allowed—and trying to get the other to laugh with the most ridiculous faces.

"Why not?" she asked. Her hair was purple today, save her dark roots, and the cut was a sharp bob just above her shoulders. She wore jean overalls over curvaceous hips and a bright green T-shirt. If I was the side table of a room, she was a lava lamp.

Devlin planned to debut his newest—and supposedly, most amazing—composition at the SOOK fall showcase. The spring/summer season had just begun, but with the arrival of the Devil of the Symphony, the gossip was already focused on the September show. This year, the pièce de résistance was to be

Devlin's crowning achievement. He wanted me to help him perfect the cello solo, and to receive private tutoring sessions.

Why me?

Erin and I stood in the corner of the room, huddled together, sipping crappy free coffee before practice. My two days were almost up. Devlin … Maestro … whoever, would need my decision today. Every time the door to the rehearsal space opened, my heart dropped to my toes thinking he would walk in and ask me in front of God and everyone what I had decided.

"I'm just not that good," I said with a glance to the door.

It was just Barry, second chair cellist, schlepping in on the heels of Carla.

"Ugh," Erin groaned. "I hear you play at night when I'm waiting for Mom to finish cleaning. I know you're so good. You come alive when you think nobody is around."

Had I been so obvious? My love for the instrument never diminished over time, even if the person playing it had.

"You're so good. You should be first chair," I said.

"Thank you. I know. Stop deflecting." She poked my shoulder teasingly.

"I just worry about—"

"Is it because he's so big and scary? I wouldn't want to be alone with him." She shuddered theatrically.

"You think he's scary?"

She looked at me like I was nuts. "Obviously."

"He's just doing that to try and seem tough. He's like those red pandas that jump up on their hind legs when they're scared." They're so darn cute.

Devlin stayed late last week to help Barry work through a particularly tricky transition without prompting. Devlin put all the chairs away after practice so Erin's mom didn't have to when she polished the rehearsal space floor. Nobody else noticed these things?

Her jaw dropped. "Red panda? No. More like grizzly bear. And I don't think it's an act. Man's got some anger issues he needs to work through."

I shrugged.

"Are you going to decline today?" she asked.

"I don't know. Maybe he forgot he asked. Want to stay here and hold my hand while I talk to him?" I joked, but a little part of me wouldn't have minded if she did.

"I think you'll regret missing this opportunity if you don't help him. You *are* amazing. You hold back at auditions." As she spoke her dark eyebrows moved up and down behind her glasses.

I frowned. "No, I don't."

"You do. You're better than you let on. Lord knows why. But this could really jumpstart your career."

An icy dread shot through me. "Yeah," was all I could mumble.

"Shit. There he is." She waved goodbye and tossed her gum in a small trash can as she ran to her seat. "Good luck," she half-whispered, half-yelled.

I completed my own mad dash back to my chair. Devlin stomped up to the podium, still in his biker boots. The scent of cold air and leather followed him as he passed.

We were all in our seats, tuned and ready before he lifted the baton. "Let's go. Where we left off last week." He tapped the stand.

There was a flurry of turning pages, and just like that, we were off. The Devil was his typical unrelenting self as we practiced Tchaikovsky's *1812 Overture* for the summer performance in July. He didn't acknowledge me. Not me personally. Nothing more than "Cellos, wake up!"

I wanted to jump up and scream, "Hey, remember how you rode your motorcycle to my ever-loving house asking for my help? Because I sure do!" But instead, as always, I sat quietly, awaited instructions, and studied him in brief glances.

At first, the mask and hat were a continued source of gossip and rumors spread of what could be hidden underneath. Disfigurement? Criminal past? But as time went on, he acted like they were invisible, and it became part of his persona. Like we were the crazy ones for noticing it. Reverse emperor's new clothes. He never brought them up. A poor trombonist casually joked about his mask, and had subsequently gotten the nastiest glare of a lifetime. Nobody had mentioned them since. To be honest, I got used to seeing them, just like anything else. It was a part of him. If anything, they made the intensity in his glare all the more unnerving and highlighted the ferocity of his movements.

At the first break, he stripped out of his leather coat. How had he even worn it this long with the lights on him and his dynamic motions? He deftly unbuttoned the cuffs of his white button-up dress shirt and rolled them up to the elbows, one at a time. The white material stuck to his damp skin. His forearms were unreal. Probably from gripping the handles of his motorcycle. A shudder ran through me.

He was the conductor, so my watching him would go unnoticed. Nobody would see how I memorized the way his forearms flexed as he gripped the baton and his other hand moved with practiced ease as it waved the brass to come in.

I shot my gaze across the practice space to Erin. Her lips were pursed around her reed and her cheeks were dimpled with exertion, but she managed a quick nod with wide eyes as though to say, "I saw it too, girl, and yes I need a towel for all this drool," or something along those lines.

I smiled and *pow, pow, bang*! There went the timpani signifying the climax of the piece. Emotion filled my chest. It was thrilling music, perfect for the Fourth of July outdoor concert just a few short months away. It was a safe bet as a crowd pleaser, and no doubt why he'd chosen it for the SOOK's first public show with him as conductor.

My heart, the ol' softy, swelled with the ringing bells as the patriotic piece built to the famous climactic ending. 'Merica, yeah! Tchaikovsky did not write this for America, but let's be honest—it was ours now. With fireworks exploding in the background, this was about as American as Chevy trucks.

The music built until we all worked up a sweat; even the gentle flutists were pink with exertion. I swayed in my seat, my heart rate clambering along with the tempo. Barry, the second-chair cellist in front of me, had a Florida-shaped sweat stain on his back.

Devlin bent forward, arms out wide, fingers beckoning. "Hold!" he screamed over the note. "Hold it! Don't dim. Strings come on! Louder!"

Grins split as sweat dripped down our faces. Arms shook with ferocity as we struggled to maintain the note. The brass section had to be close to passing out at this point.

He pinched off the note abruptly and we all stopped, bows lifted and mouths opened. The air held that last note as our ears adjusted to the sounds of heavy breaths and a few relieved huffs of laughter. He lowered his arms. We smiled around the room at each other, feeling that thrill of a job well-done. There was something absolutely magical about a room full of different instruments forming one perfect composite of sound. I pressed down the goosebumps on my arm.

We waited with bated breath as Devlin gripped the podium, head down and shoulders heaving.

"We need so much more practice," he growled, his head still down.

I shot a glance to Erin again as she slumped back, spreading out her Converse clad feet. She was obviously preparing herself for the lecture we all knew was headed our way. It hadn't taken long to learn the new conductor's habits.

"Just not enough." He linked his fingers on top of his black base-ball cap, his arms framing his head like he couldn't handle it. And I was definitely not noticing how his biceps bulged at the action, pulling the fabric to capacity, because his temper was appalling and juvenile and I would never support that. But also, daaayum.

"The violas were late coming in. The cellos lacked gusto. Don't get me started on the brass section. And for the love of God, who dropped their bow?"

I hunched, hiding as much as I could behind the neck of my cello. So much for thinking maybe he'd go a little soft on me now that he was asking for my help. My cheeks burned with humiliation. His critique of the cellos wasn't all on me, but it felt that way.

The only good thing about this rant was that it signified a break. A violinist started to loosen her bow and Devlin shot her a glare.

"Did I say we were done?" he asked in a scary calm tone.

Color drained from her face. It wasn't her fault. His lectures, typically at the end of rehearsal, were like Pavlov's bell. If ever I felt a lecture coming on, I got an overwhelming urge to pack something up. He seemed more wound-up than normal, even for him, and that was saying something.

He brought his face forward and lowered his voice. "I have an announcement." Nobody moved or spoke. Eyes flicked to gauge the reactions of the other players. "The SOOK will be re-auditioning for chair selections." Nobody spoke while we waited for more information. That couldn't have been right. "For each section," he added on.

Noise erupted all around me. I sat quietly as dread settled in. Chair auditions were common enough when there was a major change, but right before Maestro Henrich retired we'd auditioned for new chair assignments. Holding another audition this soon, for the entire symphony, was pretty unheard of. Maybe this was what had been bothering him?

Carla raised her hand. She was only a few years older than me but was married with kids, a first chair, the daughter of the SOOK's co-president, and always looked chic. It was hard not to compare all that I lacked against all that she was.

"Even the first chairs?" She spoke before he called on her. I cringed internally. "I've been practicing the Bach solo for the fall showcase." Her confidence was strong; in her defense, she'd been playing with the SOOK for many years, and had been first chair for the last two. But after the question was out and Devlin's head slowly twisted toward her, her confidence melted. She flicked a glance to Barry, who had suddenly become very interested in his sheet music.

"Excuse me?" Devlin asked.

"I said—"

"I heard your question, but assumed it wasn't for me as you

didn't address me as Maestro."

"Sorry. Maestro." She lifted her chin as red stained her cheeks.

"All chairs are required to audition," he said.

She huffed out a breath and smoothed her ponytail.

Nobody liked to be criticized in front of their peers. So that must have been why I had a momentary loss of brain function and wanted to convey some cello camaraderie.

"Don't worry, Carla. I'm sure you'll still make first chair." The words came out without my meaning them to. The different sections had already started talking and probably no one but the cellos heard me.

Her head snapped to my seat, behind her and to the right. Derision was the word you could use to describe her lip curl.

"I'm sorry. Who are you, you little toad?" she whispered with slitted eyes.

My mouth snapped shut and I focused on scraping off a piece of rosin stuck to the body of my cello with my fingernail. Well, that was what I got for talking to her. Or anybody. Head down and play. Feel nothing. Do nothing. Say nothing. That was the way to get by.

I risked a glance up. She had turned back around and was angrily flipping through her music. I told myself she was embarrassed for being chastised. That her comment had nothing to do with me. She was ashamed and angry, and I was an easy target for the feelings she couldn't take out on Devlin. Still. Pretty crappy.

"The SOOK is hiring an outside agency to coordinate the auditions. I will be working with a committee to decide who is the best fit for each position." The room quieted as Devlin spoke again. "I'm telling all of you this now because it could take weeks before this is all settled. I don't have more information at this time. Last thing. The fall showcase will be featuring my newest concerto. Take ten."

The room filled with sounds of whispered gossip. When I glanced up again, Devlin was studying Carla with a stern expression. His gaze strayed to mine and, knowing that I had caught him staring, he quickly looked away. He stomped off the podium and left the room without another word.

CHAPTER 3

THE DEVIL IS IN THE DETAILS. PAY ATTENTION.

DEVLIN

So much for a fresh start.

A few weeks in, and already my emotions got the best of me.

The farther I got from the rehearsal space, the less anxiety tied my tongue. My faults made me weak. The bandana hid my flushed cheeks, but the heat was getting unbearable. As soon as I was alone, I'd pull it down to breathe deep again. I'd go home, swim some laps, work the concerto, and everything would level out.

The anxiety management techniques came when the first symphony spread the rumors I'd been fired for my anger issues. Despite my best intentions at the start of each day, my nerves had me living up to those expectations. My inability to address the lack of respect between the musicians only ratcheted up my feelings of powerlessness. Carla didn't think I'd heard her barb. I should have called her out rather than announcing the chair auditions so bluntly. Music I could control. My own words and emotions were trickier. Rather than accept this fault in my system, I gathered my anger. I focused on the things that pissed me off.

The SOOK wasn't playing up to their potential. The previous conductor held chair auditions before his retirement simply as a way to leave his mark of authority; a final power play. Old practices and deep-seated nepotism were just some of the issues with the current symphony. If I wanted to prove myself, these would all need to be corrected.

Which brought my thoughts back to Kim. They strayed there often lately.

Kim hadn't given me her answer. *Christine*, I corrected internally. Hadn't she learned that I wasn't a patient man? I'd told her I wouldn't wait forever and that the position would go to someone else. But it was a lie. It had to be her.

My mind drifted to last week. I'd stayed behind in my secret office to work through some stress. Notes had floated in through the vents sending chills up my arms. When I'd glanced through the register, I'd seen her. In that moment, everything had been revealed to me. Who Christine Day really was. The magic in her playing was still as strong as ever. Her talents were unbounded, if only she'd share them. The music had swirled and consumed me like a cool mist. It had called me to her. She'd played with light shining out of her. It was nothing like the reserved Christine in rehearsals. It was as if my life had returned to me. Since the moment I'd first heard her play, I'd needed her with me to guide my music. That call of the music had guided my pen with a ferocity I hadn't felt in years.

I needed *her*.

The back door exit was in sight when I stopped my retreat. I had to go back and talk to her.

"Devlin, ah, there you are," a voice called out.

"Maestro," I corrected.

The second I registered that it was Dick's voice, I knew I wouldn't be leaving. I looked longingly at my motorcycle waiting for me as the door closed again.

"Ah, yes. Maestro, I don't suppose we could have a moment of your time before you run off again," Dick said.

I turned to see the twitchy man make his approach. Speak of the devil. Wait, that was me. Speak of the thorn in my ass. His hands were clasped and his mustache twitched. As always, Andy was at his side. Richard Firmin and Andrew Gill were the co-presidents of the SOOK. They were the go-between the SOOK and the board of directors for this performing arts center, where we played and practiced. Nobody else called them Andy-Dick, but as they were a package deal, it was just easier.

I pulled my riding gloves into place, drawing out the action to avoid shaking hands. "I have an appointment." It was with my piano, but Andy-Dick didn't need to know that. "What do y'all need?" I didn't bother putting my helmet on yet. I couldn't risk my mask falling loose.

Andy pursed his tiny mouth. His red-rimmed eyes and pale hair contrasted in an alarming way—like a rat in a medical trial. "You're required to come to the board meetings at least once a month per your contract. As you have missed the last two, we thought it best to catch you up." His words came out rushed.

I turned fully toward him, crossing my arms. Andy stepped back slightly in synch with Dick. There were some benefits to my reputation.

"Five minutes," I growled.

"Let's go back to our office." Dick glanced around as the musicians walked by chatting happily.

Damn, this was not going to be fun. For them. I tossed my leather coat over my shoulder. "Lead the way."

Andy-Dick shared an office made of glass that sat over the lobby —I supposed so they could watch as the money came in droves every performance.

"Listen, Devlin—"

"Maestro," I corrected. I didn't follow their lead as they sat in office chairs.

Part of the baggage that came with being one of the youngest conductors at age thirty-six in the history of the SOOK was that some people often forgot how to address me. And with that omission came a lack of respect in general. I was done playing that game.

"Right." Andy cleared his throat and began again. "Listen. We've been patient with the antics." He gestured to my face. I blinked slowly back at him. "But the chair auditions? Really. The board will not be okay with that. They wanted to make the announcement to avoid just this sort of upset."

"We know you're talented," Dick quickly cut in. "We're honored that you chose our humble symphony to debut your newest composition. Truly."

I tilted my head a fraction to acknowledge him. Good cop/bad cop was part of their whole routine.

"But you're risking upset to our most senior musicians. We need them happy."

"Their happiness is not my concern. Having talented musicians who can play my music is. The SOOK is underperforming. This needs to be addressed." I stated slowly for them to understand and to make sure I didn't mess up my words.

Andy wrung his hands. Dick's face went from pink to tomato red as he spoke. "Maestro. You're talented, but if you upset the Board they will not renew your contract. It's one thing to change up the musical numbers but now, to ruffle the talent's feathers?" He shook his head.

"Maybe the talent needs to be ruffled," I said. I looked pointedly at Dick, whose daughter Carla was on my short list to be shifted around. Her talent was marginal and her attitude was appalling. I balled my fists.

Dick straightened. "Listen. You're on thin ice already. You don't want your temper to ruin another opportunity."

"Richard, please—" Andy started.

"Well, he must be aware of it."

I held up my hand. "I'm aware of my reputation. I'm also aware that the SOOK hasn't sold out a performance in three years."

"I fail to see—"

"Tickets sales went up ten percent when I signed on. And they continue to climb. Just from the attention I've brought. Don't pretend you don't need me. This symphony is dying. You brought me in to change things up and to play my music. Don't insult me by refusing to let me do my job."

"We appreciate what you do," Andy cut in, a thin sheen of sweat now covering his forehead.

"Then let me do it." I stepped closer, looking down at the two men.

Dick frowned but remained silent.

"We're done here." I shrugged into my jacket.

I was almost to the door when Dick spoke. "The Board will only take so much. Control your temper and fill those seats. If you can't manage that, you're out."

I didn't turn around but looked over my shoulder. "Let me do my job."

Dick made one final parting shot. "We may want you, but don't get confused, we don't need you."

I nodded once before heading out to my motorcycle. They weren't wrong. My past was catching up with me. But in that moment, I couldn't have said anything else. I physically couldn't find the words. Better to let my mask speak for me. I got on my motorcycle and kicked it to life.

I was only back in Knoxville to prove myself. I'd leave this place as soon as a better offer came. For now, I had to stick through to the end. The SOOK would improve and I would conduct them. I would make that happen.

Kim Dae would help make that happen.

CHAPTER 4

END PHRASES WITH INTENTION.

KIM

Sometimes throughout the season the SOOK had performances for the investors, board of directors, or other VIPs from the community. They were typically smaller affairs, made of about one hundred super wealthy people eating an overpriced dinner while we performed like wind-up monkeys clapping symbols. It wasn't all bad—sometimes the caterers let us eat the leftovers. Tonight was one of those nights. The SOOK was performing a short showcase featuring a few key soloists, including Carla. We were meeting for a short final rehearsal two hours before the show, dressed in our typical black-tie performance outfits. My black slacks were starched stiff and my silk top trapped in the heat.

Actually, now that I looked around the room, I realized that Carla was late. Bad night to throw a tantrum. She had a habit of making a grand (read: late) entrance if somebody offended her, which happened roughly once a month. This didn't seem like the best way to prove a point to the Devil of the Symphony. Especially not at the last rehearsal before a high-stakes show. Tonight was a dinner performance where we all but begged for money from the Tennessee elite. Old money, new money—it didn't matter so long as it was big money.

Devlin stomped up to the podium. He always seemed to stomp places, like he wanted to give everybody plenty of time to stop talking about him. As always, he wore all black, matching the rest of us. Instead of a skull scarf, he wore a solid black one made out of shinier material. His closet likely consisted of nothing but perfectly folded face scarves, all different colors, sizes, and patterns. His baseball hat had been upgraded to a velvet trilby hat. Once again, instead of looking hokey and gauche, the overall effect was jaw-droppingly alluring.

Immediately all shuffling and talking stopped. Devlin was allowed to roll in the minute rehearsal started but we all learned early on that we needed to be ready, in our seats, instruments tuned and in position, because the moment he stepped on that podium he would lift his baton and tell us exactly where we were starting with absolutely no preamble or "hello, how is everyone?" A little small talk never hurt nobody, but I wasn't about to tell him that.

His eyes flicked to Carla's seat. He didn't react in any sort of way. What did that mean? He pulled his baton from his coat jacket like it was Harry Potter's wand, but instead of lifting it into the air, he held it low with both hands.

He cleared his throat and spoke. "There's been a change to the program tonight. Carla Firmin is out for the next few days and cannot perform her solo this evening."

My gaze shot to Erin who mouthed "whoa" and my eyes widened in agreement. Carla was many things, but she never missed an opportunity to show off.

He looked to Barry. "Are you prepared to step in?"

"I haven't—I don't know the solo," a very pale Barry stuttered out.

Devlin's eyes narrowed. "That's disappointing." He looked to the rest of the cellos.

We shrugged and looked from one to the other. The murmurs

grew louder around us as I sunk lower into the seat and slowly tried to make myself disappear. Of all the nights. Of all the solos. I refused to look at Erin. If I could fold myself up and slip into my F-hole I would. And that was not a euphemism.

"Maestro," a voice called out. "Christine Day can do it," Erin continued over the rising murmurs of shock. My eyes went wide and my face flamed.

"Christine? The fourth chair?" somebody to the left of me said. Mumbled speculation surrounded me, but I was too focused on not moving even an inch. If I didn't move at all, maybe I'd disappear. I had reverted to toddler logic. Someone nudged my arm. I stared unseeing forward. This could not be happening.

"Ms. Day?" Devlin asked, his rich voice flat. I couldn't tell if he was disgusted or amused at the suggestion.

"She's played the solo before," Erin said, and the world spun around me in a blur. "She's been well taught."

"I've heard her play it too," Barry jumped in.

How convenient for you, Barry.

They were right. I was a classically trained musician. I had been accepted to Juilliard. I was not some meek wallflower with no talent. But this? I didn't ask for this. I didn't want the solo. Where was Carla, of all the days? I couldn't look at anybody else in the room. Devlin studied me with an unreadable expression.

"Is that true?" he asked.

If this were a cartoon, there'd be an audible "gulp" sound from me right about now. I took a deep steadying breath. "Yes. A long time ago. I haven't played it since—"

"She was practicing it last night," Erin interrupted, sending her straight to the top of my dead-to-me list.

I tilted my head to more accurately to send my death stare her way. Okay, so I had been practicing it late at night after everybody left. The third movement of Brahm's *Piano Concerto No. 2* contained a beautiful solo that was sentimental to me. That didn't exempt Erin from my wrath though. Oh no, she was so not getting a banana cake from Donner Bakery this birthday. She'd be lucky if I made her a card. Store bought cards from here on out.

"Let's play through. I want to hear if you're qualified," Devlin said.

"Yes, Maestro."

Around me, the symphony moved into the ready position. Devlin didn't pick up his baton.

"You'll need to move," he said coolly, as his gaze flicked to the empty first chair.

Amazingly, my legs supported me despite how badly my knees tingled. The neck of my cello was tightly gripped in my fist like it was the only thing keeping me from spinning off the earth.

"We will start from the Andante movement," he called out as I got situated.

Next to me Barry gave me a brief nod of encouragement. I managed a small smile back. Playing alone at night was a heck of a lot different than feeling an entire symphony watch you. I wiped my palms on my dress pants before straightening my spine.

My nerves were shredded. I did this for a living and yet I couldn't get my bow to stop wobbling where it hovered just above the strings. My heart sputtered and cranked to a manic tempo. Carla should be here. What if something happened to her? The world began to tune out around me. Tears pricked behind my eyes. How ridiculous was that? I played with these people every day, but if I tried to speak or breathe or move, I'd start to cry.

"Hey." Devlin's voice was so soft I hardly noticed it at first. His biker boots appeared in front of my blurring vision. "Christine?"

I lifted my chin to find him standing in front of me with a furrowed brow. "Is she okay?" The question just slipped out, but I needed to know.

He dropped into a crouch to better hear me, causing me to pick up soft hints of cologne, fabric softener, and motorcycle exhaust. "What?"

I asked again a little louder but likely only Barry would be able to hear, if that.

His face was impassive like he was processing what I said. "Who? Carla?"

I nodded stiffly.

"Family emergency. She'll be back on Monday," he spoke softly.

"Oh." A weight lifted from my shoulders.

My chest rose as I took a deep breath in. I released it slowly. Surely the entire room was waiting to see what my deal was.

"I appreciate you stepping in for her." He lifted his chin to get me to look into his eyes. "I'm sure she would appreciate it too."

I doubted that, but at least I wasn't taking the performance from her. I was helping the orchestra out. I could absolutely do this. My thoughts had me worrying my bottom lip.

His focus lowered to my lips then quickly to where my hand gripped the shoulder of my cello. He cleared his throat. "Are you ready?"

I swallowed down my irrational fears. Carla was fine. It was just one show. I could do this. I got into position in answer to his question. Those dark eyes flitted around my face as though checking to see if I really was ready.

"All you need to do is watch me." When he spoke his mask hardly moved; nobody would know he'd spoken at all. My gaze was locked on his as it smoldered with intensity. "It's you and me."

As though I could look anywhere else. When he gave me his focus, the rest of the room faded away. The rest of the world.

"Ready?" he asked.

I forced my shoulders down. He got back onto the podium and I lifted my bow to wait for my solo entrance as he counted the rest of the orchestra in. The notes on the page transformed into a foreign language. The music quieted, signifying my entrance. I drew my bow along the string, but my tense arm caused a noticeable wobble. A wave of heat burned up my neck, a flush likely giving me away. Just when I thought I might lose total control, I remembered his directions. I looked to him.

His arm conducted the rest of the orchestra smoothly as they played their soft accompaniment, but his head was turned to me. He was willing me to look at him. His eyes narrowed when mine finally met his. He nodded his chin subtly. I didn't need to read the music. I knew this solo in my sleep. Instead, I kept my focus on him. I played. Everything else blurred into the background. The music came then. It flowed through me.

It was just us and the beautiful music.

CHAPTER 5

DON'T JUST PLAY THE NOTES, BLEED THEM.

DEVLIN

atch me.

Christine Day led the rest of the cellos on stage. With her shoulders back and chin lifted, the small audience gathered behind me might think she did this every day. She showed hidden courage in the face of this last-minute switch up, but underneath her cool facade, her color was off and there was a tense set to her jaw.

Just watch me, I willed.

Our gazes clashed. Each time they did, a bolt of awareness shot through my body. By the end of the pre-show rehearsal today I was jittery with adrenaline. She had watched me the whole time. Now as she settled into first chair, she preferred to look at me rather than the hushed commentary of the onlookers.

"Who is that?" someone whispered behind my back.

"Not sure," another replied. "Where's Carla?"

When Carla hadn't shown up, I'd thought my first donor dinner show would be a dismal flop. The second chair looked like he was going to lose his lunch when asked to perform. If not for Kim, who knows what the board of directors would have thought. Carla's sudden absence felt like another blow to my short career with the SOOK. So much rested on Kim stepping up, but I worried she might shy away from taking the lead like Barry had. Her reticence was written all over her ghostly-white face. She'd shocked me by asking first if Carla was okay and then after only a few moments of hesitation, she'd played the solo almost perfectly.

Now, here she sat, feigning confidence as the audience waited expectantly for us to begin.

"Thank you all for coming today." I addressed the room speaking loudly so my words were not muffled through the mask. Several of the onlookers raised eyebrows at my appearance but I was used to it. I kept my voice low and commanding, but damn I hated this part. "There has been a small change to the program. Christine Day will be performing the solo in the third movement of Brahm's *Piano Concerto No. 2.* Now, please enjoy your dinners as the Symphonic Orchestra of Knoxville performs for you, our most honored guests."

The room clapped politely as I turned back to my musicians. I took a moment to steady my hands before I lifted the baton.

Despite my worries that there would be another small act of rebellion, the symphony performed well. The first two movements went without a hitch, but I could feel Kim's nerves grow with every passing measure. As the third movement began, a red flush began to spread up the pale column of her neck. The symphony wound down for her solo. Forks stopped clattering against plates, voices dropped off. All the eyes in the room went straight to her.

Kim took a deep breath in as she lifted her bow to begin. Her gaze found mine and, just like in rehearsal, they remained locked there. Though slightly nervous at first, her confidence grew with each note. Her body swayed with her performance.

A swift check on the audience found they all shared looks of wide-eyed wonder at this new soloist. How could they not? Of course, she was beautiful, but that was the least interesting thing about her. The moment her bow pulled across the strings, her soul was expressed. She couldn't help it. Her zeal for life floated along with the notes and filled every inch of the room.

She took direction perfectly. I hardly needed to lead. She read my cues, feeling instinctually, when I slowed her down or sped her up. When our eyes would lock, my heartbeat would stutter and I was never so grateful to have my face covered. Otherwise, she'd see all the things I felt too soon. We had time for that later.

A dark lock of hair had come loose from her tight bun as she rocked with the music. She blew it out of her face before it stubbornly came back to fall in the same place. She let it be. A small smile tugged her mouth after she nailed a particularly difficult slide. The power in those delicate fingers as they flew into fifth position was astounding. Her face was sharpened with focus, her mouth forming shapes with the music. Her brows arched and flattened in turn.

Still, I sensed she'd held back. This was not the languid passion I had seen when I'd watched her play at night by herself. There was a stiffness to her that wasn't there before. Something had caused her to change from the Kim Dae I knew from the past to the muted Christine Day of today. Our rehearsals together would have to focus on that, fix whatever it was that prevented her from giving in fully. Even still. With only a spark of the fire I knew she possessed, she lit up the room.

When she opened her eyes again, they returned to me. I smiled knowing it was safely unseen behind the bandana. I hoped she felt a fraction of the pride blazing in my chest right now. I was proud for her, even if she would be too modest to accept her talents.

The movement ended with her solo and the room exploded into applause. Chairs pushed back from their tables and cries of "bravo" filled the room. My focus remained on her as long as it could, watching her take the praise with grace but not faux humility. She nailed that and she was proud of herself. Her smile lit up the room.

This.

This was exactly what I wanted. She would be the key to my success at the SOOK. She was my angel of music. Now I just had to convince her.

CHAPTER 6

RESPECT YOUR BODY AND THE DEMANDS UPON IT. COMMIT OR QUIT.

KIM

After a round of thunderous applause, all the musicians went backstage. The smile planted on my face was hollow. I had performed well and it had been fine, but the applause scared me. As soon as I'd started to enjoy the feeling of the performance, a different sort of anxiety had creeped in. The standing ovations and accolades from my peers felt unwarranted and excessive. I hadn't earned this. But I smiled and took the compliments. Carla's reaction still weighed on the back of my mind. Hopefully, we could all forget about this and go back to normal when she returned.

What had Devlin thought? Had he noticed the hyper-extension? Or the over-correction right after? Had he heard the wobble of my bow? His face had been unreadable throughout the whole performance, as usual. His eyes had been focused in concentration and his strong build filled with tension as he led us. At one point, it had almost seemed like his eyes had held a smile. Which was crazy, really. The Devil didn't smile. That was the nice part about not seeing his whole face at once. I could really tell myself that he was smiling and there was no substantive proof to tell me otherwise.

"Where have you been hiding?" Erin ran up to me and squeezed my hands.

I laughed and hugged her. We were both slightly damp from the performance, but who cared? She beamed and so did I.

"It was nothing," I said.

"A new tutor?" she asked with a glint in her eye.

"No, no." Devlin still hadn't brought up whether I planned to work with him, and I was grateful. I understood what an opportunity this was, but a larger part worried about the fallout. It would lead to attention and other … The other scared me.

"Well, you were fantastic. There's my mom—I need to go talk to her." We hugged again and Erin was off.

"You were too," I called after her.

My stomach growled loud enough to be heard over the excited chatter around me. Now it was time for food and water. I'd spent the whole day with pre-show jitters at a whole new level due to the unexpected solo. As the adrenaline wore off, my body shook with hunger. My parents had shot me big grins and thumbs ups from their seats near the front after the performance. While they were artists, they weren't musicians, so they would only ever notice a mistake if it was major.

I skulked around the backstage hoping to see a snack table or a friendly-looking waiter. Somewhere there was a whole catering area set up for the meal up front, but I would be fine with a vending machine at this point. The old back hallways smelled faintly of mildew and memories.

Eureka! Far down an old hallway near a rattling water fountain stood a well-stocked vending machine. I tapped my lip. Cookies, or something with a little more substance? Why not both? The emergency dollar I kept stashed in my bra was almost in the slot when a man's voice cut through the back area.

"Hey, don't I know you?"

I spun around to see a handsome man approaching, his highly-polished dress shoes glinting in the light. His fair skin was accented with sharp cheek bones and full lips that were quirked as though he were waiting for me to get the punchline. His almost-white blonde hair was slicked back with gel and was as sophisticated as his tuxedo. His eyes though? I'd know those sky-blue babies anywhere. As my recognition grew, so did his grin.

"Roddy?" I shook my head.

Roderick Chagny. My first love. I blinked and took in his appearance. He was more handsome now as a grown man. So handsome. His features had gone from cute, almost feminine, to strikingly masculine. He could have been a model for Scandinavian vodka.

"It is you." Snacks forgotten, I stepped toward the reminder of my past.

"Yo-Yo, I can't believe it." I shook my head at the nickname he'd called me most of my adolescence.

I threw open my arms and wrapped them around his neck. He held me tight. He was muscles, sharp bones, and expensive cologne now; such a different feel than the thin frame I used to hug all the time. I started to pull back, but he held on a second longer. He tucked his head into my neck and groaned a little as he squeezed me tight. Him being back and knowing he saw my solo tonight added to my already muddled brain.

"God, look at you." He finally released me, his eyes glinting as they moved over my face. "You haven't aged a day."

We held each other's hands and grinned like children as we shared looks of happy disbelief.

"What are you doing here?" I asked finally.

"I'm in town visiting my folks. They wanted me to see Carla's solo. They want me to represent her." He grimaced. "But then you came up. I knew it was you the second I saw you. My God, you're even more beautiful than I remember."

I blushed. It was Roddy, all these years later. Roddy from orchestra camp. First chair violin. Adored by all, and my first boyfriend. My guardian angel. He'd been the one to keep me going with his words. Even after Jethro and the time at the retreat. It was his notes I had pulled from my memory to keep me going.

He interrupted my thoughts. "You were amazing tonight. Perfect. Nobody could tear their eyes away from you."

"Thank you." I shook my head. I hadn't been perfect at all. I was sloppy from nerves, especially at first.

It was hard to be complimented on my talent. I took it with a combination of modesty and deflection. "I've been practicing a lot lately."

"It shows," he said. "I can't believe it's you."

"I can't believe you're back. You're so huge now." I took a deep breath to calm my nerves. "I mean successful." I had heard that Roddy had left playing music himself to manage soloists instead. "I've heard of some of your clients—Markus Savagno and Caroline Tetch. She's touring Asia right now, isn't she? So impressive."

His dimple appeared with a sheepish grin. "Just lucky."

"Luck is timing and preparation," I said quoting one of his notes from so many years ago.

I quoted them all the time, but only I knew that.

He shuffled with hands deep in his pockets and smiled at the ground. "You're right. Thank you. They're amazing clients. But tonight is about you. That performance. You should hear the buzz … I can't believe you're Christine Day. When did you change your name?"

"My parents thought I should have a—a stage name after …"

He cut me off. "We don't have to talk about all that."

Most people never wanted to discuss the darker parts of my past. It was a blip on the radar and people preferred to ignore it. Christine Day was all that mattered now. But maybe Roddy and I could talk about it. Maybe he was back to finally help me move on with my life. My chest lightened for the first time since Carla had missed practice.

"We should go out."

"Now?" I glanced longingly again at the snacks.

"Are you too busy to celebrate?"

"Celebrate what?"

"Your successful solo."

I frowned at that. It should have been Carla's solo. My stomach growled loudly, and I made a face.

"I was actually about to get a snack." I thumbed behind me to the vending machine.

He grimaced. "Don't eat that. Come back to my box. My parents had it all set up. I have real food."

Roddy tugged me away down the hall and I mourned the trail mix still in the snack machine. By the time we climbed back up the flights of stairs, made small talk with a few acquaintances, and wound through a pressing crowd, I was pretty dizzy. With how regularly I worked out and practiced, my blood sugar tended to be an issue. I knew better than to wait this long to eat and drink. I was highly susceptible to coquettish fits of fainting. It was pretty embarrassing actually, so I was diligent about snacking regularly.

Roddy's box, or rather, his parent's box, sat just left of the stage, high up with an amazing view. The room spun a little as I plopped into one of the chairs. I'd never been so grateful to stop moving.

He handed me a glass of champagne. I held up my hand and shook my head. "No thank you. I don't drink."

"Not even to celebrate your fantastic performance?" he asked.

I didn't feel like arguing. I just smiled and accepted the glass.

"Cheers." He tinged his glass against mine and took a hearty gulp. He eyed me closely, raising his eyebrows. I brought the glass to my lips and took a tentative sip.

"Cheers."

Even the small drop in my stomach seemed to burn. Rationally, I understood that one tiny sip of fancy champagne wasn't going to set me down a path of self-destruction again. But it was best if I steered clear. I set the glass back down and smiled.

"You don't seem as happy as you should," he said with a concerned frown. "You're probably just in shock from everything. You just found out today you were going to play, right?"

"I'm happy. It's been a lot really fast, and I think I just need to eat."

He glanced around the box suite lined in red velvet curtains with gold tassels. "Looks like they cleared the food already. Let me go track some down. You drink that champagne." He pulled me close and kissed my cheek with a little growl. "I'm so happy to see you again."

I nodded and smiled.

As soon as he left, I sat back into the seat and pressed my palm to my forehead. The skin there was clammy and cool to the touch despite how I burned up. I needed to eat. I needed to breathe. For the past ten years, I had followed the same strict schedule and now all this change was all too much, too soon. I bent forward, holding my knees and taking big gulps of air as best I could as the doctors had suggested.

Something snagged my attention on the floor near the opposite seat. A folded piece of paper.

My shaky hand reached out and snagged it.

It read: Don't let nerves make you sloppy. You're better than that.

I smiled and gripped the note to my chest, still in that same familiar handwriting. Never had a critique felt so good. Roddy was still leaving me notes. He may have upgraded his lifestyle, but he was still my best friend from camp.

I re-read the note, gripping it with trembling fingers. Roddy wanted me to be happy and successful. I picked up the champagne and stared at it for a long minute. I could relax and have a nice time. I took a big sip. The past was the past. I would be okay.

The note was still gripped in my hand when Roddy returned a few minutes later wearing the charming, easy smile of the kid that I knew. Maybe it was the high of night or the buzz of the champagne, but I felt like it had to be fate that we'd met back up like this. I'd always wished I could end up with the one who had given me all those treasured notes. Obviously, I was just getting to know Roddy again and I didn't want to rush anything, but still, what if he had been the missing piece all these years?

"The bad news: I couldn't find food. Good news: I pilfered a bottle of Dom Pérignon from the VIP bar." He held up the contraband as he walked into the box and closed the door behind him. "Finish that glass and we can get this party started."

I handed him my empty glass. My stomach burned but the effects of the champagne muted my hunger a little. Maybe I'd regret this later, but a piece of my past had been returned to me and I wouldn't overthink it.

I smiled at him wondering if I looked as foggy as I felt.

"You seem more relaxed," he said.

He popped the cork from the bottle. It fizzed over and I clapped.

"I'm just happy to see you again. Look what I found," I whispered and leaned in with a grin.

His gaze moved to my hand and the note I held up. He patted his pocket. "You found that."

I nodded and waited to speak until the room stopped moving.

"You're not mad?" he asked hesitantly.

"No. I love your notes." I wanted to tell him how much they had meant to me, how it helped to think that he was out there somewhere rooting for me. I bit back the words; I knew the champagne was loosening my tongue and I didn't want to come on too strong. "I missed them. I missed you."

He grabbed my hand with the note and squeezed. "I missed you too." He tried to take the note back, but I pulled away.

"Nope. I want to keep it. I still have all the other ones."

"You do?" His smile faltered for a moment before sliding back in place. Maybe my intensity had freaked him out after all. I slid the note into my pants pocket, letting it go for now.

"Tell me about your life these last few years." I changed the subject putting on a relaxed tone.

"Busy." He grinned as he stood and grabbed my glass to refill it.

"I messaged you online. After … camp."

"You did?" He held up the glass to the soft lights in the walls to check the level then poured a little more.

"Yeah. Just a few times. I knew you were romping all over the world, making it big. But I thought maybe you'd want to catch up."

There was so much left unsaid after camp. Maybe getting closure on that time of my life was more important than I'd realized, because his reappearance felt like hope.

He sat in the chair across from me and spun us so that our knees almost touched. "My assistant might have thought it was spam. He helps manage all that. It's been a whirlwind since graduation."

"I'm sure. You're so successful now. I'm not mad. I'd just wanted to let you know I was thinking of you." I shrugged. I'd gotten over being mad and upset. A lot of people disappeared from my life after I lost my scholarship. I had gained the SWS. They were true friends. I'd traded up and I had no regrets. Except for Roddy. His sudden disappearance had hurt the most after everything we had gone through. Then again, grief hits everyone differently; he had coped as best as he could.

He leaned forward and rubbed a thumb over my cheek. "If I had known you'd reached out to me ..." His gaze dropped to my lips. "I thought of you a lot. I regret not finding you sooner."

Though it was crazy, it really felt like he was about to kiss me. I brought the glass to my mouth and took a long sip of champagne.

"But I'm here now. We're together again and that's all that matters." He leaned back in his chair and smiled at me. "You're so beautiful."

I shook my head and studied my hands in my lap. It wasn't that I wasn't flattered; I just didn't know what to say. I had little control over my appearance, which was totally subjective. Exterior beauty was never a good indication of the quality of content inside.

"Tell me about you," I said, hoping he'd go with the subject change. "Where do you even live now?"

"Oh boy, where do I start? I lived in LA for a while. Too fake." He grimaced. "Then New York. Too jaded. Then I traveled for work. Now, I use my folks' house as my permanent address to keep it simple."

"Are you going to be here in Knoxville for a while?"

He held up his glass. "I'm starting to think it would be nice."

I sucked in my bottom lip. The little bit of champagne hit me suddenly, and I was ready to call it a night.

"I should probably get going. This has been so great—catching up. But I have an early morning." I tried to stand but I moved too fast and got a head rush. I sat back down to steady myself. "Can I have some water?"

"Of course. But let's not wrap this up just yet. We've hardly talked."

"Yeah." I shook my head. "No. I mean that sounds good, but I think I need to go find my parents. They'd love to meet you. I told them all about you every time I got back from camp."

"I can't wait to meet them. They're probably wonderful. Of course, how could they not be? Look at their daughter."

"Yeah, they're great." I smiled. He said everything just right. "Roddy, can I have some water?" I thought I had already asked but maybe I hadn't. "I don't feel great."

"You always did have a sensitive constitution. Remember that one time we stole peach schnapps from the camp counselors and snuck out to the lake at midnight? That was a great night."

"We had some great times." I smiled even though the thought of that lake only added to my nausea. "Water. Please." I knew my voice sounded firmer than I meant it too.

He let out an exaggerated sigh. "Okay. I'll be right back."

"Can you find my parents too? I'd like to go home."

He chuckled. "Sure, lightweight."

I had my head back and eyes closed before he was even out of the room. I just needed the room to stop spinning. I heard the door open and his steps recede. I must've fallen asleep because it seemed like he was back in the room only a second later. The door opened and shut softly.

"Did you find my parents?" My voice sounded slurred even to my own ears. I *was* a lightweight. I shouldn't have drank at all. I knew better than that. Why did I let myself get talked into doing things I knew I would regret for the sake of other people's comfort? My eyes wanted to stay closed.

Roddy didn't answer. I startled when arms wrapped around me;

one under my neck and the other behind my knees. He scooped me up with no problem.

"I can walk. I'm fine." I nuzzled into his shoulder, putting no feeling behind the words. My cheek brushed the starchy fabric of his suit coat. The flexed muscles were tense with the effort to hold me. Talk about a real-life glow-up.

It was nice to have Roddy back in my life. I hadn't been looking for change, but maybe I wouldn't have to feel so alone having somebody who knew the dark truth of what happened at camp. I stopped trying to fight the drowsiness, and let the darkness take over.

The last thing I heard was, "Kim," in a deep rumble. My real name. I didn't even realize how much I'd missed hearing that name until it was whispered in my ear.

CHAPTER 7

PULL YOUR SHOULDERS BACK; YOU ARE NOT A HUNCHBACK.

DEVLIN

It wasn't kidnapping if her health was at risk. It wasn't kidnapping if I was taking her to a place where she could get some help. That imbecile was pretending to care while plying her with alcohol on an empty stomach. Couldn't he see how pale she was? How her face was misted with sweat? I saw him watching her like a predator after her performance. When he followed her out of the backstage area, I made it my mission to keep an eye on him.

I waited until he left his parents' box before walking inside. I didn't owe him an explanation for my concern. And it appeared I had been right—she was passed out in a chair. Anger thrummed against my skull, battling a wave of fear. Her hand was curled under her chin and her smooth skin was frighteningly colorless. Her chest moved up and down lightly and she let out a soft sigh. The fierce musician of an hour ago seemed so fragile.

I picked up her glass and sniffed it. I didn't smell anything, but I've never seen someone fall asleep so easily either. Maybe she had spread herself too thin. Maybe the solo tonight was too much, too soon.

Roderick Chagny's sudden appearance back in town was an unfortunate complication. If ever there was a person who could ruins my perfectly laid plans, it was him. He represented every user and abuser in the industry; an agent who saw dollar signs instead of people. I took a steadying breath. I didn't want to do something I would regret in a moment of anger.

Then I saw the empty bottle of champagne. I took out my phone and shot my brother, Wes, a text. He had already planned to come over after the show. My new plan required his help. He responded immediately, just as I thought he would.

Maybe I was acting impulsively. But I wouldn't stand around and watch her get taken advantage of. I scooped her into my arms. Holding her settled a feeling of rightness deep in my bones. She needed to be kept safe from toolbags like Chagny. It scared me. She was stronger than this. It was unnerving to see her so defenseless and trusting. Didn't she know what people were capable of?

"Kim." I hadn't meant to say her name, but she seemed so fragile in my arms.

Kim Dae was a creation of curiosity. I had surreptitiously watched her enough to know that her eyebrows would constantly move with all of the questions that flowed through her mind. All that questing for knowledge would crinkle her flawless skin, while intelligence would flash in her dark eyes.

In contrast, her pseudonym, Christine Day, stood back from the crowd and mirrored the cold beauty of an instrument waiting to be directed. Her dark hair was always arranged artfully while she gazed at me during rehearsals. Every muscle would pause as if my slightest wish would move her to the creation of beauty.

But this woman in my arms, she was all of that and more. Her beauty was breathtaking when she was at peace like this. I'd seen her heart-shaped face, a younger version, in my dreams. Now, her long brown hair was twisted in a tight knot that looked painful, with a few loose tendrils breaking free. I wanted take it down, but I wouldn't even know where to begin. With her eyes shut, her face was a flawless canvas, save for the two dark slashes of her eyebrows. She looked so much the same still, yet older. Mature. Sharper features, but with a delicate bone structure. I wondered what she would think if she saw me without the mask.

I stepped out of the room, but not soon enough. I ran directly into Mr. and Mrs. Dae, led by Chagny.

"Chagny," I said flatly.

"What's this?" He gestured to Kim.

I didn't respond to him. My focus went to her parents who shared similar looks of worry. "She's dehydrated."

"Oh my, she's so pale," Mrs. Dae said to her husband.

Chagny stepped forward. "She didn't say she was unwell. Quick. Take her to my car. The hospital is only a few miles away."

Again, I ignored him and spoke to the parents. "The hospital wait time will be hours. Dr. Thurston lives near me and can be at my house by the time I arrive home."

"To your house?" Mr. Dae frowned.

"You're welcome to follow me," I said and tried to step around Chagny.

"I'll go with him, honey. You meet the guests," Mrs. Dae said to her husband. Then turning to me she added, "We're hosting a small soiree tonight. I'll make sure she's okay and then bring her home."

"This is crazy. You can't take her to—"

"I have many spare rooms," I cut the dirtbag off. "She's more than welcome to stay at my home until the morning when I can return her safely."

"It will be very loud at our house and she needs rest. Today was such a big day," Mrs. Dae said. "Honestly, if this wasn't fairly common for her, I'd be more worried. Most likely she just needs to eat and sleep."

Kim shifted in my arms with a soft moan. Her parents exchanged another worried look.

"You're right." Mr. Dae glanced at his watch. "Okay. What about the car? How will you get home?"

"Oh shoot." She frowned. "I didn't think about that."

"I'll drive you, Mrs. Dae," Chagny insisted. "I have much I'd like to discuss with you."

"Oh, that would be lovely, thank you, Roderick."

I glared. "Not necessary."

"I insist." He smiled with all his teeth at me.

"No—"

"Excellent. So it's settled," Chagny spoke over me. "Let's go. Devlin must be getting tired, holding Kim like that."

Mr. Dae kissed his wife goodbye and headed out. The rest of us started toward the exit.

After I gave my address, I walked away from the group, not waiting to ensure they would follow. When I was a few feet away, Chagny said, "How unfortunate for Carla that she missed tonight."

"Oh yes. But good for our girl," Mrs. Dae replied.

"Somebody mentioned rehearsal had been intense today. The Maestro is very stern with the musicians. Maybe she just needed a night off," Chagny said with saccharine sweetness.

I kept my focus on breathing and not punching him in the face.

What game was he playing at? I put more distance between us. Wes's car sat idling waiting for us. A minivan wasn't my vehicle of choice, but my brother had it ready and waiting.

"Is she okay?" Wes asked.

"She will be. Help me get her in," I responded.

He opened the passenger door for me. I placed her in the seat, leaning it all the way back so she could get comfortable. She curled up, still more out of it than anybody should be after just a little bit of champagne. She mumbled incoherently—something about food and notes.

Once she was situated, Wes cleared his throat. "I'm not aiding and abetting criminal activity, am I?"

I shot him a look.

"Don't answer that. Just give me the keys to the bike and we can pretend this never happened."

I tossed him the keys and he caught them happily.

"I'll see you back at my house," I said.

Once in the driver's seat, I finally smoothed the loose strand of hair out of her face, tucking it behind the soft shell of her ear. Electricity shot through me.

I balled my fist and pulled it away.

Kim could help me with my music. Nothing more. I wouldn't let old feelings get in the way of new goals.

* * *

"It's not kidnapping," I said to Wes. Wear a mask and people automatically paint you as the bad guy.

"You keep saying that like it's true." My brother closed the door behind him as he came into the front hallway to whisper-yell at me.

Kim was still asleep in the guest bedroom upstairs. I didn't think Beethoven's *Fifth* would wake her right now. Though I did keep my hat and mask on just in case.

"Thanks for the car and for bringing my bike back."

He made a gesture like I was dumb for thanking him. "Just don't tell Kelly."

I made a gesture like he was dumb for having to say that. But yeah, I would definitely tell Kelly at the earliest opportunity if it meant I got to see my brother smacked upside the head by his pint-sized wife. "And you don't have to whisper. She's fine. Just tired."

"That's good. Still weird that she's here."

I sighed pointedly at him. "For the record, her mom followed me here." And left again at the soonest opportunity. Chagny, too. Every second he was in my company he would subtly undermine me in passive aggressive ways. They guy was smooth. I'd never be able to charm her parents like he did so effortlessly. None of that it mattered as much as her health. Thankfully, Wes had arrived shortly after and could out charm a used car salesman. When Chagny realized he was outmatched, he cleared out. Mrs. Dae seemed eager to return to her party, and Chagny relented as soon as she'd made it obvious she was ready to go.

"I didn't just whisk her away in the night. They agreed that it would be better if I took her here and called the doctor rather than wait four hours at the ER."

"Sure, this is all a totally normal thing to do. Nobody will think anything of it. Rumors won't start." Wes made his way toward the kitchen and I followed. He helped himself to my fridge and snagged two beers.

"Could you not lay into me? I'm exhausted." I rubbed my eyes until white spots danced in my vision. I grabbed the beer he nudged me with and leaned back against the counter.

"You're exhausted?" Wes clinked my beer. "You just made Dr. Thurston drive all the way up here to your creepy mansion by the lake, just to find out she was tired and needed food. That man's too old for this. What's this really about? Is she the reason you're back here?"

"He lives five minutes away. Don't be so dramatic." I pulled the gaiter mask down under my chin and swallowed four deep gulps of beer. After wiping my mouth on my sleeve, I said, "I told you why I'm back."

"Yeah. You did. How will staying through a season at the SOOK prove you're hirable?"

"The last three symphonies fired me for my temper, right? Just ask anyone." I glanced to the side. "I need to show I can play well with others."

"And what's with this cellist?" He shook his head. "There's something here I'm not buying."

I picked at the label on my beer bottle and debated unloading on him.

"It's gonna break Ma and Dad's heart if you up and leave again with no warning." He leaned on the counter next to me and crossed his ankles. "The girls too."

"That's dirty. You know I'm defenseless against my nieces' dimples."

He smiled and I saw a copy of my own face. Or at least my face when I had smiled. In front of actual people. Mask free. Wes had the same almost-black eyes and matching dark curls, though he kept his hair trimmed short. We shared the same intense glare that our mom said could get us out of anything as kids. The difference was Wes wielded his with an easy smile to charm, and I used mine with a frown to intimidate.

"Can you take off the hat? At least you pulled down the frickin' mask." He gestured to my face. "I can't even remember what you look like."

"Like your reflection. But better looking." I cleared my throat. "I can't. If she comes down—"

"Yeah, yeah. I get it." He cracked open two new beers against the counter like any good ol' boy learned to do by the age of fifteen. "You built this beautiful home and you're hardly ever here. Short visits only. Now, you're back for at least six months and you're telling me this has nothing to do with the woman currently sleeping in your guest room?"

I swallowed. It was complicated. She herself didn't know of our connection in the past and if I brought it up too soon, it might push her away. I would need to talk to her first. Eventually. I set down the beer to wipe my palms on my pants before picking it up again.

"I needed to be back home and back in these mountains to feel inspired. To finish something through to the end. Kim, that's her name, is going to help me. Though she goes by Christine now, actually."

"Okay." Wes shook his head and blinked rapidly like he was trying to make sense of everything.

"I heard her practicing after rehearsal a few times." I explained. "She has incredible talent. But it's not about her." I held his gaze.

His eyes narrowed. He wasn't buying it but sensed I wasn't saying any more about her.

"What's that other guy's deal? The one hovering over Kim's mom?"

"Roderick Chagny." My voice was heavy with distaste. "I'm not sure why he's back. I don't like it."

"I don't trust him. Too charming."

"Said the pot about the kettle."

"Yeah, yeah. I'm sincere though. I can't help it." Wes's eyes drifted over as I spoke. "Wait. Chagny … I know that name."

"His parents are rich." I forced cool indifference into my voice. "Big donors to the SOOK performance center."

"How would I know any of that? Wait." Wes snapped his fingers. "He was that kid that you hated from camp."

"You can't remember your wedding anniversary, but you can remember some kid a lifetime ago?"

He threw his arm around my neck. "I remember people that mess with my little bro." He tugged off my hat to give me a noogie before I could stop him. He was two and a half solid inches shorter than me and had gained a post-football season gut about fifteen years ago, but he never passed on an opportunity to show me he was the older brother. I pushed him off and put my hat back in place.

"He didn't come after me," I growled. "He just got under my skin. I was a counselor when he was there, and his parents' wealth made him untouchable."

"Didn't he do something? Some drama?" Wes asked.

"Not officially," I mumbled. "He managed to never get caught doing anything. He's just one of those people. Everybody loves him. He says just the right things. But I would always catch him in these little lies. For no reason. Always claiming something that was small, almost harmless. But blatant, pointless lies."

"Yeah, I know the type. Like 'I've got four parakeets,' when you know for a fact they don't, but also who the fuck lies about having birds?"

"That's a real specific example, but yeah, exactly. And you can't call people out on stuff like that or you look like the jerk." I took another slug of beer.

Wes nodded and gulped down the rest of his bottle. "I hate guys like that. Don't worry. If you want, I'll kick his ass." He flexed and kissed his biceps. "These guns haven't lost their bullets."

"It amazes me that we're related."

Wes pushed my head and I pulled a punch to his gut.

"I better head out. The girls are probably threatening to tie Kelly up and break out the cookies."

I laughed and walked him to the door.

"I'm glad you're back. It's nice being able to stop by like this." Wes squeezed the doorframe, checking the sturdiness all while avoiding my gaze.

"Yeah," I said, sniffing once before stuffing my hands deep in my pockets. I wouldn't be here for long. I didn't have the heart to tell him that. Not right now.

"I hope you find what you're looking for." He held my gaze. "With the SOOK," he added.

"Me too."

CHAPTER 8

LET THE MUSIC CALL YOU.

KIM

I wiggled deeper into the sheets. I would let myself have just a few more minutes. Practice could wait. Swimming could wait. Just for a little while longer. My eyes wouldn't open anyway, so if they went on strike, I was at their mercy. My head rested comfortably on a pillow that must work part-time as a cloud, and the heavy down comforter smelled like fresh laundry and sunshine.

I went back under with a contended sigh.

The next time I woke up I was a little more concerned about where I was. My eyes shot open and blinked away the sleep rapidly. I frowned at a vaulted ceiling I'd never seen. My fingers splayed out to grip a majestic duvet that wasn't mine.

"Curious," I said.

I turned my head to the side and spotted a few pieces of furniture. Too homey for a hotel, but lacking in personal touches. Guest room? It was lovely and comfortable, but it was still distressing not knowing where I was. I fought sleep to recall the events of the night before. My phone sat on the bedside table. I picked it up and found it charging. Next to that sat a plate of delectable looking scrambled eggs, with toast and orange juice.

I unplugged my phone and squinted at it until the screen came into focus. It was almost ten in the morning; much later than my usual wake time of five a.m.

I had one text.

"Eat the food. Drink the juice." It was Devlin.

I sat up in bed with a racing heart. Wait, wait. Was I at Devlin's house? The Devil of the Symphony himself? Cloudy bits of nonsense started to return to me … the solo … Roddy … the champagne … ugh.

My hands trembled as I navigated to the group message with my parents to search for clues and let them know I was alive. I couldn't imagine what they thought. To my immense relief, I saw that they had sent a goodnight text.

"Everything is good at home. Rest up. Call us later tomorrow after you talk to the Maestro." They *knew* I was with Devlin. They were *okay* with it?

More hazy memories floated back in bits and pieces. Being carried away. Hearing my parents discuss a plan. Doc Thurston with a stethoscope checking my heart and shining a light in my eyes. Gosh, I had been so out of it.

I tossed my phone aside and scrubbed my face awake. Had Devlin carried me out? Imagining the hulking conductor gently carry me away sent a thrill through me. Next to me, the curtains were drawn on a large window. I looked down to discover I was in a set of comfortable cotton pajamas over the bra and underwear from last night. I remembered changing now, too. I let loose a long sigh and calmed myself down.

My stomach rumbled, and after making use of the attached bathroom, I dug into breakfast with no qualms. Maybe it was because I had grown accustomed to most of my choices being made for me. Maybe it was because I'd woken up in far worse rooms without any clue as to where I was. And this was certainly better than a hospital bed. Or maybe it was just knowing that

Devlin was here. The Devil of the Symphony clearly cared if I could perform.

I felt a thousand times better with food in my stomach. My head still pounded, but I didn't feel as awful as I thought I might today. I warred with myself over what to do next. I would have to tell Devlin my decision sooner or later, and that was a weight on my chest I couldn't shake. First, I needed to find him.

Still in my pajamas, I crept to the door and cracked it open. Soft notes of a piano greeted my ears, far away but alluring. The melody was unfamiliar. It was gentle and flowing like a trickling stream, and it sent goosebumps down my arms. The music compelled me to walk down a hallway that ended with a banister overlooking a large open space. I was on an upper level. Below was a luxurious living room with expansive windows stretching from floor to ceiling. Tall pines lined the property outside, but beyond that, a heavy fog and overcast sky blocked any further views. It gave the chilling effect of being in a dream where there was no world outside the immediate area of this house. The drifting, seductive notes only added to the surrealness of this whole situation.

The haze of sleep still clouded my brain. I debated staying there until somebody found me, but the melody was too captivating. It floated up from a wrapping staircase off to my left. I followed the notes down, wondering on some level if I was still asleep. Once I reached the main level, I caught a glimpse of a gleaming gourmet kitchen branching off behind the stairs. To the right, a massive dining room bled into the living room I had just been looking down upon.

The music was closer, but still came from another floor below. I would need to descend farther into the foreign house.

A door tucked away past the modern chef's kitchen seemed to be the source of the music. When I pushed it open, it led to yet another set of stairs leading straight down. These stairs were not plush carpet like the set I had already descended; they were wooden and narrow. The air was cool and damp and smelled faintly of earth. My feet carried me forward before I could fully process how odd this all was. Or maybe I understood the weirdness, but I couldn't stop now.

My only goal was to get closer. I had to find the source of that song. The melody had transformed, coaxing me onward with a staccato beat. Each step seemed to fall in time with the short, loud notes. Cement cooled my feet when I reached the bottom.

Dim light illuminated a long hallway that stretched farther than it had seemed when I'd first descended. The few side doors branching off were locked—I checked. I was being led, called by something that tugged on my chest. Rational thought remained upstairs; now I was driven solely by instinct. Maybe I should have been scared, but I simply wasn't.

The hall ended with a heavy metal door. Just on the other side, the music rang clearly. I went in.

It was unlike anything I'd ever seen, greater than any rehearsal space. Cavernous and huge. Guitars hung in neat lines along the walls. The ceiling and any unoccupied wall space were covered sporadically in red foam soundproofing panels. A door off to the side looked like it led to some sort of recording booth. Various instruments, some I recognized and some exotic and foreign, were showcased around the room. Thick Turkish rugs lined the floor, stacked and frayed in some spots. It was like a recording studio and rehearsal space made a glorious love child. It was the wet dream of every musician, ever.

In the center of the room, slightly raised on a platform, was a grand piano more beautiful than anything I'd never seen. Glistening black and sleek.

And there, lost to the music, was Devlin. It was a breathtaking sight. His fingers moved dramatically over the keys, seemingly without effort, his shoulders hunched.

He was totally shirtless. And honestly, from this angle I could not tell if he was wearing pants. I could see a glimpse of a definitely hairy leg and bare feet. Maybe I shouldn't have come here. Was this some weird musical-slash-sexual thing? Was I being intrusive? I should definitely leave.

Except.

His muscles. My goodness! Ropes of muscles bunched in his

back and arms. They flexed and released with every movement. I thought Thor brought the godly muscles, but Devlin could absolutely wield Mjölnir or any other massive hammer. I was intrigued and curious and really, if he didn't want to be caught naked in his super-secret music lair in the middle of the day by a guest in his house, then he should have locked the door. That's on him.

I crept closer. Okay, he was wearing jeans. And of course, as always, the bandana and hat were on. Shirt? No. That's too much commitment, but a hat and bandana … those were essentials, apparently. Today the mask was a solid red and in the dim light it was haunting. He didn't notice me come in. He was too lost to the music, which was now a dissonant, almost irritating piece that was somewhat reminiscent of Scriabin's atonal scales.

What would he do if I walked up and took off that mask? Would he be mad? Maybe I was even mad for thinking it. Would he kick me out of the symphony? Would he no longer want to work with me? Why was I suddenly so curious to see what was underneath? It wouldn't change anything, would it?

Something about the mystery of it called out to the darkest part of my soul—to the part that always got me in trouble.

I moved closer, step by step, soundless in the cacophony. Just a peek. Who was he? What was he trying to hide?

Closer yet. My hand reached out. My heart slammed in tempo with the music.

I grabbed the fabric where it hung loose.

Just a peek. What was the worst that could happen?

CHAPTER 9

PRACTICE EVERY DAY; MUSIC WAITS
FOR NO ONE.

DEVLIN

My hand shot out and grabbed hers just as her fingers grazed my neck, where the scarf was tied. The abruptly cut-off notes trembled in the air. Chills shuddered down my skin from the contact and goosebumps spread down my arms and chest.

She gasped and reared back trying to squirm out of my grip, but I didn't release her. Instead, I twisted my body on the piano bench, bringing her around at the same time so we were face-to-face. Even sitting I was almost as tall as her.

"I'm sorry! I was just—"

"What?" I demanded. "Wanted to see under this? Want to know what sort of freak wears a mask?"

"No! I wasn't … I wasn't thinking. I'm still all foggy. I'm sorry!"

I tugged her closer to me so that my face was inches from hers. She was rambling. I'd never heard her talk this much in rehearsal. She always sat quietly, watching me, glancing away any time I focused my attention on her. Her eyes were wide. Her mouth formed a perfect, horrified O shape.

"You knew exactly what you were doing," I said.

"Please. I'm sorry. I'll go." I gentled my grip but didn't let go as she carried on. "I just woke up. I'm in this big, beautiful house without any clue as to why. All while creepy music fills the house all around me. And you're just down here playing like … like a maniac from a scary movie!" She stopped her rant to press fingertips to her cheeks. "I feel hot. Do you feel hot? It's definitely hot." She tugged at the collar of the too-big pajamas I had left for her.

I placed my other hand over her mouth. A headache pulsed at the back of my skull. I had brought her here. That was my choice, yet I was embarrassed at being caught in such a vulnerable position. What if she saw the truth about me? It was too soon.

"Stop talking," I said.

Her quick breaths warmed my palm covering her mouth. Her eyes widened at the unexpected contact. Bursts of sensation shot through my body.

I glared hard enough that my annoyance would come across even with my bandana in place. I dropped her hand that had been reaching for my bandana. Holding her hand had unwanted consequences. It was best to avoid touching her at all. I released her mouth too, slowly, in case she started up again. Her full lips closed to suck in her bottom lip, actively fighting the words that wanted to spill out, no doubt.

Her skin was colorless this morning. Her dark hair was pulled back in a tight ponytail, fuzzy on the side she slept on. As I'd checked in on her throughout the night, she'd remained sound asleep in the same exact balled-up position. Her chapped lips and bleary eyes concerned me.

"Did you eat?" I asked her.

She looked at me as though this were some sort of test. After a moment, she nodded.

"And drank some water? You don't look so good."

With that, her eyes narrowed, but she held her tongue. Now that she had quieted, the lack of rambling made me feel self-conscious. I didn't like to be the one required to make conversation. It never came easy for me like it had for Wes. Her silence made me uncomfortable. Being uncomfortable made me angry.

"Are you done pawing at me?" I asked.

She nodded once. So this was the game.

"You can speak," I said.

"How kind of you."

I stood to tower over her. "At rehearsal, you rarely talk."

"I'm respectful."

Somehow, I doubted that. I saw the looks she shot the clarinetist, Erin. I crossed my arms to mirror her stance.

"Right," I said.

Her eyes kept darting to my body and after a pointed look she blurted out, "I'm not the one that's basically naked save for a mask. It's very misleading. Either be naked or put more clothes on."

"Am I bothering you?"

"No … I'm not bothered. This isn't … I don't care." With every protest her voice grew an octave higher. "A man's body. Pfft. It's whatever." Her gaze moved from my chest to my face to the ceiling to the piano and back to my chest again in a second. At least some color rose to her cheeks. Maybe that was key. Distraction from the oddness of the situation.

"You seem flustered." I stepped closer, purposely invading her space.

Even now, as she pretended to metaphorically clutch her pearls, her gaze had trouble staying still. Her tongue popped out to lick her lip and her swallow was audible. I flexed my pecs, a quick jump. Her eyes widened a fraction before refocusing on my face.

"I'm not flustered. A body is a body. My mother is a painter. Naked people constantly traipse through my house." She frowned as what she said sank in, like she hadn't meant exactly that. I had to admit, I was having a little fun now.

"Hmm." I stepped closer. My voice rumbled lower. "You're totally comfortable?"

"Yup. Mm-hm." Her focus returned to the ceiling.

I leaned lower. She smelled amazing for having just woken up;

like a sun-warmed blanket on a summer picnic.

"And now?" I asked lowering my voice to a growl.

"Well, I mean, typically my personal space isn't violated like you're doing."

I bit back a smile. This was more like it. "Are you saying you feel uncomfortable with me getting too close?"

"I'm not intimidated by rock hard abs and imposing biceps."

"Clearly."

She lifted her chin and poked my pec. Like a pebble thrown against a rock face, I didn't react. "You don't scare me," she whispered.

"I should."

"You think because you grumble and wear a mask that you can intimidate me?"

"No." I stopped my tactic and used my work voice. "But as your Maestro and composer, you should show some respect." Her jaw swayed in the wind, so I kept talking. "And how would you like it if I came up to you and tried to take off your shirt?"

"That's hardly the same," she said with haughty disdain.

"It's not?"

"No, you're half naked and—" A blush burned her cheeks as she spoke.

"Because I'm not fully dressed, I deserve your unwanted touches?"

As soon as the words processed, her face drained off color and her shoulders slumped. Okay, maybe I'd gone too far, but I had a point to prove.

"No, I would never blame … I wasn't trying—"

"I know you weren't," I said to take away some of the pain I inflicted.

Her brows drew together in seriousness. She took a deep breath as she stepped back. The cool air rushed in between us, immediately leaving me surprisingly cold.

"I'm sorry." Her focus shifted to the floor. "You're right. I apologize, Maestro."

The words cut as they'd intended to. I had gone too far. I was still learning the balance of authority without hurting people. Typically, I failed. This was why face-to-face conversations were troublesome.

"You can call me Devlin." I glanced to the side. I didn't want animosity between us. I only wanted boundaries. "While we're here. Away from everyone at work."

"Okay. Why do you call me Kim?"

I knew what she was really asking—how I knew her as Kim and not Christine—but I played dumb. "Tell me what I should call you."

She hesitated. "Christine is fine." She lifted her hands to smooth her ponytail. "Or Kim. It doesn't matter. I answer to both. But honestly, whatever. You pick." She laughed nervously.

"What do you prefer?" I asked.

"Oh, I don't care."

"Pick one." Her indecisiveness was frustrating. If she was going to help me, she had to learn to stand up to me. I stepped closer.

She stepped back. "It's not a big deal."

"Kim or Christine?" Closer.

Back. "Fine. Kim. Kim is good."

"Wasn't that hard, was it?"

But it was for her. Her chest heaved up and down and the exposed skin at her neck was splotchy with stress. The same as it had been when she had performed her solo. Even her eyes were glossy. I'd gone too far once again. I felt like a jackass. I had only been trying to get her to push *me* back.

"I'm sorry—" I stepped forward to comfort her.

The action had her lurching back again, but she had reached the end of the short platform. Her heel was off the edge. Her arms windmilled for purchase where there was none. In slow motion, she started to fall backward. I reached out as her arms shot forward to wrap around my neck. Our bodies slammed together. You couldn't slide a piece of paper between us.

"Oh dear!" Her hands shot to her mouth, causing her to fall back again. I had to twist with her in my arms to keep us both from losing purchase. Her face buried into my chest to hide. I thought her humiliation was the reason, but after a second, her shoulders began to shake and it seemed alarmingly like …

"Are you laughing?" I asked, with skin still searing from our contact.

"I'm sorry." She choked out a laugh-snort.

"You *are* laughing." The sweet sound instantly soothed me. I found my own smile start to grow.

"I don't mean to be. It's just so inappropriate. I molested you. How am I supposed to ever look at you in rehearsal?"

"You're laughing harder." I wondered if she could hear my matching smile.

Her whole body shook in my arms and started to crumple forward.

"I'm sorry—I'm nervous. This is me freaking out."

"You're an odd duck," I said softly.

"Said the man in the mask." She laughed harder. "God, I shouldn't have said that. I'm sorry. I don't know what's happening."

She fell so that she was crouched, almost hugging her knees, and I was forced to let go of her. I carefully pushed her back from the edge of the platform. I knelt down to see her bright cheeks unsuccessfully hidden behind her hands.

"Are you going to be okay?" I asked in a teasing tone.

"I'll survive somehow." Her voice was muffled. She looked up and dropped her hands, revealing a dazzling smile. The air was sucked out of my chest. I blinked away and rocked back to give her space.

There was an assumed reputation with conductors. Especially younger male conductors. We flew all over the world depending on where our agents got us the best positions, and we were known for "cellos in different codes," as it were. I, however, had a strict and relentless no-physical-relationships policy. No relationships, period. The mask was not only to protect myself, but also to keep a very specific barrier between myself and those who played for me.

"Okay." She gained her composure with a deep breath. "Maybe we should talk about why I'm here."

CHAPTER 10

IF YOU TRIP THROUGH AN ENTRANCE, GET THE HELL BACK UP.

KIM

At first, I thought maybe the weird exhaustion from the night before was to blame for my odd actions. Now I'd clearly lost my damn mind. Devlin had always intimidated me. More than anybody I had ever worked with or for. But he'd never scared me. I knew that was what he wanted with the mask and the cranky-pants temper, but all it did was make me want to get to know him more. He was a puzzle that needed to be solved. Sadly, my attempt to not show fear while simultaneously being completely embarrassed and confused came out as nervous laughter. I was officially a hot mess.

Maestro.

He had reminded me. There was a dynamic. And not a kinky, fantasy role-playing sex dynamic. Gah! Why did I even make that analogy? Okay. Focus. No more fumbling, just answers.

"Have you made your decision?" he asked avoiding my own question.

"No. Not yet."

He blinked at me. It was really hard to read someone's emotions when they only showed a quarter of their face. It was either squinty eyes or wide eyes. That being said, weren't the eyes supposed to be the windows to the soul? In Devlin's case, his window was closed. Or winterized. No. These windows were covered in blackout curtains. Okay, I needed to stop making analogies.

Thankfully, the mask faux pas seemed to have been forgotten. His words weren't so terse. Why was he wearing that damn mask? Why was I so drawn to it? Why was I so desperate to take it off? I had always been at the mercy of my curiosity. *No. Focus. Maestro could fire me. Be a good cellist.*

"I was hoping to discuss what you had in mind," I said but with a rise at the end, like it was more of a question. "Do I need to call for a ride home? Do you want to put on a shirt?"

I like to think I saw the smallest hint of a smile in his eyes with that one.

"No," he stated blankly. "You're staying here."

"What?" I asked. Maybe I was still dreaming.

"Today will be a trial run. To help you decide. As you were supposed to do yesterday."

"Oh." That was a fair offer. But I barely made it through the last five minutes unscathed. How would I handle almost a full day of his undivided attention? The thought of having to make a choice, having to decide right there and then, caused panic to cramp my insides. I couldn't just decide. I just woke up. I was still half asleep. There was nothing I could do except stall.

"I need to check my schedule." Though I already knew it. It was Saturday, so swim, practice, and a free afternoon, which on this Saturday happened to include a SWS meeting.

"Your schedule was cleared." His gaze flicked to the side then back to me.

I was beginning to feel the smallest hint of irritation. For many years, I'd let my parents and therapists make my choices for me. I'd grown to rely on it. But here was a new person in my life that was deciding things for me. The choice to accept his offer was mine. Even though it caused me panic, it was mine.

"I don't remember okaying that," I said.

"You were there." He cleared his throat and his hands started to ball. His own irritation was obviously growing. But what right did he have to be annoyed when I was the one whose life had to change?

"Were my eyes open? Was I snoring? Was a tiny dribble of drool leaking from my mouth? Because those are all strong indications that I was, in fact, not capable of making a decision."

His eyebrows furrowed. "It's one day."

I muttered. "What about my SWS meeting? That was supposed to be at three. At my house."

"What organization is that?" Again, his gaze flicked to the side, avoiding me. Almost like he felt guilt. "I didn't know about that."

I sucked my teeth as I thought. "Mm, it's a book club of sorts. But more than that."

I propped my hands on my hips. I wasn't exactly sure how to explain that we were all Jethro Winston's exes and we got together to drink and talk shit about him as an excuse to try different activities. It was harmless fun, but admittedly, from the outside some saw us as a bunch of bitter rejects.

Devlin wiped his palms down his jeans as he stood. "I'll take you home. I thought that—"

"Wait." I stepped closer to him. I wasn't sure what changed my mind. Maybe it was the flash of hurt that crossed his eyes. "I just need more time to decide. I'll have a cup of coffee and think, okay? We will practice today, and I'll decide?"

His glare returned. His shoulders bunched. "What's to decide? Other qualified people would love this opportunity."

"It's a big decision. It'll take time, commitment. I just need to think." I was bristling too. "If other people are better suited, then why do you want me?" It was the question that had been burned into my mind since the beginning. Why me? Carla was far more qualified that I was. Or even Barry. I would have thought it was the solo that sold him, but that happened after he approached my parents. None of this made any sense.

"I didn't say you weren't good enough." He shifted his weight from foot to foot. "You just lack practice. Hence the request for additional practice on the weekends."

"Gee, thanks."

"It won't be every weekend. We can break if we have a performance or a holiday, but we only have eight full weekends remaining. My house is large enough to accommodate you if that's the issue. My staff as well."

My eyebrows shot up involuntarily. I hadn't seen any evidence of anybody else. My parents were wealthy. I knew all too well that I grew up with privileges that few people enjoyed. But we didn't have staff. Was I in a Turkish soap opera?

"You have staff?" I asked.

"Yes."

"Wow, conducting pays. Who knew?" I shook my head. "Okay, so." I cleared my head and got back down to business. "Hypothetically, the plan going forward would be I come here on the weekends?"

"Saturday and Sunday mornings. As the schedule allows."

That was a lot of time to spend with him. I'd have to learn to keep my curiosity locked down. I still had so many questions, but Devlin didn't seem like he was going to answer them. He was so closed off. I needed answers, but I only got anger or deflection when I pushed.

"And then by September, you think you'll have finished the *Smokey Mountain Suite*? How do I help?" I asked.

"I'm stuck on the cello solo in the second movement."

I waited for him to explain more but that didn't happen. "You just need someone to play it?"

He hesitated but after a moment said, "Yes. I'll need you to play through it so I can make tweaks. But it's more than that. This composition is my crowning achievement. It will put me in the same league with the biggest contemporary composers. It will ensure I have a career no matter where I go. It will—" He scratched under his mask. "It's very important."

"Great," I said. "So no pressure."

CHAPTER 11

KEEP YOUR CELLO WHERE YOU CAN SEE
IT. BE READY TO PRACTICE AT ANY
TIME.

DEVLIN

"*L*et's get started," I said.

Kim had been digging for information on why I chose her. I couldn't tell her all that just yet. She needed time. She held so much back; I had to be able to show her through the music, and then she would understand everything. I needed time to play with her, to remind her of her own skills. Only then I would reveal our history.

Her eyes widened. "Right now? I don't have my cello."

"I brought it with us last night." I pointed to her purple sparkly hardcase that was tucked safely in the corner. As much as the minivan had been an eyesore, the automatic pop up trunk had been mighty convenient. But I would be taking that bit of information to my grave.

She smiled and said softly, "Looks like you've thought of every-thing." Her gaze then moved down to her pajamas. "Can I have some coffee? Maybe wake up fully and process?"

"There's some in the kitchen. I don't have any other clothes to offer you except for what you wore last night. Or my own."

She swallowed. "I can change into what I wore last night."

"You have ten minutes, and then we start." It helped me focus to assume the role as conductor.

"Very good idea, Maestro." She smiled cheekily at me, ignoring my instructions. "We should both put on clothes first."

My scarf hid the smile she coaxed out of me. Maybe I wouldn't get dressed just to mess with her. But no. This was business, and though it did seem like September was a long way off, I was anxious to get started.

"Like that would stop you from undressing me with your eyes." The joke slipped out. Or at least I hoped she'd see it as a joke.

Thankfully, she chewed her cheek to keep from smiling. "I don't suppose you could show me where the kitchen is? Or how to get out of this room even? I feel like I walked a mile to get here."

"This room is far underground. It stays cool year-round that way, which protects the instruments." I could go into the acoustics and sound proofing as well, or how it had taken me years of fighting for approval from the Green Valley council to build it. I needed a place to always come home to—a sanctuary—and this was it. It was something I was extraordinarily fond of. I wished I could have seen her face upon walking in here.

"Let's go." I held her arm and led her down from the platform without thought. So much for my short-lived vow to not touch her.

Twenty minutes later, not ten, she all but skipped happily back into the room. I had gotten dressed after all and she was in her clothes from last night. She had a surprising amount of pep. She smelled faintly of wintergreen and her hair was no longer ruffled. The haziness in her eyes had been replaced with intense focus. Again, this was not the Christine of the performance space. She sat in the chair where I had set up her stand and music, but had left her cello in its case. Unpacking that felt too personal.

She unsnapped her case and set up her instrument, and as she did, she slipped back into the professional persona that I was most familiar with. Her posture went rigid and her face smoothed with cool focus. Once her bow was tightened and she sat in a ready position, I struck a note on the piano and she tuned her instrument to it. All this was done with the unspoken comfort of people familiar with each other.

"I'll play through what I have written."

I flexed my fingers, feeling a slight rush of nerves. I began to play for her. Obviously, it was not the full symphonic arrangement; just the piano sonata so we could rehearse together. It was a little rough around the edges still and I wasn't happy with the third movement. It felt lacking. That was where her solo would be, and while I knew I was close, I wasn't there yet. As I played, I shot glances at her to gauge her reaction. Artists had fragile egos that bruised easily. She held her bow, slack in one hand, leaning forward to rest her chin on her instrument as she listened. With every glance, I noticed her gaze growing more distant. Eventually she closed her eyes and subtly rocked to the melody as though it couldn't be helped.

By the time I played the last note she sighed wistfully. "That's beautiful."

It took her a minute to come back into her head, I could see the moment she did. She blinked rapidly and sat up straighter. "Just lovely."

I cleared my throat. "Let's start at page eight, where your solo, I mean the cello solo, begins." I glanced over to see if she'd caught my error, but she was busy flipping the pages of her music. "The intro is pretty standard."

She waited for my cue, then began. We played like this for a few hours. Every once in a while, I'd stop her to listen to me play a specific part at half tempo until she could get it correctly. When the muscles in my neck protested from constantly looking at her and her cheeks grew pale, I stood.

"Let's break for lunch," I said.

Kim quietly set her cello down on its side. She had performed adequately but stiffly, like in rehearsals. As I feared, her performance skills had rusted over and she had formed bad habits that would need to be broken in order to be reset.

Only after standing to stretch my neck side to side did I notice she was unnervingly quiet. And in fact, upon replaying the last few hours in my head, I could not remember the last time she bit out a snarky comment. Her eyes were low and focused on the task of loosening the hair of her bow. She would not meet my face.

She sniffed and I reared back. Was—was she crying? Why?

"No," I said, short and unexpected as a gasp of surprise. She shouldn't cry. She should never cry.

"I can't do this," she said quietly, still not lifting her head.

"Do what, exactly?"

"This. All of this. I'm not to this level." She gestured to the cello. When she finally brought her face up, her eyes were glossy and her pale skin grew splotchy. Her attention was focused behind my head, not looking directly at me. "I don't understand why you asked me to do this."

"Don't cry," I snapped. "We've only just started."

"I'm not crying." She shot back, her bottom lip jutting out and quivering. "If it seems like that it's only because I'm angry and my stupid face makes me look like I'm crying." She sniffed.

I didn't like that she called her face stupid. I didn't like that she was acting like this. "Where did this come from?"

"I'm humiliated. I'm not at this level." She took a deep breath in. "Did you bring me down here just to show me all of my shortcomings? To remind me that I'm a second rate professional?"

"I would never do that." Inexplicably, my heart started slamming against my chest, rattling me like a gong. I could handle ego and temper tantrums, but I couldn't handle Kim's self-doubt. I didn't recognize this person. I stood, aware that my hands had fisted at my sides.

"Just explain it to me then. This isn't an attempt to fish for compliments. I genuinely do not understand why I'm here."

My heart was now racing at climactic tempo, slightly erratic and running away. I couldn't hold her gaze.

"I don't pretend that I'm not talented. But Maestro, you have to see that I'm not the best for this."

"This is why you practice," I growled the words.

She gripped her bow brandishing it like a knife. "Why not Carla or Barry? Why not audition people for this? There are thousands more talented than me."

"You're right," I agreed.

Her nostrils flared even as the rest of her face started to crumple in dismay. How did I communicate this to her? With every second she questioned me, my panic grew.

She took a deep breath and held my gaze. "I can see that you're frustrated with me," she said. "But getting angry isn't helping me understand. I hate that I sound so unsure of myself. There was a time —" She shook her head. "But you have to give me something more to understand."

She was humiliated. I was too, but she didn't see that. She only saw the anger. I needed her. My heart hammered. I had to give her something. I couldn't risk her saying no. Rejection from her of all people might break me.

"It's not always about talent. It's about potential." I began tentatively, trying to explain some without giving too much away. "You're dedicated. You're punctual. You're available." These were all facts that were true, but they weren't selling her. The trepidation was still there in her quivering lip. I lifted her chin, touching her again before realizing it. "Some people have a spark in them. I've heard you practicing at night when you think nobody can hear you. You have that talent, but more importantly, you have passion."

Her eyes widened.

I went on, "There is something locked inside of you that is desperate to be free. When I heard you play ..." I swallowed down the fear in my dry throat. "You inspired me—my music. That's why I need your help."

Her mouth closed as she processed. My heart raced as though I'd confessed all my sins. Her head just shook like she wasn't sure of any of it.

I swallowed. Go big or go home ... alone. "I can't do it without you. I need you. I've tried and failed on my own. I'm stuck. This is my last chance." The confession sent me into a tailspin. If she walked away now, after I admitted all this to her, where would that leave me? I regretted saying so much. I should have just forced her to do it.

But then her features smoothed and she nodded. It was just like the night of the solo, when she understood that she was doing it to help and not to take. "You need me to help you. This is for your success. I understand that now."

CHAPTER 12

FEEL THE COMPOSER'S MEANING.

KIM

*D*evlin needed my help. The choice was mine. After he'd admitted to watching me play, I'd left the room under the guise of needing a break and come back to the guest room to think. I was too floored to process. Well, let the processing commence. If I was alone and at home, I'd change into my softest sweatpants, make a cup of tea, and binge-watch crappy TV. But no. There were no distractions to aid in avoiding the thoughts and fears that caused a downward spiral of self-doubt and panic.

I was curled in a ball on the window seat watching the heavy rain fall outside. It had been an exceptionally cold and rainy start to spring. The dreary weather only added to my melancholic state. All that was missing was Adele to sing along to, and my self-indulgent pity party would be complete.

I inspired him. Those words were on a loop in my head.

It would be easier if he demanded from me. If he told me I had to do it and pointed out everything on the line. I wanted the Devil of the Symphony as he presented himself; demanding and sure of everything. He seemed convinced that I was the key to his success, and more alarming than that, vulnerable to my rejection.

I longed for the safety of home and my strict schedule.

My phone buzzed with a text. I jumped at the sight of Devlin's name popping up. It was still so weird to get messages from him. A tiny frission of something happened in my body.

"Lunch is ready."

I blew out a long breath through pursed lips and tossed the phone to the side. I wasn't ready to see him. But I was super hungry. My stomach grumbled and I acquiesced. I dramatically rolled off the window seat and shuffled to the door. If nothing else, eating always helped motivate me.

I kept my ears perked for sounds from Devlin as I made my way down to the dining room table. My jaw dropped. Heavy wooden blocks were stacked high with several types of olives. Hard and soft cheeses with waxed edges had been laid next to fat, dark purple grapes and little green ones. Almonds, cashews, and Brazil nuts piled in small mounds were tucked between decadent chunks of dark chocolate topped with flecks of sea salt. Slices of fatty hard salami and prosciutto were splayed next to whole grain round crackers. It was a Caravaggio painting come to life with rich colors, abundant textures, and enticing smells. My eyes could hardly register all the treats spread before me.

My stomach growled loudly in approval.

Next to a stack of plates were three silver buckets of ice with bottles in them at the end of the table, along with toothpicks and napkins. I was happy to find a sparkling cider that I could drink. The rosé I would avoid. Geez Louise, how many people were joining us?

My phone buzzed again. Devlin. What did it mean that a little spike of something flooded me when I saw his name?

"I have work and won't be able to join you."

Yes, I had just been distressed at the idea of seeing him again, but truth be told, his message evoked a small pang of disappointment. I was alone a lot. My parents were so close and their love for each other so strong that I had always felt like a third wheel. Well, at least I was excellent company.

I still had the phone clutched to my chest when it vibrated again.

"Enjoy." The follow up text said.

"Thank you. The food looks amazing," I sent.

The message showed as read but a second later my phone was forgotten.

"Hello? Hope it's okay we just let ourselves in—Holy cannoli!"

I spun around at the exclamation to see Gretchen LaRoe, looking as fabulous as ever, standing in the doorway. She nodded with approval at the food piled high behind me as she shrugged out of a floral print raincoat and hung it up on a hook.

"Gretchen?" I ran to meet her at the door, tears almost immediately filling my eyes. I didn't even realize how badly I'd wanted company until she'd arrived. I squeezed her so hard she wheezed.

"Okay, okay. Girl, I need to breathe."

I loosened my grip but I didn't let go. "What are you doing here?" I looked up to her face, situated above her ample cleavage. My chin quivered, giving me away. Her cat-eye black liner was perfect, and her flaming red hair was styled in its typical boho-retro chic. Whereas I looked I'd jumped out of bed to wrangle a rooster— and lost.

"We heard there was a last-minute move of the SWS meeting." Her smile melted as her gaze moved over my face. "Are you crying?"

I shook my head. "We?" Hope filled my chest and I let her go.

On cue, Suzie Samuels, Blithe Tanner, and Roxy Kincaid filed into the room wearing bewildered looks.

I ran to each of them and squeezed them until their backs popped. Even Suzie, who was the newest member of the SWS and who I had only met one other time. I didn't care. I needed all the hugs today. Each hug was welcomed warmly. When I was finally done, I wiped my eyes with a sniffle. I was a sap; I owned it.

"Here." Gretchen pushed a duffle bag into my arms.

"What's this?" I asked.

"Provisions," she explained. "We thought maybe you were in danger, but I see we were way off base."

Suzie's dark hair was styled in a sleek bob with the left side shaved close to her head. Her eyes were wide as she took in the massive living room with floor-to-ceiling windows. "This place …"

Suzie's mouth hung open, her head swiveling to take in the room. With the massive windows and trendy—and no doubt expensive— interior design, this was no average home, to be sure.

"When you hear 'cabin in the woods' you think chainsaw-wielding serial killers and half-naked teenagers. This is …" Suzie trailed off.

"Unreal," Blithe finished for her. Her long, pale, blonde hair fell straight down her back. She stared at the ceiling before shaking her head and turning to the buffet. She squeaked in excitement when she found the rosé and began opening it.

"This place is insane. I equally want to rescue you and knock you out to take your place." Gretchen moved toward the table of food and we all followed. "I could totally learn the violin."

"Cello," I corrected.

"Listen, I'd learn the fracking harp to stay here."

I set the bag on the floor and knelt to rummage through it. As hungry as I was, I was desperate for comfortable clothes. Starched pants were fine for a performance but there was no give to the waist-line, and I was about to eat my weight in cheese and crackers.

I almost cried again, tears of relief this time, when I spotted my favorite pair of yoga pants (which were, incidentally, never worn for yoga).

"Thank you so much guys. Oh yes, you got my favorite moisturizer too! You're everything a girl could ask for." I held up a cotton T-shirt that said, "Baby got Bach" and rubbed my face into it like the Snuggle bear. "Mmm." It smelled like home and comfort and lazy days. Another outfit, a better bra, thank God, and—

"What's with the baseball bat?" I lifted out a heavy Louisville Slugger.

Gretchen winked with a knowing nod. "I gotchu, boo."

"We've been concerned," Roxy added. As always, she was dressed in all black, including heavy black eye liner and a leather coat covering her tattoos. She had been the last to leave the Wraiths and the life that came with Jethro Winston. She was the sharpest-edged but easily the most fragile of all of us. "We heard there was weirdness last night after your concert and suddenly you're off the map and this random number is texting us. I don't like this shit."

"Someone texted you?" I asked, placing the bat back into the bag and taking out a fresh outfit.

"The number was unknown but mentioned the meeting with a time and address. We figured we'd check it out," Suzie said.

Blithe grinned as she grabbed a batch of grapes. Her almost-see-through eyelashes fluttered with excitement. "We were stoked that you were being assertive and taking the lead for the next meeting."

I shook my head. "It wasn't me."

"That's what I said." Roxy made a told-you-so face at Gretchen, her dark rimmed eyes squinting at her. "Didn't sound like you. You're never that decisive."

"That feels sort of judgey," I said.

"I didn't mean it that way. You're very go-with-the-flow. It's a compliment," Roxy amended.

The words were out there though, stuck in my mind like burrs in socks where I'd be picking at them hours from now. I didn't think I was indecisive. Was I? I was careful. Was that how they saw me?

"Anyway, we knew there was a risk because it was all very cloak and dagger. We all came together just to be safe." This from Suzie. "Anybody that chooses to mess with us gals is planning their own funeral."

"And I have reinforcements in the car." Gretchen made the shape of a gun with her fingers.

"Where they will stay," Blithe said pointedly.

I smiled and warmth spread through me again. No time for over-thinking. I was so happy to see these ladies and have some non-music time. No ruining it by being a grumpy Gretchen. Plus, we already had a Gretchen. I couldn't believe Devlin would do this. I had only mentioned the SWS meeting a few hours ago, and he had somehow managed all this.

"This is Devlin's house," I explained.

"The Devil of the Symphony," Blithe gasped.

"Your conductor?" Gretchen raised an eyebrow.

The girls all looked at each other like this information made no sense. To be fair, this information made no sense.

"Okay, you have got to tell us what is going on." Blithe sipped some pink wine and did a shoulder shimmy of happiness.

"Of course," I said. "But first, stretchy pants."

* * *

I walked in to find the girls had created a pile of blankets and pillows in front of the massive fireplace that was the centerpiece of the luxurious room. I filled up a plate with a little bit of everything I could fit on it.

"Okay, so if a dolphin is such a lame choice, what animal would you be?" Blithe snapped.

"A shark, obviously," Gretchen said without delay. "Everybody knows sharks are awesome."

Roxy rolled her eyes at their antics but spoke to me as I joined them on the floor. "This place is beautiful."

"I know," I said. This place was so big and beautiful. It was a shame he lived here all alone. "You should see Devlin's studio in the basement."

"What's his last name, anyhow?" Suzie asked.

"No last name. It's a stage name. Like Madonna." Gretchen sniffed the cheese in her hand before taking a nibble. "I looked into him when he started at the SOOK but there wasn't much. He just sort of appeared on the classical music scene a few years back."

I thought about that. I would have to ask him his real name. Sure, and then he would just take off his mask and reveal all his secrets to me.

"Okay, now that we are full and more agreeable. Spill it," Roxy demanded.

In as succinct a manner as I could, I replayed the events of the previous night, and a little before. I started with Devlin showing up at my house unexpectedly, then Carla's sudden absence, the solo (pause for *woot-woot*s of appreciation), Roddy showing up, and then finally waking up here.

By the time I was done talking, I think an hour had passed and the wine was gone. I sipped my cider and eyed them over the rim as they took in my story.

Gretchen, of course, was the first to speak. "I can't believe love note guy is back."

I winced. I had sort of been hoping to keep that part out of the story. But when you only have two exes, and one is Jethro Winston —who obviously wasn't the one dropping love notes—it wasn't a surprise that she made the connection.

"Dang it, I hate being new. Who's the love note guy? What's that about?" Suzie's cheeks were flushed, making her emerald eyes sparkle.

Roxy set her empty glass on the granite hearth in front of the fireplace and pulled a blanket to her chin. She yawned sleepily around her sentence. "It's not just you. I don't know who he is either."

"You tell it, Kim. It starts like this, 'This one time, at band camp …'" Blithe giggled at her own joke and rested her head on the pillow next to Roxy. With Blithe's pale coloring and Roxy's edgy-dark look, they were like a yin-yang.

The room had grown warm from the fire despite the chilling winds whistling outside. Our full bellies gave us all a lethargic peace, melting our limbs into wherever the nearest pillow was. I scanned the girls and couldn't help my contented smile.

"To start, they weren't love notes. Some were even harsh criticisms, actually. Also, I will have you know it was an orchestra camp—far less phallic-shaped instruments," I said. "More F-holes, though. And wood." We all laughed. "My parents basically sent me every summer growing up. Camp Hickory was for the kids of senators and super-fancy old-money types. It was tough to get into. People came from all over the world," I explained. "You still had to apply, and some really successful people came out of it too."

"Ohh, like who?" Suzie used the back of her hand to stifle a yawn. "Anybody I know?"

"Well, like Francesca Belia and Karl Norman." I threw out the names of some of the biggest up and coming classical musicians only to receive blank stares.

"Oh, and YouTube boy … Gah, what was his name? You had the biggest crush on him," Gretchen ratted me out. Again.

I scrunched up my face. I had really been hoping she'd forgotten about that.

"Who?" Blithe tilted her head in thought.

"You know, the one. He had that huge song and then fell off the map," Gretchen said. "'*Thoughts of you, my soul on fire,*' uh, something, something, '*I look at you, but*

you—'"

"'*You're looking at him …*'" All five of us sang the rest of the chorus.

"'*Can't Look Back*?' Oh, I loved that song!" Roxy burst out excitedly before calming herself. "Not that I would ever admit it," she added flatly. She reached for her phone. The white glow from the screen illuminated her face. "'Erik Jones had a U.S. number one hit for ten weeks,' blah blah, 'Trouble with manager.' Hasn't been heard of since." She lowered her phone. "I totally remember that guy. He was so hot."

"Did you know him?" Suzie asked me.

"Oh, gosh no. He was older—a counselor by the time I went. Then he got so huge. He was already on his way to being somebody, but after that song happened, he exploded."

"Crazy," Blithe said.

"You were obsessed with that song."

"Oh my God. Shut up, Gretchen." Heat flooded my cheeks. "No more booze for you."

"Come on, it's adorable. You would listen to it all the time back then."

Truthfully, I still did from time to time.

"First of all, he was only eighteen when that song came out, but he was super talented. He was a musical virtuoso at camp. Also, we aren't talking about this. When will you let my embarrassing tween obsession die?"

Not tween—teen. And if I was being honest, I'd still probably squeal and flap my hands with big sloppy tears if he held a concert.

"Never. I will never let that die. That's what friends do. They keep you humble by rehashing your most embarrassing memories. Preferably at the absolute worst times." Gretchen blew me a kiss.

I tilted my head with a wry smile. "Gee, thanks."

"Will someone play the song before I lose my clucking mind? Otherwise, it'll be stuck in my head all week." Suzie's voice got higher with impatience.

"I haven't heard this in forever," Roxy said as music from her phone filled the air.

As though we'd rehearsed it, we all started singing the chorus and throwing our arms out. "'*But you, you're looking at him.*'"

Instantly, I was filled with a soothing reassurance that only thinking of your most adolescent feelings can resurrect; when everything felt so bright and shiny and possible. It was hokey and angsty—everything a sixteen-year-old girl needed. We all had that song that lifted us in our darkest mood. That song will forever remind me of the happy times before camp ended the way it did.

"It's all very dramatic," Roxy said over the song.

"Oh, you love it." Blithe poked her shoulder.

When the music stopped, I had hoped the previous topic would have been abandoned. Not likely with Gretchen around.

"Okay, the notes. Explain." Like a hound dog on scent, that one.

"Fine." I made a face at her. "Roddy was first chair violin and basically the quarterback of the symphony."

"Hch. Nerds."

I shook my head at Gretchen.

"He was very popular—everyone loved him. They were drawn to him, really. He'd play Oasis on his guitar at night around the campfire and we'd all swoon. He was just inherently cool, you know? When we started hanging out, I felt like somebody. It was just in the summers, and totally innocent. Though I did get to second base with him once on a boat." I wiggled my eyebrows saucily.

I kept my tone light, leaving out the memories I preferred not to think about. I never talked about the dark side of my last summer there. I didn't want to be the one that still felt broken.

"Summer love," Roxy said dryly.

"What about the notes then?" Suzie asked.

"Oh. All the time, he left me these notes about my playing in my cello case."

Gretchen had gone a whole two minutes without talking so she felt the need to say, "She still has them. They're mean."

"They were helpful," I corrected. "He was the only one who didn't suck up to me or treat me like this delicate flower. I liked it."

"She was obsessed."

I had a shoebox with all of them still in my closet. It would be a toss-up between that box and my cello if the house caught on fire and I could only save one. Honestly, the cello could be replaced. Those notes though? They got me through the worst times. Through rehab. I knew it was silly. I knew I was a romantic, but there was something about always knowing somebody believed in me that gave me strength.

"So romantic," Blithe said on a yawn. "And now he's back."

"He said he wants to get to know me again," I explained.

"Is that what you want?" Roxy asked.

"I think so, but I need to focus on helping Devlin first."

"I'm glad to see you doing this," Gretchen said with rare sincerity. "A little change of pace might be good."

"I know we didn't know each other until after high school. But I knew of you. You were so motivated back then. I was always so envious that you knew exactly what you wanted. I didn't even know what shampoo I liked yet." Blithe frowned at her empty glass.

I smiled but dread coiled deep in my belly. The Kim I was in high school was long gone. I hadn't been her since before Jethro and rehab. I hated sounding whiny. I was fine being where I was. I was pretty happy—mostly.

"I'm just glad that you're safe," Suzie said.

Suzie had been taken by a violent biker gang once and, understandably, still carried that with her. I squeezed her foot. She looked up and we shared a smile.

"Me too. I mean, I guess I was taken, but platinum style," I teased.

"I had my doubts," Roxy said. "Who just whisks you off to their mansion in the mountains with a large underground crypt that was converted to a lair?"

"It was never a crypt, and it's not a lair now. It's a music room. It's amazing," I said.

"Po-tay-to, po-tah-to." Roxy flipped out a hand.

"Still, I doubt a kidnapper would invite your closest friends to hang out and eat fancy finger foods," Gretchen said. "I have more questions."

"Of course you do," I said.

"I thought we hated Devlin?" Gretchen said.

"I never said that. I said he was tough."

"And he's not anymore?" Suzie asked.

"No, no. He's still prickly." His tough guy act had always seemed so thin to me. Even when he yelled, it was like he was scared.

"But?" Roxy asked.

"But what?"

"I felt a 'but' coming," she said.

"Me too," Blithe added.

"There's a joke there that I'm not gonna touch." Gretchen picked at a cuticle.

"Okay, buuut," I dragged out the word. I debated sharing what he said about me inspiring him, but was worried it wouldn't mean the same to them out of context. "It's nice to be challenged sometimes. If that makes sense."

"Totally," Suzie said on a wistful sigh.

Gretchen threw a grape at Suzie's head. "Ugh. Nobody wants to hear from you."

"Why? What did I do?"

"You're all fresh and in love and it's a little much, to be honest." Gretchen's words were sharp, but she had been the one to push Suzie when Ford was fighting for her.

"Haters gonna hate," Suzie said.

"Taters gonna potate." Blithe nodded.

"I feel like we are talking about potatoes a lot tonight," I said.

"We are all so very classy," Suzie said. "We definitely deserve to be here."

The room filled with laughter. Having the girls here was just what the doctor ordered. I couldn't keep the smile off my face. I thought again about what Devlin shared with me earlier, and how he needed success. It wasn't just about what held me back anymore. After all, what's the worst that could happen? Me helping him wouldn't really change anything for me, but it could change everything for him. Give him what he wanted. Maybe I owed that to the universe.

"Time's up, ladies."

We all turned toward the hall where Devlin's voice boomed out of nowhere. The hallway was shadowed so it was hard to make out anything except a gray man-shaped silhouette taking up most of the doorway to the hall.

"It's getting late," he finished in a slightly softer tone.

He looked and sounded intimidating, but that was what he did. That was his whole shtick. The girls all shared equal looks of shock and awe. He stepped forward so the light from the fire illuminated his mask. He was wearing the skull one again. It was decidedly ominous in the soft light of the night with the rain falling outside.

"Holy frijoles," Gretchen muttered next to me.

After a moment I cleared my throat and slowly the girls stood and collected their things.

His gaze seared the side of my face. How long had he been

standing there listening? I was desperate to see if he was looking only at me or if he was studying any of my equally lovely friends.

"Kim, you pick the next activity," Roxy said.

"I don't care. Whatever y'all pick is fine," I said. "I just don't know what my schedule is going to be like for a while," I explained.

"Well, don't lollygag too long." Blithe hugged me. "We need updates about your beau."

"Wait, another Winston brother?" Roxy said.

"No. Beau like boyfriend. Roddy," Gretchen clarified.

"He's not my boyfriend."

"Yet." Blithe smiled sweetly.

"Thank you for coming," Devlin said stiffly.

"Thanks for having us," Suzie said. The others added to the sentiment.

"I'm happy to housesit anytime." Gretchen pulled out a business card and handed to him.

He glanced over it before sliding it in his pocket with a nod.

"I'll walk y'all out," I said on a laugh, and brushed past Devlin.

CHAPTER 13

NEVER LET THEM SEE YOUR NERVES.

DEVLIN

As the women gathered up their things, silence finally descended like a blessing. Even in my music room, twenty yards below ground, I had heard their chatter for the last few hours. Their laughs and yells leaked in as though carried through the pipes. I couldn't think, let alone focus on composing. And then that damn crap pop song ... in my house.

The room looked like a group of hobos had camped there for a weekend, not a few hours of chatty women. A whole pack of them.

Kim led the guests to the door, and chatted happily with the blonde.

"You didn't mention the mask," the blonde whispered.

I stilled in the shadow of the hallway as they retreated.

"He wears it all the time?" another asked.

"I sort of forgot about it," Kim said.

"He's a little scary."

"Isn't that the point?" the redhead shot back, loud enough to be heard. "Let us know about Roddy. I'm so happy for you. I know how much he means to you."

I didn't growl. At least, not very loudly.

Chagny. The second a star started to rise, people like him grasped the coattails and held on for dear life. The second she lost favor, he would drop her. But to play with her heart in addition to her career? That was obscene. I'd be having words with him. There were professional lines that shouldn't be crossed.

Kim shut the door quietly behind her friends. My ears rang in the heavy silence. She turned around slowly.

"Okay. I want to warn you." She lifted her head and met my eyes. She extended her arms out and took a tentative step toward me. "I'm going to hug you."

I froze. "Why?"

"As a thank you. For bringing them here. Is that ok? Are you against hugs?"

I tried to relax my body.

"Hugs are fine," I said.

She stepped closer.

"It's the being accosted that I had an issue with," I said lightly.

I worried that my teasing tone wouldn't come through, but as her eyes narrowed, a small smile teased the edge of her mouth.

"You're not going to let that go any time soon, are you?" she asked.

There was no need to answer, because as I was focused on the delicate shifts in her facial expressions, she removed any space between us.

"I'm going to hug you so hard." She said it as a threat.

Awareness shot through me with that simple taunt. Like a music box wound up, I was suddenly filled with undeniable tension and had nowhere to release it. Then her arms wrapped around me. Her head rested on my chest. I wrapped my arms tightly around her back in return.

A small surprised gasp escaped her. "Oh."

"I'm not against hugs." My chest filled with sudden tension; the drum of my heart raced to an unheard tempo.

"Good to know," she said.

How long was an acceptable time for a hug? I wasn't sure. Probably a few seconds ago. I wasn't about to let go. Nobody hugged the Devil of the Symphony. Not outside my family. This was nice. Unexpected. We should stay like this until the sun came up. She smelled a little like cider and camping. I breathed deeper. And maybe lightly of peonies. That scent, captured in a symphony, would make listeners feel the same warm comfort engulfing me now.

We broke apart slowly like the last note fading into the air.

"That was nice." Her candidness was surprising, as she normally seemed so restrained.

I would try the same thing. "It was nice."

She let out a long yawn. "That was a lovely evening. Thank you."

"You're welcome. You're not a prisoner here. We're helping each other."

But did she think that? As much as I wanted to use my power to strong-arm her into playing for me, it would never work that way. The choice had to be hers. The music had to come from her.

I'd given her the space earlier. Brought her friends over in hopes of cheering her up. Now, I faced the very real possibility that she might pass on the opportunity. But I had to let her be strong enough to let me down.

The air was heavy, thick like the bellowing notes of an oboe.

She took a deep steadying breath. "Okay. I want to help you." She filled her diaphragm a second time. "I will do it."

I didn't need to ask for clarification. We'd been having the same internal dialogue. "Are you sure?"

"Yes." Her eyes hardened with resolve.

"Okay. Good." The words fell painfully flat considering the relief that coursed through me. "I think we'll do really well together." I swallowed thickly. "But you have to really want it."

Her eyes moved around the room and she chewed her bottom lip. Then a decision was made behind those dark eyes. "I do." She focused on me. "I want it, bad."

We held each other's gaze. We were professionals. I was a

professional. But that last sentence stayed in my mind long after I took her home, haunting my thoughts as I fought to sleep.

* * *

I would not break my music stand on that trombonist's head. I would not be the devil they painted me to be. I had restraint. I was a professional.

I kicked a chair instead.

My gaze went to the first chair cellist where Carla sat once again. Kim caught my eyes. She frowned and looked quickly away. Shame crept over me. She had to see that they weren't listening to me. They weren't respecting me. I needed every note they played to be brilliant, but if the musicians didn't trust my vision, the symphony would fall flat and the critics would roast me.

They were sloppy and chatty. I didn't care if it was early Monday morning. We only had so many weeks until our first show together as a symphony. They needed to play better.

"Break for ten. And when we reconvene, I want you all to pretend that this is your career and that you give a shit."

The room was silent after my outburst. I was working on the bursts of anger. My therapist said outbursts like that would only diminish their respect for me, but I found it therapeutic—and better than violence toward the closest musician. That first chair violinist would snap like a twig if I so much as looked at him too hard. Their eyes were on me as I left the room. I didn't look at Kim when I passed. As far as I was concerned, she was Christine while we were here, and nothing had changed.

My temper was only increased when Chagny appeared outside the rehearsal room door with a bouquet of flowers and dumbass grin on his face. He stepped slightly in front of me as I left the room.

I looked pointedly at my watch then said, "Chagny."

"Aren't you being a little hard on them?" he asked with cool affability.

How much trouble would I be in with Andy-Dick if I punched

him in his smug face? I saw right through his nice clothes, styled hair, and manicured hands to the slug underneath.

"Rehearsals are closed," I said.

He grinned like my silly rules had no control over him. "I'm here to see my dear friend, Christine."

Since when? I almost spat.

"This is a rehearsal, not the Front Porch on date night."

He winked. He actually winked at me. My fists balled. I rocked my head from side to side to pop my neck as I took a cleansing breath in.

"I'll only be a minute." He clapped me on the shoulder. As if we were fucking pals. "My parents are excited for the showcase. They can't wait to see this new composer taking the world by storm."

When he was met with silence, he continued, "Just have to learn to control that temper. How's Carla doing, by the way?"

What exactly was he insinuating?

He laughed with a small shake of his head. "Great talk. As always."

Everything about him was smooth confidence. His face was relaxed, and a loose smile tugged the side of his mouth. But his words were a warning. His parents were some of the biggest donors to this symphony. He was reminding me that for all my power, they considered me to be no more than a lackey.

The urge to warn him away from Kim was right on my tongue. But he'd love that. He'd see it as a challenge. Instead, I brushed past him without another word. Let him think it was a win. Despite my short temper, I knew the long game. There was no way Kim would fall for a tool like that.

"Nice mask, by the way."

I barely heard the words before he stepped into the rehearsal room.

That pasty son-of-a-bitch. What a fine nose; it needed character. Maybe a surgical reset after I punched it into his skull.

The muscles of my neck and back were rigid. Distantly, the voices of Andy-Dick came from around the corner. They were the last thing I could possibly handle right now. Instead of heading to my office after all, I made my way up to a long-abandoned storage room on the second floor. It was my secret place nobody knew about. The small and dusty room provided a safe space.

I tugged down my mask down and threw my hat on a stack of broken chairs from the seventies. I scrubbed my hands over my face and hair. I hated this shit, but it was necessary. Breathing came freely for the first time in hours.

The punching bag in the corner took the brunt of my frustrations until my knuckles were close to bleeding and the adrenaline faded. Once my breathing quieted and my heart wasn't hammering in my ears, I stilled to listen. There was another advantage to my secret space. The venting system led directly above the rehearsal room. This was where I first heard Kim playing solo.

I moved to the register in the corner and flicked open the vent. From my position a floor above, the back of the bassists and cellists were just visible. Kim was in her seat smiling at Chagny who squatted in front of her. Her face was deep in the bouquet, inhaling. What a showy way to mark her as his in front of the whole symphony. Carla stood close to the vent talking to her father. Dick had come into the room, as I suspected he would.

"He wasn't in his office," Dick said.

His other half was discussing something with a group of musicians in the corner.

"He needed to go pout. He's such a diva." This from Carla. She pulled out an e-cigarette and took a long pull blowing the smoke into the air. They were strictly prohibited.

Her father lowered his voice. "I know you don't like him, but he'll be out soon."

I stilled. The room around me hummed as I strained to listen.

Carla rolled her eyes. "You keep saying that, but he's still here."

"He can't control himself. The donors will only allow so much brash behavior. His showcase is going to be a disaster."

"What about the chair tests? I'm first chair. Everybody knows that. I shouldn't have to audition again."

"I know. Don't worry about it. I will fix it."

The anger returned inside of me. So that was how it was going to be?

Another musician walked up. "These antics are getting a little ridiculous, aren't they?" He too pulled out an e-cig and inhaled.

My focus shifted behind them when Erin walked up to Kim just as Chagny kissed her head and made his way over to the group.

I brought my attention back to the gossips.

"He won't last, even if he pulls off the performance of a lifetime. He's not worth the trouble. My parents aren't pleased." Chagny picked up on the conversation seamlessly.

Carla raised an eyebrow. "Oh?"

"They wanted him to bring in the revenue, but he won't last. He'll burn out. His ego? The antics? The mask? It's all a little juvenile. He's a ticking time bomb."

"The rest of the symphony can't stand him," Carla added. "They're close to rioting. He treats them like children and they'll only stand for so much. He's gaining a reputation all right, but probably not the one he wants."

"Listen, I like the guy." Chagny pulled a pitying face. "But he can't maintain a career anywhere. This will be his, what? Fifth conducting position? In as many years. It's sad."

The worst part about eavesdropping was hearing ugly truths about yourself.

The clarinetist left Kim's side, and after several worried looks, she joined the gossiping group. "Be careful what you say."

Carla rolled her eyes. "Or the Devil of the Symphony will get me?"

Erin frowned. "He's our Maestro. He should be respected."

Behind the conversation, Kim was now listening, though she tried to hide it. Her profile showed a worried frown, but she didn't speak.

"Time to get back in our seats," Erin warned, looking at the screen of her phone.

"He isn't even here," Carla said. "He's off throwing a tantrum."

"You have no idea where he is. You better be mindful of what you say."

With that, I left the room. As I made my way back to the main floor, I debated as to why was Kim so intimidated by that foolish cellist. I still had a hard time accepting this quiet version of Kim. No, not Kim. Christine. The Kim I was beginning to know spoke her mind easily. Christine hid behind her instrument and played it safe. It was like she had split herself into two completely different people.

Well, I'd had enough.

I stalked into the room and cleared my throat at the podium. Carla and a few others were just getting back to their chairs.

"Chair auditions begin this week."

The room went silent. I'd show them who was in control. I'd show them what happened when they crossed me. I would keep it until the end of the season, but that didn't mean I had to make it easy on them.

I was the Devil of the Symphony.

CHAPTER 14

KEEP YOUR INSTRUMENT IN ITS CASE
WHEN NOT USING IT.

KIM

*D*evlin's house was a bit of a drive even in the light of day. Yes, I had lived in Green Valley most of my life, but I'd never really paid attention to this area of the Smokies. I had almost turned the wrong way three times. I took my time and drove about fifteen miles an hour around the sharp back roads. It didn't help that the rain was falling off and on in thick sheets and the temperature was falling rapidly. Seriously, wasn't it supposed to be spring? Devlin's house was at the top of a super steep hill with a treacherous driveway and even Mom's brand-new BMW fishtailed a bit after a particularly sharp turn. By the time the car slid into his driveway, my palms were slick with sweat.

This past week had been exhausting. I couldn't even think about the chair auditions. I'd done a thousand of them in my life, but they never stopped being terrifying. This audition had been before the Maestro and the board of directors. Thank goodness the rest of the symphony was not allowed to listen.

Tension had hung over the symphony as each musician took their chair test. Devlin's temper had only ratcheted up with every passing

97

day until there were talks of walkouts. All week, I'd come home and given cello lessons to my students. I was so exhausted by the time I ate dinner that I could barely make it to bed.

Anyway, it'd been a long week. I wanted to go home and binge watch bad TV until my brain melted. But first, I wanted to drop off my cello at Devlin's house for our lesson the following day. I had made plans with Roddy when he'd brought me flowers to meet at Daisy's Nut House the next morning and I felt weird about bringing my cello with me to the restaurant, or worse, leaving it in the car. Green Valley was mostly trustworthy but if an Iron Wraith strolled by and a ten-thousand-dollar cello was just sitting there unwatched … well, the good Lord only expects so much. And since I didn't want to have to drive all the way back to my house to get it before I met with Devlin for our first official rehearsal, well, long story long, here I was at his house.

The only other time I had been here, I had been carried in mostly unconscious. Putting it that way didn't sound fantastic. But now, having parked and stared up at the elaborate contemporary cabin without a real plan, an extreme case of nerves bubbled up. The house was really more of a small mansion. What's in between a mansion and a house? My years of playing MASH as a child had not properly equipped me to answer that. It was bigger than my parent's home, and they weren't particularly modest when they built the 4000 square-foot home so far outside of Green Valley, it was almost to Maryville.

I hurried up the fancy slate stairs that lead to a solid-cut steel door, my cello on my back blocking me somewhat from the down-pour. As I rang the doorbell, my finger slipped and didn't push the button exactly in the middle. I spent the longest ten seconds of my life debating whether I should push it again and potentially come off as an eager beaver, or just drop my ten-thousand-dollar cello and run.

Thankfully, the door pulled open before I did something stupid. Stupider? More stupid? An attractive man in his late thirties tilted his head at me.

"Hello," he said like we already knew each other. He was

dashing like Chris Pratt—circa the *Parks and Rec* years, not all ripped like in the *Jurassic Park* movies—but with darker hair and eyes. His kind eyes flitted over my face and an easy smile formed. He was handsome enough that direct eye contact was difficult. Also, there was a familiarity to him. A furious blush spread on my cheeks. This was why I needed to get out more. I was a grown woman. This was ridiculous.

"Hi," I said.

His eyes moved to the massive case I was carrying on my shoulder.

"Hi," I repeated. "I'm Christine. Well, Kim, I guess."

"You guess?" he asked with a wry smile.

"Yes." I shook my head and started over. "I'm here for Devlin."

"I gathered as much. We've met once. You probably don't remember." He stepped back, gesturing me in. "Come on in. It's getting nasty out there."

I smiled and entered the house, noticing two surprising things: the sound of voices carrying in from the kitchen, and the smell of onions and sauce. My mouth instantly watered.

The handsome man paused just inside the door.

"I'm Wes. Dev's brother."

Devlin had a brother? Why did this information come as such a shock to me? It conflicted with the image I had of him as a solitary grump that sprung from the earth and dwelled in the cold basements of buildings.

"Nice to meet you." I glanced down at my jeans and plain green T-shirt and suddenly wished I had dressed a little better. "I didn't mean to intrude. I just came to drop my cello off before our session tomorrow. He told me I could bring it by."

His smile was so easy and quick that my mind couldn't process the fact that this man shared the same DNA as Devlin. If it weren't for the same brown eyes and bushy eyebrows, I wouldn't have believed it. Though to be fair, Devlin could be a big smiler; there was no way of knowing.

"You're not intruding. It's just Friday family dinner. Please set that down—it's almost as big as you." He took the cello from my shoulder and set it gently near a hall tree.

Friday family dinner? The mind-blown emojis just kept coming.

"Well, I'll let you get back to it …" I moved to leave, but he started walking toward the kitchen, assuming I'd follow.

"You can't leave without at least saying hi. He's just fiddling down in his man cave—sorry, music room."

"I guess. Just for a minute," I mumbled.

He stopped abruptly and I almost ran into him. "Actually, can you go down and tell him that dinner is ready?"

"I don't think—"

He placed his hands on my shoulders and pushed me toward the door that lead to the stairs.

"Uh, sure. I feel like I'm imposing." I looked over my shoulder.

He was still so relaxed. "You're not. Just tell him to come up. He loses track of time and won't see if I text him."

"Okay but—"

"Great, thanks."

The door shut behind me. No way out but through, I supposed.

No music drifted on the air this time as I descended the stairs. I checked the rehearsal space with all the padding, but it was empty. None of the rooms got a response when I called out. There was a door I hadn't noticed before off the main room. Maybe some sort of recording booth?

I knocked but got no response. For the second time in ten minutes, I debated the awkwardness of knocking again or just tucking tail and bolting. Like ripping off a Band-Aid, I tried the door only to find it unlocked. I pushed it open and a plume of steamy air punched me in the face. The realization that this was in fact a bathroom sunk in as I belatedly registered that a person stood hunched over the sink, gripping the basin, head hanging. Not just any person. A painfully sexy, naked, male person.

Let me repeat that for those in the back. Naked man. Standing nakedly without clothes on his undressed figure … bare. The man who was my Maestro, and composer. YUP. That one.

Somehow, maybe by some supreme act by God or the universe, he didn't seem to notice my entrance. Or maybe time had simply stopped to give me a moment to fully appreciate the sight before me. Muscles. Muscles everywhere: big ones, little ones, fat ones, skinny ones too! They popped up in mini waves near his neck, they emphasized his flexed triceps and ripped forearms as he gripped the sink. His flanks were that of an Olympic swimmer. His bottom was so toned it could deflect bullets. My gaze travelled down his massive thighs, his calves, his bare feet. My god. Bare feet.

The leg that had been slightly raised lowered to the floor and then, fully available for my viewing pleasure ...

Whoop! Whoop! Penis alarm! This was not a drill!

Yes, I should respect his space. True, I should not make a big deal about male anatomy. But it had been a long time (pun intended) and I was hard up (more punning) and he was beautiful. I'm sorry. Not really. Typically, these things don't do it for me but the turned angle of his body highlighted the cut of his abs down to the thick black curls and fine form of his cock and balls. My God. That was a lovely penis to look at. I never thought I'd say that, but some cave-girl instinct wanted me to club him over the head and make babies with that specimen.

My gaze slowly dragged back up and the delayed realization that he was fresh from the shower sunk in. His face wasn't covered.

I've always been drawn to curiosity and danger. If I was told not to do something it was as good as telling me to do it. Maybe I'm disturbed and attracted to the taboo or macabre—like watching serial killer documentaries—but yeah, I had to see more.

My eyes shot to the mirror hoping for a peek at his face but unfortunately, the steam defeated me.

Maybe I had let in a blast of cool air that finally reached him or maybe I had squawked like a bird, but I'd been spotted. With a start, he suddenly pulled the towel that had hung loosely over his shoulders to cover his fricking face. It wasn't his modesty he protected—it was his face.

Well, I couldn't help that my eyes drifted over his shoulders and neck, now fully on display.

"Kim!" he was yelling.

Sounds filtered back into my brain.

I swallowed and found his face, the lower half still covered with the towel. His dark hair was curled and glistening; it had lines like he had just run his fingers through it. But a few stray curls fell forward. It was longer than I'd thought. I loved how the ends were wild. Every section, every scene, was a million frames per second that uploaded to my mind, memorized for mental gifs later.

"What are you doing?" he yelled again.

"Sorry! I knocked!"

"I didn't hear you!"

"I see that now!" My eyes noticed his dark little nipples surrounded by a decent smear of thick black curls matching the ones I had seen south. Was I also into body hair? All signs pointed to yes.

"Get out!"

"I'm going." I backed up.

All this felt as though it happened both over the span of a year and in a split second. My eyes drifted over him again. Not on purpose! That was probably the final straw though, because he growled and moved toward me, towel firmly in place.

"I'm going." I held up my arms. "I'm going."

But my feet weren't actually moving. He was right in front of me. His chest heaved in rage. His gaze was fiery.

That towel was awfully tiny, and he was just, like, two inches from me. My eyes—again, not my own fault—started moving down.

"Get. Out."

He reached behind me for the door handle. Now that my sight wasn't the only thing working, a clean, evergreen scent wrapped around me as his damp arm brushed mine. My other senses went from slowly waking to high alert and every nerve felt like a live wire.

I backed up enough to exit and the door slammed in my face.

I studied the wood grain for several seconds. My heart and body hummed. I was so physically aware of him now. Pieces began to slide into place. An understanding. My body felt too heavy and too light at the same time, like I'd float away save for the heat planting me in place. I was so physically attracted to him. I'd buried the feelings since he'd started under the assumption it was the kind of crush kids developed on their teachers, or like, your dad's sophisticated friends. The type of crush you get for someone you respect because of their expertise. It was totally harmless, and you were perfectly safe in liking them from afar.

This was not that.

This was a game changer. This was genuine grown-woman-on-man, full-on, insane attraction. My body wanted to slam on his body. My arms longed to pull him close, desperate to feel his weight on me. In me.

I let out a long, slow, shaky breath.

But that wasn't the only thing that had me studying the door for far too long, feet firmly planted in place. It was the other revelation that slipped in. It hadn't clicked at first. The startlingly handsome grown man in front of me didn't match the memory of the teen. I was so sidetracked by his body, my brain had stalled out temporarily. But when you spend enough time looking at someone, they're permanently implanted in your memories. Honestly, the most surprising thing about all this was that I hadn't placed those mesmerizing eyes sooner.

His beard was another distraction. Thick and full. Long enough to tug my fingers through but not scraggly in the least. It was another layer to hide the face behind it. But I saw it. And once I saw it, there was no unseeing it. The glass had shattered.

Despite his best attempts, I'd seen his face and what he'd kept hidden. I saw the truth of what he hid. I understood so much more now.

Devlin was Erik Jones.

Oh my God.

CHAPTER 15

PERFORMANCE IS VULNERABILITY.

DEVLIN

I couldn't move, immobilized by shock and horror. My body felt rigid with icy fear. It coiled in my gut, ready to bite like a viper. Had that really just happened? I glanced at the shut door. I examined my still naked body, the towel held in place over my face. Had I really chosen to cover that over my ...

"Jesus," I swore out loud.

This was not what I needed. I had tried to set boundaries and expectations with her last weekend. All tossed out the window in a matter of three seconds. And now this.

I did a double take down at my naked body. I sported a half-woody.

"Seriously?" I asked it.

It jumped in response.

Why did she have to look so pleased? The shocked "O" of her mouth. Those blushing cheeks. The greedy gaze that kept flicking back over me. My cock jumped again. I clenched my jaw and threw the superfluous towel to the floor.

Outside the door, the shadow of her feet remained.

I flicked off the exhaust fan. The fan that had blocked out her knock. I could almost feel her standing right outside the door. Somebody else might have closed their eyes and left in a hurry, maybe a dramatic squeal, but not Kim. No, she mentally ate up the real estate of my body like it was the last thing she might ever do.

I closed my eyes and rested my forehead on the door. I was rock hard now.

"Ahem," she cleared her throat and knocked.

Go away, go away.

I wasn't sure who, or what, I was talking to at this point.

"Um, Devlin?"

I let out a long slow breath. "Yes?"

"I just want to apologize." Her tone was far more composed than how I felt.

"Okay."

"I did knock. And I didn't mean to barge in. Down here or on your family dinner. I was just dropping off my cello, like we discussed. I was about to leave but then your brother sent me down—"

Brothers were overrated. I was going to murder Wes.

"But he said I should tell you that dinner was ready. Oh, yeah. That's what I was gonna say. Dinner is ready," she added with a nervous laugh.

"Okay."

"Also."

Oh God.

"You should know that I saw your penis." Her business-like tone distracted me for a flash before the words sunk in. My eyes popped open. I hadn't expected her to own up to it. Couldn't we ignore the elephant—or rather, the eggplant—in the room?

"I didn't mean to do that either." But her voice lifted, and I could tell she was fighting a smile. "I mean, not at first. But you know. Penis. In your face. How are you not going to look?" She laughed again.

"Are you laughing?"

"Yes. Sorry." As second later she gasped, "No. Oh, God—no. Not at your penis. You have a lovely penis. You should know. I've not seen too many penises … penii? But anyway, it was a very nice penis."

"Please stop saying penis."

"Should I say cock? Or dick?"

I was wrong before. Now I was rock hard. I bit my lip to keep my hand from lowering to stroke. This was torture. We were maintaining boundaries. We weren't supposed to be thinking about physical attraction. I roused some anger to help find a balance. It was either get angry or pull open that door and kiss her.

"You can go now. I'll be upstairs in a minute," I growled.

"Okay."

The shadow of her feet remained, and her internal debate was audible.

"What, Kim?"

"It's just … I think it's important to talk about these things. Clear the air before it gets awkward." Her tone was cautious, almost clinical.

"I don't see how you constantly mentioning my dick makes it less awkward."

"Heh. Yeah, true. Well, just so you know. I'm fine. And this was one hundred percent my fault. I don't want you thinking anything … um, weird. It's just a body. A nice body, a very nice body. You should know that. You probably do know that. You have eyes …"

"Kim."

"Okay. Sorry. Again. Leaving now."

I let out a long breath. My hands braced the door. I was fighting a lot of different feelings. I could rip the door open to let her look her fill. Or punch the mirror to distract myself with pain, an easily identifiable sensation.

I groaned. "Kim. I can see you're still there."

"Right. I know. Just one more thing …" Her voice went up an octive higher.

"Yes?"

"I saw your face." She said it so quickly that the words ran together.

Anything else I'd felt was instantly drenched with ice cold dread. My throat closed so tight I couldn't take a breath in.

"And, um. I understand now. I mean, not that you need me to understand. But I get it. And I want you to know. I would never tell anybody your business, okay? I'm not like that. I know how it feels to have everybody know the worst about you … ugh, not that your face is the worst. I'm going to stop. Okay, in summation—you have a lovely body, and I won't ever mention this again. So there's no reason to feel uncomfortable."

"Right." Not uncomfortable at all.

She sounded genuinely concerned, but I couldn't think of anything past my own fear in that moment. Dread made me sick. What did this mean for us working together? Her voice was peppy and light, but what were her real thoughts about seeing me fully? If I could see her face, maybe it would be clearer. I wished so many fucking things had gone differently in the last five minutes. Any vain sense of pride I'd found in her words were instantly squashed.

"Okay. Well, I'm going to go home. I'll see ya in the morning." She kept her tone light, but I sensed her wounded feelings in the clipped words.

Finally, her shadow moved from beneath the door. I couldn't hear her retreat, but it felt like a warm blanket being tugged off in winter. I took a deep, steadying breath. She had talked to me when she could have cowered and pretended it never happened. She was trying to be mature about a ridiculous situation. I was in a position where I should follow her example.

I scrambled to wrap a very large towel around my torso and pulled open the door. "Wait."

She stopped halfway down the hall and spun towards me. The backs of her fingers had been pressed to her cheeks and she dropped them like she had been caught doing something bad.

"You're right. This doesn't have to be weird," I called out to her.

Her eyes were wide. I couldn't tell if she was trying not to move her eyes over my body, still half exposed, or if she was trying not to react to my face.

"Good," her voice went higher. She wasn't blinking. Her hands were fisted. She was trying so very hard.

I couldn't help but smile.

Her eyes widened.

"What?" I asked.

"Nothing. I just … I was thinking you looked like your brother just then."

The smiled fell back off my face. "Makes sense."

We both took three mirrored steps toward each other.

"Right. Heh. Brothers."

I swallowed. "And I appreciate your promise of discretion."

"Of course," she shook off the comment.

"You should stay for dinner," I said.

Her eyebrows shot up. "Really?"

"Do you like stuffed shells?"

"Yes." She swallowed thickly. "That sounds good."

I ran a hand through my hair, her gaze focused on the action. She sucked her bottom lip in.

"I'll change and be up in minute. Tell my folks?" I asked.

She nodded and turned on a heel and skittered to the stairs leading up. This was fine. We had worked through it. She was unaffected and professional. Things would be fine.

But first an ice-cold shower. Again.

Despite our discussion to not let it be weird, I fully expected the opposite.

By the time I joined my family in the dining room, Kim was chatting happily with my mom as she set the table. My dad and Wes carried two large dishes of pasta to the table.

"Hey honey," Mom said.

I kissed her cheek and hugged my dad.

"Kim was filling us in on the Fourth of July show you're doing," Dad said.

"Sounds fun. Fireworks!" Ma added.

"It's kitschy," I said.

"People like kitschy. And families like coming to outdoor concerts. Never too soon to get kids exposed to the symphony," Kim said as she lined up forks on linen napkins.

"That's why we are doing it," I said with purposeful dry sarcasm.

She smiled at me, taking me so by surprise that I smiled back without thinking. We stood there grinning at each other for two beats too long. This was why I needed to wear the mask.

I ran a hand over my face, checking for the bandana that was not there. It seemed pointless now. I never wore it around my family anyway unless other people were around.

"Okay, let's eat," Ma said. When she passed me, she lowered her voice and said, "Glad to see your face tonight."

I shrugged.

After saying grace, we dug in. For a few minutes there was only the clatter of spoons against dishes and chatter of passing items. I tried to picture how Kim saw my family after meeting them for the first time. And studying my parents it occurred to me, oddly, how much older they were now. I had been gone for so long that they had transformed into grandparents while I was away. My mother's hair had grayed near the temples and the skin around her eyes was wrinkled from so many years of smiles. My dad, too, wore more wrinkles than I remembered. But it was hard to not see them through the filter of my life. Her thin lips still quirked up to the side while she listened to someone speaking. Dad's gleaming bald head would crinkle with every belly laugh.

Wes still looked like the same dumbass, only a little chubbier.

Once we were all a glass of wine in, except Kim, who'd had water, conversation flowed as though we'd done this a hundred times. With every passing minute, the tension from downstairs melted into warm contentedness.

Kim was ... surprising. She was eloquent and cultured, but boisterous in a way I hadn't expected. She was so quiet in rehearsal that I'd assumed she was shy. But that was Christine, apparently. Kim knew so much about music and art and literature. Her parents were two successful artists, after all. She adapted to conversation easily. Even though my parents and brother were self-dubbed blue-collar, hard-working, salt-of-the-earth people, content to drink beers and watch Sunday football, she shared her knowledge in a way that was casual and charming without an ounce of condescension.

We spoke freely of our favorite pieces and shared some of the funnier stories from rehearsals. Like the time her friend, Erin, challenged a bassist to a freestyle rap battle and wiped the floor with him. Once or twice our gazes met and held a beat too long, like we shared an intimate secret. I caught her staring openly at my face a few times, but she'd smile and I'd be utterly disarmed.

Her knowing my truth still made my skin itch, but there were perks too. I wouldn't have to mess with the damn masks during our weekend rehearsals.

My parents clearly adored her. Of course. And even my brother turned his charm on all the way to eleven on her. They shared a witty banter that bordered on flirtation without being inappropriate. Still.

"Did you know Wes is married with two little girls?" I said.

"That's true, I am." Wes grinned and pulled out his phone. After a few clicks he turned the screen toward Kim. "That's Ellie, the older one. Rose is the baby. Though, she's almost four now."

"Oh my goodness! Those cheeks." Kim's face melted as her gaze moved over the photos. "Where are they now?"

"Ellie has a stomach bug and Kelly, that's my wife, didn't want to bring them and risk spreading germs. They're having a girl's night."

"She's beautiful too. Looks like Wes won the lottery," Kim said to me.

"Ha!" Wes guffawed. "I'm wounded." His hands smacked his gut that protruded over his jeans. "I'll have you know I was quarterback back in the day. Prom king, too."

"Oh, I stand corrected," she teased.

"You two will hit it off. Next week," he said leaning to the side to slide his phone back in his pocket.

"What's next week?" Kim asked.

Wes gestured to the meal they all currently shared. "Friday family dinner."

"I'll be cooking a lamb recipe," Dad said. "I've been wanting to try it."

"Y'all have dinner together every week?" Kim asked.

"Of course," Ma answered. "Since the boys were little. It's something we insisted on since the beginning. Every Friday."

"If we can," Dad said, buttering some fresh cut bread. "When Devlin travels, it's trickier. There're months at a time we don't see him."

"It's hard," Ma said at the same time Wes said, "It's great."

"Sometimes we go to the Front Porch. Or Ma and Dad's," I said.

"We figure, you did so much to fix up this place, we should come here as often as possible while you're still in town," Dad said.

"Next time," Wes said to Kim.

"Well. I don't know …" A blush spread over Kim's cheeks.

"Kim plays in the symphony. She's helping with the fall showcase," I said, hoping Wes would take my point.

"Great," Wes said without missing a beat. "She'll be here a lot then."

Kim and I exchanged another glance. She opened her mouth to protest again, but I gave a quick shake of my head. Wes wasn't worth the effort.

Talking around a full mouth, Wes added, "Light years better than some of your exes."

Kim frowned at her plate. Now he was just putting her on the spot. Trying to sniff out something between us.

"Wes. I already told you Kim isn't here in that capacity."

Kim raised her gaze to mine, and I gave her an apologetic smile.

"Stop trying to stir things up, Wes," Ma warned.

"You're making her uncomfortable," Dad added. Which only made the whole thing even more uncomfortable.

"I'm not uncomfortable," Kim insisted with a blush.

"Just saying you're better than those plastic bimbos," Wes spoke to a frowning Kim. Back to me he said, "I'm not trying to imply that you and Kim are … less than professional." Wes's ears were tipped red and his eyes glossy from the wine. "I'm just trying to compliment Kim. I like her, is all," he added.

I started to speak when Kim spoke. "I appreciate that you like me. But don't do that." She held his gaze, her face impassive. This look was unfamiliar. It was steady, no shame or smiles. Just focused.

"Do what?" Wes drained the rest of his wine.

"Don't insult his exes."

That startled me. I hadn't expected that. I thought … I don't know what I thought.

"His exes? They're forgettable," Wes said.

Ma and Dad turned their attention to me, likely trying to gauge my reaction.

"So then detail why. But you don't need to use their appearances as a reason to dislike them. Especially don't put them down to try and give me value. And don't group them together. They're individuals."

Wes blinked at her. "I wasn't—"

"I know you were trying to compliment me. But I also know how it feels to be only ever referred to as so-and-so's ex. Me and a few girls. A lot of the town sees us as no more than that. But we're all complicated, living, breathing women." She took a deep breath before turning to my father. "Can you pass the shells?

He passed it with mild shock.

"I wasn't trying to—" Wes tried.

"It's not your fault. Somewhere along the line men learn that the best way to compliment a woman is to insult another. But maybe reframe your thoughts. Because if you would have told me something like, his ex liked to kick puppies, then I'd be like, 'Yeah she does not sound awesome.' But blanket statements about all women just end up hurting us all in the end."

Kim was not argumentative. She wasn't angry. In fact, she

seemed totally in her element—borderline fired-up—discussing this. She scooped another shell and brought it to her plate. "Seriously, these are so amazing. It's just ricotta, right?" Her focus went from my mother back to Wes. "All I'm saying is, think about the *person* before you make those comments."

"That's a good point. I never thought about it like that," Ma said, wheels turning behind her eyes.

Wes's ears were entirely red now. He was the charming one who got away with saying whatever. It wasn't that I thought he was particularly offensive in general, but he did have a sense of humor that didn't always vibe with my own.

"I wasn't trying to start something here," he said.

Finally, Kim noticed we were all staring at her.

"What do you mean?" she asked.

"Did I upset you?" Wes asked apologetically.

Kim's head turned to me, her hands spread out. "I'm not upset at all. I thought we were just talking? I'm just saying we, as a people, need to learn how to compliment women without making it about something as superficial and subjective as looks or by tearing down other women. But I'm not mad at all." She smiled and shrugged.

"We don't really talk about this sort of stuff at dinner," Wes said.

"Oh, you should. Dinners are the best time. Especially when your wife and girls were here. Think about what they hear and pick up on. It adds up."

"That's true," Ma said with a thoughtful nod.

"Ma, did you make dessert?" I asked, shooting a very clear look at Wes though I spoke to her, effectively ending the topic.

"Of course," Ma said.

Kim's eyes widened. "Fantastic."

CHAPTER 16

ROSIN IS NOT A CONDIMENT; APPLY WITH RESTRAINT.

KIM

"*D*id I seem preachy?" I stopped wiping the dish to survey Devlin. It was a reflex to shutdown causal misogyny when I was comfortable around people. "I just get defensive of women being clumped into a set category. I hope I didn't offend your family. I loved them."

Devlin grinned with a blush. I would *never* get tired of having full access to his face.

"You didn't offend. My mom seemed pleased. She asked me to have you send her the links to those TED talks." He set down a plate and turned to me. "Wes'll lick his wounds and be okay. He's just used to being the guy that everybody likes. Typically, only Kelly challenges him that way. I certainly liked it."

We stacked up the dried dishes. I was stuffed from the stuffed shells; turned out you were what you ate. His parents and brother left after dessert and, all in all, I'd had a wonderful time. It was long dark by now and I couldn't see out the window in the kitchen—only our reflections in the slowly fogging glass—but the wind whipped loudly through the pines, making the house whistle.

"My parents always have the most random variety of people over. Their debates are so intense. Everyone yells and talks over each other, but in a friendly way. It's sort of like that with the SWS, too. I forget not everybody is like that," I explained.

I had the warm glow that accompanied good company. Granted, when I came back upstairs from the encounter, I was in total freak-out mode. I had done an incredible job, if I could say so myself, of containing my internal screaming all through dinner. Now, it was just a matter of not drooling openly at his handsome face every time I looked at him.

All the years I had stared at his poster in my room … how could I have not seen it earlier? I couldn't blame the beard, though that was a surprising new addition. I had thought Wes was handsome but after seeing them side-by-side, it was evident that Wes was the copy/pasted version of a low-quality screenshot in comparison to his brother. Devlin had matured into the sharp angles of a man's face. His nose was strong and proud. His beard full but trimmed. Every time our gazes clashed, I thought I might scream, "Erik Jones is here!"

"It was a nice dinner," Devlin said. "He shouldn't have been trying to grill you anyway. He got a little taste of being put on the spot."

"Yeah. I guess I just felt really comfortable." I sighed and leaned my back against the kitchen counter.

He reached up to put a clean plate away. His shirt lifted to reveal a thin flash of muscular abs. I needed more time with those abs. I wanted to be able to sculpt him from marble just from my memories. Thank goodness he couldn't hear my thoughts. I was doing my best to not be weird, but I was still shook. Every time I thought about his body … every time I looked at his flawless face … *SHOOK, I say.*

He'd been watching me watch him. I was being obvious, wasn't I? Shoot. But I had to ask. I needed to understand why he hid from the world. There was no reason. Unless being too beautiful was a crime? "Devlin, I—"

"Tell me more about these dinner parties your parents have?" He turned away to wipe off the counters. "I'm envisioning the art world's who's-who, bottles of wine, and late-night heated debates over political and social issues."

So, we definitely weren't talking about it then. Okay.

"You're not far off, actually." I yawned. "My whole life, they've attracted some real characters. I've always been ..." *Nosey.* "In search of knowledge. Older than my age, if that makes sense. So, I used to listen in. Finally, at one point, my parents told me if I wanted to be a part of their dinner discussions I had to learn to discuss things civilly. I started debating with adults at the age of twelve. More than once I fell asleep at the table, trying to hang."

A soft smiled spread along Devlin's face and it made my knees tingle. I wondered when he would let me address the elephant in the room, but I'd follow his lead for now.

"You seemed surprised by our weekly dinners. But it sounds like your parents had them too," he said.

My heart twisted a little at that. "No. Not really. That's why I learned to argue. It was some of the only time I got to spend with them." His brows creased. "That sounded worse than I meant. It wasn't that my parents ignored me. Not by a mile. But they were very much their own unit until they had me. Both in their forties and so in love." I took a deep breath trying to find the right words. "I was this bonus gift, but not necessarily something they'd always dreamed about wanting. I guess I'm just surprised you're so close with your parents. Like, what do y'all talk about, if it's not politics and art?"

He scratched at his chin. "Everything. Sometimes we do talk about that sort of stuff, but mostly they just want to know what's going on. When you know someone really well you have shared stories. That's why the dinners are so important to them. They want to always be a part of our lives. They're just like friends. I mean, it wasn't always like this. And obviously there are some things we don't discuss. We obviously don't go into the lurid details of my sex life, but I mean, most things we talk about."

Lurid details? "Let's unpack that," I wanted to say. Instead, I said, "Huh. I guess I never thought of my parents as friends. Especially not friends that I'd choose to hang out with. They're just … family."

"I guess," he searched for the right words. "I don't know what I'd do without my family."

Swoon.

"My parents don't know me. Not really." It was my own fault. I kept so much from them. "They know the person they have in their head. I'm not that person anymore." I sort of trailed off. I wasn't sure if Devlin knew anything about my past.

"Have you tried talking to them?" he asked softly.

Now it was my turn to change the subject.

"The SWS is my family. But your family are your people," I said.

He nodded. "When I'm with them, it feels like comfort. Like I don't need to be 'on.' I don't have to be anything for anybody. I don't think about what I say, I just speak," he said.

"The man behind the mask?" I asked.

He dropped my gaze. "Something like that."

A pang of jealousy cramped my stomach.

This was all just so much to take in with Devlin. It was so far from the image he portrayed day to day at rehearsal. But I supposed the same could be said for me.

"Why didn't you tell me who you were?"

His body went rigid. It was a minute before he answered me. "I guess I didn't want you to see me differently."

His confession hit home. His fears were justified. I had already started to see him differently. Internally, I had been obsessing over Erik Jones and not Devlin. I turned toward him, and he mirrored me. It was just us washing dishes, but it felt so intimate.

"You're a gifted musician. I'm doing this because I want to help *you*. Nothing has changed," I said. I vowed to myself that I wouldn't bring it up again. I could only hope that when he felt ready, he might share more.

He nodded but didn't add anything else. We'd been holding each other's gaze again. All night we had been staring at each other like we were trying to figure something out.

He blinked and pushed off the counter. "I'll make some tea."

We chatted as he got out the kettle. I found the teacups and set them up. He told me about his struggles with his composition and how close he felt to breaking through. Hearing him talk about his music was something akin to magic. I wondered if the great artists of the past had people that they talked to like this. Did Beethoven have a partner he shared his work with over cups of tea on cold evenings?

When we finally stopped looking at each other, I said, "I guess I'll get going."

He pushed his empty mug away. "I'll walk you out."

At the door, I got unaccountably nervous reaching for my coat and ended up fumbling a bit.

"Here." He wrapped me up in my jacket and I liked the way it felt to be buttoned up.

"Thanks." I blinked up at him.

"It was pretty cold when my parents left." His hands remained gripped in the collar of my coat, fussing with it to keep it closed.

"It was supposed to storm," I responded. Were we talking about the weather or was he stalling? Maybe I just hoped he was.

He finally broke away to open the door. Without warning the wind pushed the door all the way open and out of his hands. A punch of frozen air sucked the breath from my lungs.

"Whoa," I said.

We stared out the door. The tall pines surrounding the house swayed back and forth in the icy sheets of rain falling sideways from the sky. Cold drops of water pelted my face, stinging my cheek and exposed hands. The porch and steps were covered in what looked frighteningly like black ice.

My palms instantly started to sweat. My hands shook as I pulled out my phone to check the roads.

"Thanks again for dinner and everything." I took one step forward, and in a flash, I was going down.

My foot shot forward as my upper body fell back. Turns out, black ice did line the steps. Before I could even think about the sound of my head hitting the slate stones, strong arms caught me from behind.

"I got ya," he said.

I looked up into his face and his surprised eyes stared back. He held me like a soldier kissing his bride before going off to war. His gaze moved over my face.

"I guess you're staying here tonight." His words warmed me from the inside out despite the assaulting rain.

I gulped.

* * *

Sleeping had never been easy for me. Actually, I slept fine if I wasn't alone. Up until an embarrassingly late age in life I'd sneak into my parent's room almost every night. Many mornings they'd find me curled up in a ball by the foot of their bed. After that last year at camp, it had gotten worse.

By the time the phone alarm went off the next morning, I'd gotten maybe three hours of turbulent sleep. I brushed my teeth and checked in with my parents. I got ready for my next lesson with Devlin in a fog. I missed my early morning workout, but from the scent filling my nose, I would at least get coffee before we got to work.

I had a few missed texts from Gretchen and Blithe. I quickly replied to our group chat: *Can't talk now, but have I got a story for y'all.*

The texts back were not sympathetic, as expected. Patience had never been Gretchen's strong suite.

Obviously, Roddy and I weren't able to meet up. The roads were still iced over and Green Valley just wasn't equipped with enough trucks to salt the roads very quickly. No one would be leaving their homes today unless it was absolutely necessary. He wasn't surprised but sounded convincingly disappointed, nonetheless. He wanted to know if I wanted to meet up another time to discuss a business plan. I felt a little less fluttery by his texts than I'd expected. Maybe because I couldn't tell if was interested in being my business partner or being my kissing partner. I put a proverbial pin in that, so I could come back to it later.

For now, practice.

Forty minutes later, and any warm fuzzies the coffee had fostered were burned to ashes by the total assholeness that was Devlin during practice. No, he wasn't Devlin. He was the Devil of the Symphony now.

His fingers slammed the same chord six times on the piano. "Listen to what I'm playing."

"I'm trying." Embarrassment tightened my throat. We'd only just started the second movement, and already I was failing. It was better when he wore the mask. God, I never thought I'd miss it, but at least it set clear boundaries. I saw the mask and I knew who I was dealing with. How could this same man be the one who had smiled at me over pasta?

This guy was such a dick.

"You aren't though." He swore.

"Maybe if you did something other than yell at me." The words spilled out. My filter had apparently never got out of bed.

No matter that I'd spent the night, eaten dinner with his family, and seen his fantastic manhood, this dolt was my teacher. I needed to respect him. I would not lose my ever-loving mind on him.

He cooled his tone. "You're holding that cello like you're dismantling a bomb. Your whole body is tense."

I couldn't imagine why I looked tense.

"I've been playing my whole life. I think I know how to hold my instrument," I said.

"That's the problem, isn't it? You *think* you know."

My skin burned from anger; I was boiling from the inside out. "Is there any way you could be more specific? Because I *am* listening and quite frankly, I have no idea what you're talking about." I gripped the neck of my cello so hard the strings cut into me.

"I'm talking about listening to the message. Really listen. And play that. You are a conduit."

I shook my head. I had no clue what he thought or what he was trying to convey. I was a human, not a "clucking mind reader," to quote Suzie.

"Your way isn't working. You're the professional," my words flew out. I'd never been so short with somebody before. He brought it out in me. I demanded more than being yelled at. "Try something else."

Something about that sunk in. Wheels turned behind those dark eyes.

"Stand up," he demanded.

I shot up. The neck of my cello was in my left hand, the bow in my right, once again wielded like a weapon.

"Put your cello down," he said with steady calmness, but anger flashed in his dark eyes.

I felt a wave of uneasiness but listened.

He stood from the piano and cracked his neck by tilting his head side to side. He shook out his hands. Next to him, without the protection of my cello, I was reminded of his massive size.

He took the bow from my hand and hung it on the music stand so the rosined bow hair wouldn't be ruined from the oil of our hands. Then, in the world's most surprising switch up, he took my right hand in his. My hand felt tiny and cool against his large hand, calloused with the knowledge of a dozen different instruments. His thumb pressed circles into my palm. It moved to the thick muscles of my thumb pad.

"Wh-what are you doing?" I asked stupidly, because he was very clearly giving me a hand massage. And oh my, it was amazing.

"Your instrument should be an extension of you." His words were low and rumbling. "Not a weapon you aren't comfortable wielding. Relax."

Sure. Relax. Please, tell the woman ten feet under water to breathe deeply.

I took a deep breath in and out and worried if my coffee breath reached him. I worried about what to do with the other hand. I worried how to stand in a way that looked comfortable when, in fact,

I was freaking out. He was so close that if I leaned forward a little, I would collapse against his chest.

"Close your eyes," he demanded with a harsh edge.

Maybe he sensed I couldn't get passed the fact that he was currently giving me a massage that made me tingle all over. With my eyes closed, I could pretend the hands rubbing mine were those of a professional's at a spa.

It was amazing. #MagicFingersDevlin could be trending on Twitter. I hadn't realized how sore and tight those muscles were. He lowered my right hand and did the same thing to my left. His thumbs dug into the aching muscles of my forearm. He found a muscle that made my middle finger jump as he rubbed it. Tension that I hadn't even been aware I'd been holding melted out of me. I sunk into sensation. It was heaven, but I couldn't fully relax, because what if I made an embarrassing groan of pleasure?

He released me, and I let out a long breath. Thank goodness maybe we were done, because my heated cheeks couldn't take much more. I was already panting way more than a relaxed person should be. But then, to my utter horror, he stepped behind me.

"You're rigid," he whispered. I heard it clearly because he was so close to my ear. The air tickled my neck and goosebumps spread down my neck to my chest.

He was slow but deliberate as he pressed down the muscles connecting my shoulder to my neck. Sweet Lord, I was gonna die like this. Let me go this way. It was a good life.

"Relax," he said again.

I wanted to relax but the second his hands touched me again, a different sort of tension took over—sexy-man-proximity tension. His scent encompassed me. He smelled like cooking dinner, and relaxing by the fire, and good conversation. He should smell like death and regret; that would make this easier.

The image of his naked, glistening skin popped back into my mind. It had been there most of the night while I'd tried to sleep. It was the first thing I saw behind my eyelids when I woke with the blankets tangled between my restless legs. Wow, this was not the best time to remember that. But, well, since we were here …

"It's a little hard at the moment," I said to break the tension. When he went stock still, I realized my mistake. "To relax," I added as quick as possible.

"Hmm," he rumbled out.

Dear God, did he feel anything close to this on his end? This spark? Was it because I was a hard-up horn dog with a totally indecent crush, or was this heat between us a real thing that would exist outside the roles we played? You couldn't force or fake attraction, but sometimes two bodies rubbing together was enough to stir our most ancient needs.

"Roll your shoulders," he said.

Then he took my head in his hands and gently pressed his thumbs into the base of my skull while his fingertips spread through my hair. Goosebumps spread over my skin and my breasts screamed out for attention in the only way they knew how. My nipples hardened and grew heavy with want. *Play with us, squeeze us, twist us, suck us,* they called out.

"You're a string tuned to high. A second from snapping," he said softly.

"I am not," I said. It came out as a half-hearted whisper.

He tilted my head side to side. He moved to the deep tissue of my upper back and neck. As a cellist, I had almost perpetual back pain and what I called "cello butt"—a constant ache in my tailbone from sitting stock-straight on the edge of a chair. I wondered if he was aware of cello butt. Maybe those muscles needed to be worked.

I coughed out and cleared my throat.

He didn't notice and continued my three-hundred-dollar massage. As he rubbed, an amazing thing happened: I actually started to relax.

"Ohh," I moaned. I didn't even care.

I did notice that his body pulled back away from me slightly. Maybe I freaked him out. But he was the one rubbing me down telling me to relax; what the heck did he expect?

He pressed my shoulders down away from my ears. As he did, he said, "Years of playing incorrectly have locked them into a hunched position."

He rubbed his thumbs deep into the tension. My body felt delicate and tiny under his touch. He could easily toss me around, bend me, break me …

CHAPTER 17

BELIEVE THE STORY THE MUSIC IS TELLING YOU.

DEVLIN

Finally, she started to relax into me. She was pliable. She took instruction perfectly. I could spend my life instructing her into various positions. She melted into me and it grew more difficult to ignore the heat radiating between us. Sweat broke out along my brow. The air puffed out of my nose, too hot.

She had to feel it too. What would she do if I slid my hand forward and across the expanse of her delicate collarbones? Felt all her softness under my rough skin? How would she respond?

I cleared my throat. "Pick up your bow again."

It took her a minute for my request to sink in through the layers of relaxation. Eventually, she blinked rapidly and picked her bow back up. Her hand clamped it into a rigid C-shape.

"No. Hold on to that relaxation. Feel the balance of it." I grasped her hand so that I almost completely embraced her from behind. "The bow should feel weightless. There. Good. Middle finger and thumb. That's all you should use right now."

"I know this. This is all first-year stuff." Her defenses were down but I could tell this still frustrated her.

"Exactly. You think you know. But we need to start here."

My arm moved out and in, mimicking the draw along a string.

"See. That. The pointer and pinky only provide direction. They aren't demanding or crushing. Let gravity help you," I said.

Her head fell back against my shoulder in relaxation and then she went still when she realized it.

"No, shh. That's okay," I whispered, and she stayed in place.

We played an invisible instrument, our right arms traveling out and back in perfect tandem. We played the same piece of unheard music.

My left arm wrapped around her so that I grasped her left shoulder. "Now this is the neck of your cello. Place your fingers on me."

Her fingers were tentative as they grasped my skin. "It's too big."

I swallowed with difficulty, briefly shutting my eyes against the barrage of images that accompanied that soft sentence.

"It doesn't matter. It's about balance again. Relax your grip."

Her fingers moved up and down my forearm and a shudder I hoped she couldn't feel ran through me.

"Your arm is much hairier than my cello." A smile came across with her words.

My own smile followed, as always, without will when I was around her.

"Your thumb is flat. You should have a cupped hand, using the tip only. Keep your hand loose and it will travel distances faster," I said.

"I know."

"Then do it."

She grumbled but obeyed. Her fingers danced delicately up and down my arm. It was tricky but with our right arms still bowing, she played me perfectly.

Her scent and the unheard notes floated in the air around us. The soft sounds of our shared breath and rustling clothes filled the space. I joined her closed eyes and lived in this moment.

My instinct was right; together we would play beautiful music. She was perfect to play my piece.

Eventually, I started to pull away. When she made a sound of dismay, I said, "Stay like that. Don't even open your eyes yet."

I carefully led her back down to the chair. I replaced my arm with the neck of the cello, placing the bow on the string.

"Now, just play."

She kept her eyes shut tight; her dark lashes fanned out against her pale skin. Her face was smooth in relaxation, and her cheeks flushed with color. Her mouth was relaxed and slightly open. She looked devastatingly beautiful.

She played the last piece we had been working on without being able to see the music. She was gifted, but somewhere over the years since camp she had lost faith in herself. She had been changed and filled with nonsense.

"Good," I whispered. If she'd heard me, she made no sign. She wasn't aware of anything outside what she played in that moment. As it should be. "It's that space between the notes. Feel it. Touch it. The music is all around you."

The music flowed from her. It wasn't my piece of music; it was a snippet from the July show we were performing. She was perfection though.

She played and I sat on the bench of the piano listening, elbows on knees, fingertips steepled and my chin resting on them.

She played until she reached the end and when she did, she lifted her bow off the string and the last note hung in the air.

Several long seconds later she blinked into awareness. Her gaze moved around until it found me watching and listening intently. Her eyebrows raised in question.

I tried to speak, cleared my throat, then started again. "Better. Much better."

"Thank you," she said.

"Remember that feeling when you play. Block out the years of mechanical lessons and tap into that feeling. Well done."

A smile broke out on her face. Perhaps I could be a little more generous with positive feedback. She responded better when I showed her, taught her. I'd just grown so used to snapping and taking. That wouldn't work with her.

She had me questioning so many things I thought I knew.

* * *

"Look!" Kim's voice broke my attention.

She stood at the kitchen window, leaning over the sink, to look outside. How nicely she filled out her pants was of no interest to me. I cleared my throat.

"What?" I asked as I went to her side.

I was sore and tired. My stomach grumbled. We'd been playing so long we'd both lost track of time, and now the house was dark again. The storm had not relented overnight; it had worsened.

"I've never seen anything like this," she said.

Outside, it was the picture of winter at the end of April. Ice covered every inch of tree and earth. The driveway was an ice luge. A few large tree branches littered the ground, glittering with ice.

"It's bad," I said.

I pulled out my phone and searched road conditions. "All the roads around Green Valley are closed. There are weather warnings not to drive for any reason."

Kim's eyes were wide. "I can't believe this spring." She walked to the fridge and pulled out last night's leftovers. "I'm starving."

Without discussion, or even manners, she grabbed a fork and started eating straight out the container. "Wanf som?" she asked around a mouthful of food.

I shook my head at her.

"What? No? And I'm sorry. I shouldn't be telling you how to write your own music. It's your decision."

"Kim, stop. It's good." I took the container from her hands. "I wouldn't have asked for your help if I didn't want input."

I wouldn't make a big deal about it, but I liked seeing this side of her. The side that offered glimpses of her assertiveness, like I saw at dinner with Wes. It was what was missing at practice. She was not overthinking. She was just being herself.

We dug back in, chewing in silence, occasionally tearing off hunks of bread with our teeth from the loaf of French bread we passed back and forth.

After a few minutes we sat back with sighs against the sink. We hadn't even made it to the table. In our defense, the clock read almost five. We'd played almost six hours without a break.

"I guess we were hungry," she laughed, wiping her mouth. "I feel like I ran a marathon." She rocked her head back and forth to stretch. I debated offering another massage but the last one had sucked years from my life.

"We're making progress," I said.

"Don't hurt yourself with all that praise, over there." She rubbed her slightly protruding stomach. "Look, a food baby." She turned the side and stuck her stomach out even more, rubbing her hand over the area like a proud mother-to-be. The vision sent a weird warmth through me and an unsettling sense of déjà vu made me dizzy. I shook my head with a laugh and looked down.

"I think I'll name her Ricotta," she said.

"You look Prego."

She looked up at me shocked. "You made a pun."

"It's less funny when you point it out."

She crackled with laughter. "That was a good one."

"I can be funny," I complained, acting out a wound that I felt deeply. The price I paid for playing the bad guy.

"You *are* funny. You should show it more." Her eyes widened as she realized what she said.

"Humor doesn't get results," I said. My smile fell.

She chewed her bottom lip and refused to meet my gaze.

"What? What are you trying so hard not to say right now?" I asked and crossed my arms, turning fully to face her.

"Nothing?" Her voice lifted at the end.

"Just say it."

"You could soften a little at rehearsal."

I growled.

She faced me now as well and her arms came up as though to settle me. "Hear me out. You're so much more than this image you portray. You're funny and nice and sometimes even a little patient. You come across as such an—"

My eyebrows raised at her abrupt stop. "An asshole?"

"Your words."

"Your thoughts," I said.

"To me, it feels like you're trying to make them respect you. But there's a chance you're pushing people too far the other way. People aren't bending. They're about to snap."

"They need to be better." Heat crawled up my neck.

"I understand a little bit more now." She gestured to my face. "Because you want to …"

"Get to the point, Christine." I regretted the words as soon as I'd said them, but if she were about to lecture me about presenting a different face to the world, the hypocrisy had to be pointed out.

Her eyes narrowed. "You don't have to be anything you're not. But let them see your humor. It might get you better results. There's talks of people—"

"I know what they say about me. And I couldn't care less. They have no power. They don't like things the way they are, they can leave. I'm not changing who I am to make them more comfortable. They're all replaceable."

A look of hurt crossed her features. "Me too? If I left, you'd easily replace me?"

I went to the cabinet for a glass. "This isn't about you. You committed to me. To this September showcase. If you can't handle the pressure, tell me now before we go any further." I filled the glass of water and immediately chugged it down.

"So quick to anger." She shook her head, still leaning against the counter. "I'm not saying that. But treating people like they're instruments, and not living, breathing, feeling humans will only make them hate you."

My heart hammered in anger. A horn sectioned blared in my ears.

I growled. "Being funny and wearing a mask are sort of contra-dictory."

Her gaze moved to my fisted hands before she looked up at me through her lashes. "You don't have to wear the mask."

"I think you're forgetting, I'm the Maestro. The conductor and the composer. Sorry if I made you think anything else."

Her face drained of color. "I haven't forgotten. Not for a second."

CHAPTER 18

LUCK IS TIMING AND PREPARATION.

KIM

*O*ur next practice was considerably less awesome.

My comments about his behavior had gone too far. I regretted relaxing so much around him. The veil between here and symphony rehearsal often felt so thin I forgot it was still there. My thoughts flowed so freely. I shouldn't have made comments about who he should be in rehearsal. So many lines were crossed this weekend.

We rehearsed and I did my best. When we got to the area I had mentioned working on, I had lost the courage to bring up my suggested changes. There was disappointment on his face, but I didn't have the emotional energy to defend myself.

I didn't get any feedback when we broke around nine that night. It had been a long time since I'd played that many hours in one day and my body felt it. And though it would make sense that my body would be exhausted, I was filled with anxious energy after dinner—cold cut sandwiches. Separately. He shook off my invitation to share a meal under the pretense of having calls to make. Maybe that was true, but it likely came back to boundaries. Message received.

My body hummed with extra energy that needed to be dispelled. Between the storm trapping us in the house, the rehearsal, and that massage earlier—which I absolutely refused to think about—my mind felt like a caged bear. But not the peaceful sleeping kind; more like the kind left starving and with a raw steak just out of reach.

I went in search of adventure.

The halls of the house were endless. Every turn down a new hall led to more empty rooms and closets. And yet, not a home gym in sight. A body like Devlin's in a house like this had to have one.

"Can I help you?" His deep, brusque tone cut through the air.

A yelp escaped me. My hand shot back from the door handle to the next room. It was as though he'd materialized by my thoughts alone. Thank God, I didn't actually have that super-power, or he'd pop up embarrassingly often.

"I was looking for a gym. Since I'm stuck here another night, I need to work out," I said, sounding short to my own ears and with just a pinch of salt. It wasn't his fault we were trapped another night and yet …

Sticking with the bear in the cage metaphor, him waltzing up to me right now was like a random hiker jabbing a stick between the bars.

"I don't have one," he said coolly, his hands tucked deep in the pockets of his jeans.

His biceps sort of winged out to the side. His chest muscles were stretching the capacity of his T-shirt. The man didn't get that body just through conducting the symphony.

Maybe I accidentally stared too long at his body, or maybe he was messing with me, but he added, "I swim."

My eyebrows shot up. "Me too," I said too quickly.

"I have a pool downstairs. You can use it if you want."

"I didn't bring a suit," I sounded disappointed to my own ears.

He crossed his arms. "You want to swim or not?"

Ten minutes later, he was in his swim trunks and I was in my bra and undies. That had escalated quickly.

Here was the thing: I did not wear sexy underwear these days. I'd gone through a thong phase during my Jethro era, but then I'd discovered the comfort of laser-cut satin full-coverage panties. Same idea for the bras. The point was, that if I wanted to rationalize this situation, I could say my granny panties and full-coverage bra were far more concealing than many swimsuits.

Rationally, that should have helped. But it didn't. I was in my skivvies. Devlin basically was too. We were just a few feet apart with only Jesus and a couple of flimsy layers between us. Forget eye contact—I could barely look at his nipples. There was no safe space to focus on, so instead, I dived directly into the pool. Maybe he had been looking at my body. What would it mean if he had been? How would I feel depending on what I saw on his face? Best to not find out.

The water was uh-may-zing. Perfect temperature. Was it saltwater? My body felt deliciously buoyed.

The whole room was insane. At this point, cherubs could lower from the ceiling with tiny little harps and I wouldn't even be surprised. It was an underground grotto, seemingly cut straight from the rocks of the Smokies. It could be a natural hot spring, for crying out loud. Natural rock formations were all around us, complete with stalactites and stalagmites.

Devlin smiled at me from next to the pool when my head bobbed back out of the water.

"What?" I asked, squinting the salty water out of my eyes.

"Interesting."

"What?" I asked, drawing out the word.

"I didn't peg you as the jump-right-in sort of gal."

"Don't paint me with that brush. And don't you dare say that I'm not like other girls. Because if you do, I might go off on you like I did Wes," I said all this while kicking softly to stay afloat, aware that my nude color bra was now just plain nude right under the surface.

He held up his hands. "You surprise me is all." He shook his head with a laugh before lifting his arms above his head to stretch side to side. My own personal Colin Firth as Darcy. Back here again. Me staring, him existing. I let myself sink until my head was under water. Unfortunately, I didn't stay there because … saltwater. I popped right back up like a fishing bobber.

A second later the water splashed into my face as he cannon-balled right next to me.

When he came back up, he shook his head once to dispel the water. His dark hair sprayed a stream and formed a peak over his forehead. Almost immediately it started to curl. He looked as happy as a goofy puppy with a chew toy.

"Oh, I would have never pegged you as a cannon-baller," I mocked.

"I'm a total baller."

I groaned at his stupid joke. The weirdness of earlier seemed to be dissipating but I still struggled with his idea of boundaries; one minute they're firmly in place, the next he's suggesting swimming together. It was a complicated situation, and I got the impression he wasn't even sure how to handle it. I'd follow his lead.

My hand gripped the edge of the natural stone and I kicked softly, enjoying the lightness of the water. He came up next to me. His dark lashes were clumped together in little spikes and a drop of water ran down his face to his neck and continued lower. Ah, to be on that journey …

"I'm sorry about what I said while we were playing earlier," he said.

"I did not expect that," I said honestly. "You surprise me too."

"I don't think you're replaceable," he added seriously.

"Thanks," I said.

His gaze moved from my hair to my chin and cheeks and nose and back to my eyes. "I'm trying to keep strict boundaries between us. The symphony and me. I didn't mean to take it out on you. Favor is too easily swayed. One second, you're loved by all. The next, you're totally forgotten."

"I'm sorry I stepped out of line. I didn't mean—"

"You didn't. I asked for your help." He shook his head. "Let's move on."

My heart constricted with his vulnerability. I wished I could assure him that nobody would care about the man behind the mask, but I couldn't promise that at all, could I? I ached to reach out and hug him but instead I said, "Race you?"

"What?"

"On your marks." I braced the wall.

"I'm not racing you …"

"Chicken." I got my feet ready to push off.

"… because it wouldn't be a fair race. I'd obviously wipe the floor with you," he rushed out.

"Get set."

"Your funeral."

"Go!" I ducked under the water and shot off the wall. He scrambled in the water next to me. I focused on my perfect stroke. It was like practicing scales, done enough times to come naturally.

We met again back at the wall where we started. We were both panting and grinning like fools. What was it about a swim race that brought out the child in a person in the best way?

"It was a tie," I panted.

"Only because you cheated. If you hadn't, I would've won."

"Whatever helps you sleep at night."

He leaned on the wall with arms crossed. "Okay. You're a solid swimmer."

"Oh my goodness," I said clutching a hand to my chest.

He put his hand on my shoulder, his eyes searched me. "What's wrong? Cramp?"

"No. I just—I think you just gave me a compliment."

He dropped his hand slowly into the water as his face formed a scowl. "I rescind it for unsportsman-like conduct."

"Too late. I heard it. It's going to my head as we speak."

Using a cupped hand, he splashed water in my face. I sputtered and kicked him.

"Ouch! Is swimming your workout of choice?" he asked as he backed out of kicking range.

"Yes."

"You work out a lot?"

"Yeah." I felt weird talking about it, but it was so crucial for me. I added, "It helps to focus on something. If I don't work out, I get—" I hesitated.

"I get it. Me too. Mental health."

"Yeah. My parents were pretty strict after ..."

"After you got out of rehab?" he asked bluntly. There was no pity or judgement in his tone. Just as though he were asking about my last dental checkup and not the worst year of my life.

"Uh, yeah. I wasn't sure if you knew about all that."

"I've heard some things." His gaze moved to his own arms, crossed and resting on the edge of the pool.

"Ah yes. Kim, the wild child who ruined it all." Emotion cracked my voice. I wanted one person who knew me as me and not my past.

"What actually happened?" He returned his gaze to hold mine. No judgement.

My face scrunched up. "Are you sure you want to hear?"

"I wouldn't have asked," he said sincerely.

"I was on a set track since birth. I'd always been uber-motivated. Great grades. Acceptance to Juilliard. Everything was going great. Until it wasn't."

He nodded. "It's a lot on the shoulders of a kid."

"Yeah, and I skipped a grade, and with a late birthday too. So, I was sixteen and had spent a whole lifetime up to that point focused on that one goal. Graduate and become first chair of an orchestra like the New York Philharmonic or somewhere huge."

He didn't say anything, just listened. My goodness, a man who listened. Call the church, we had a miracle on our hands.

"One day, at the start of my Senior year, it all just felt like too much. I'd just gotten home from school. I had to get ready for my private lesson and it suddenly it felt like I couldn't breathe. Like I couldn't get off my bed and even grab my cello. That weekend I went to a bar I knew wouldn't check IDs. I was looking for trouble, and I found him. His name was Jethro. I fell hard and fast. He was beautiful and charming and so sweet." I sighed with a little blush.

Jethro hadn't loved me, but he had loved my body. The fallout of my disastrous choices overshadowed so much of the greatness of those short few months, but there were revelations too. My body had been a mystery before Jethro, something I used to accomplish a goal. After that, it was like I had this super-power. I could feel pleasure whenever I wanted. More than that, another person could bring me pleasure. I'd felt so many things. The man had opened me up. And he'd been damn good at it. I'd discovered what I liked and didn't like.

Thinking about all this reminded me it had been a while since I'd had that with another partner. I was … well, I was the bear in the cage and sex was the steak. You know what? Forget the bear thing. Truth was, Jethro had given me an appetite and I hadn't been sated since.

"Unfortunately, he moved with a fast crowd—a terrible motor-cycle club. He was a lost soul then too. His daddy was bad news. Anyway, I got hooked on the feeling of riding with him. That unpredictability and wildness. I skipped lessons, and then school. I was absolutely addicted to not having any plans." I closed my eyes and remembered the vibration of the bike as it rattled my chest. The open road ahead with nothing to do. That feeling like my whole life was ahead of me, and I didn't have to make a single damn plan.

"But this story isn't a happy one." He didn't quite ask.

"No. I started doing drugs. At first, I told myself it would help with my grades and relieve the pressure. But it quickly became apparent that I was no longer in control."

He frowned with a nod.

"I was lucky that my parents caught on fairly early. Some of the kids I partied with didn't have anybody looking after them and never got out. But my parents found some drugs in my cello case. From there, it was off to rehab for the rest of my senior year. No more scholarship. No more first chair. I'd messed up. My whole reputation was ruined for a few months of fun." I let out a long breath.

It was a while before he spoke. Maybe I had unloaded too much, too soon. I didn't tell him everything, but it was nice to get this much off my chest. My filter was clearly gone around him.

"I think the past is tricky. It shapes so much of who we are. Mistakes, especially. But they're necessary, you know? It's a fine line between learning from them and being indebted to them."

I held on to his every word.

"But you can't let it hold you prisoner. It was just a lesson, not a life sentence."

Goosebumps trickled down my neck. "That's true. It's hard, because my whole life changed after that. I didn't really feel like I could trust myself anymore."

He shook his head. "You can trust yourself. You just have to listen first. Listen when your heart tells you what it wants."

The air between us grew charged. What did I want? My body seemed to want something that my mind wasn't ready for. My heart hammered and I felt so heavy for somebody floating. I focused instead on why we were here: his music. Outside of that, I wasn't sure. I had lived so long in fear of dreaming too big. I wasn't ready to think about all that.

"Thank you," I finally settled on. "For letting me talk about it. It's this big black spot on my life. Most people ignore it or actively change the subject because it makes them uncomfortable."

"Take it from someone who also has a big black spot. The opinions of those people don't matter. It's just your people that matter. The people who love you as you are. The real you."

The SWS immediately came to mind. They couldn't care less about my success or failures. They just loved me.

"You're right," I said. "So wise for a masked man."

"Har har."

I wanted so desperately to take the focus off me and move it back to him. I wanted to learn everything about this man.

He must have sensed my body tensing. "Don't you dare," he said.

I wiggled my eyebrows. "On your marks."

We grinned at each other.

"One more lap," he said.

"Fine."

"And one more thing, and this is really important—" He dunked his head and shot off the wall.

"Cheater!" I yelled, but he was already gone.

CHAPTER 19

FEAR HOLDS YOU BACK.

KIM

The swim with Devlin was cleansing. When we were relaxed around each other it felt like we were old friends. That's how it felt being with the SWS. The girls and I could go months without meeting up—once we even went almost a year—but then the second we were back together, it was like no time had passed. With Devlin too it was as though our souls were old friends. Only my evolving desire for him felt new.

The shower that followed our swim melted my bones. I fell into bed in a pair of his sweatpants and the T-shirt I'd worn the night before. I was just on that happy verge of sleep when a bang rattled the house. It cracked through the air out of nowhere.

My eyes shot open with my heart pounding in my ears. My arms gripped the comforter as though they could keep me from whatever danger approached. My sleep-addled brain couldn't comprehend the sound until a second later when the room lit up as lightning flashed, followed immediately by a clap of thunder that rattled the windows.

I flipped over to scream in the pillow, kicking my legs. I was so tired. My body was desperate for sleep but—

CRASH!

It wasn't that the thunder scared me. It just stirred up memories from that final night at camp. Normally, I'd just crank up the music or put on headphones. But I didn't have my headphones.

A second later, I chucked off the blankets and ran into the hall. The lights flickered with the next flash and crash. I yelped and gripped the wall. I wasn't scared. It had startled me. There was a difference. This was fine. I was totally fine. I might just wander the house to see if Devlin was awake or go to the music room and play. Not that I needed company but—

Another flash and rattling boom.

"Eep!" I quickened my pace. The living room was the central point of the house. I'd make my way there and decide what to do next. Where did Devlin sleep? Not that I was going to bother him; I just wanted to make sure he was around.

He had to have a bedroom. An image of him hanging upside down like a bat in his music room flashed through my eyes. But no, if anything, he probably didn't sleep. He probably just hunched over his giant piano composing brilliant music while the rest of us mere mortals slept.

The living room was cold and dark. The fireplace sat empty. The whole room loomed large in the dark. Thankfully, his fancy house was full of motion detecting lights. The first few scared me but after feeling my way into a couple rooms the automatic lights brought me comfort. If I could find the remote for the sound system, I'd play some loud music and wait for the storm to blow over. It wouldn't be like I was alone at all.

Despite the lights coming on and the sound of crashing rain against the windows, I was still very aware that this was a huge house. Somebody else could be living here, and I wouldn't know. Devlin had to have people who cleaned and cooked while he locked himself away for hours at a time. What if he had a humpbacked assistant that would come lurking around a corner, dragging a leg behind him?

Chills wracked my body. Seriously, where the cluck was this

man's room?

I hated how scared I felt. I hated that I was basically a little child. I hated that I wished more than anything I was home where I could knock on my parent's bedroom door. I was an adult, for crying out loud. An adult who was so sick and tired of being alone.

A loud thump somewhere behind me injected me with adrenaline. The lights flickered again. Back-up generator. It would be fine. I wouldn't be in the dark. I made my way back to the fireplace and picked up a fire poker. Gretchen had instilled the comfort of wielding heavy objects in me.

Another thump and soft shuffles.

"Oh my God," I whispered.

My fear ratcheted up to brain-clogging hysteria.

Something was getting nearer. I backed up until I was tucked behind the corner of a long hallway. Only one way in. Along with a wicked sense of curiosity, I had been cursed with an overactive imagination, and now all I could picture was a serial killer that had been hiding in the house for months headed toward me with murder on their mind.

I gripped the poker tighter, ready to swing. My body rocked forward, ears pricked and desperate to catch the serial killer's arrival.

More footsteps. I held my breath. The element of surprise was all I had on my side now. When the stranger was right upon me, I took a deep breath in. I jumped out and bellowed like I was facing off a mountain lion, the poker straight out in front of me.

"ROAR!" I yelled.

I wasn't sure actually saying the word roar counted, but it got the job done. My assailant jumped a foot in the air away from me.

"Ah!" Devlin screamed.

I screamed.

We both screamed … but there was no ice cream. We took each other in. He squinted at me with one eye closed, and his T-shirt was on inside out and backwards like he'd gotten dressed in the dark. He wasn't wearing pants. Boxer shorts, yes, but that was it. He was practically Porky-pigging it.

The lights were on. I wasn't hiding. We made eye contact. He *had* to know it was me.

But surprising us both, a full second later, he screamed again.

It was not a manly shout. It was a high-pitched scream that some might say resembled that of a little girl. It's me. I am some. I would say that.

I dropped the poker out of pure shock at his terror. As my heart slowed down, a smile grew. Laughter bubbled up from deep in my chest.

Devlin clutched a hand to his chest, his eyes wide. Backing into the wall behind him, he bumped into a short ornamental table, jostling a potted plant and knocking a small figurine over. Startled, Devlin yelped in fright and jerked away.

At this point, my arms were wrapped tight around my middle. The laughter came so hard, I was silent.

"Kim?" His voice was ragged and sleepy. "What's going on?" After what felt like years of blinking at me while I laughed my face off, he finally seemed to fully register it was me. I couldn't handle it. He was so dopey. Not at all the broody Devil of the Symphony now.

I shook with silent laughter. I just couldn't stop hearing his girly little scream on a loop in my head.

"Are you—are you laughing at me?" he asked.

"Your scream—" I gasped out.

"You scared me." He scratched his head, drowsy with sleep.

"Yeah, but then you screamed again." My voice went up as I spoke. "Even after you saw it was me," I gasped out, still fighting the giggles.

"I was confused—" he said.

"Like a Disney Princess."

The corner of his mouth lifted. "That's sexist."

I sobered long enough to say, "You're right." I nodded seriously. Then on a tight, controlled breath I added, "Disney princesses are made of tougher stuff these days."

I breathed deep. No more laughing.

"Okay. Okay. I was sound asleep. I'm so glad you find this hilarious." His voice was fake-stern but his eyes softened with amusement.

"And again when—when you hit the table. Don't forget about that. You yelped!"

His voice took on a wry, self-deprecating tone. "Well. You can never trust these tables. They jump out of nowhere."

That was it. I was lost to another fit. My back slid down the wall until I rested my head on my knees. The post-terror adrenaline and Devlin's unexpected reaction had made me a little loopy. Every time I thought I had my laughter under control, I'd picture his oh-so-manly jump and the cycle just started again. My cheeks hurt from so much smiling.

Devlin chuckled a little as he shook his head. He slid down the opposite wall until we were facing each other in the hall. One lone light shone above us.

"I'm not used to company," he said.

My face muscles twitched with the effort of composure. Finally, I collected myself enough to breathe deeply and wiped the tears from my cheeks.

"I'm never going to forget that for as long as I live," I vowed.

"I'm here to entertain." He had his back to the wall, one leg bent to his chest, the other leg sprawled out in front. He watched me like he thought I was the funny one. He looked half-asleep and wholly adorable. "If you ever tell anybody I screamed like that, they'll never find your body," he said, his tone dead serious.

"Five minutes ago, that might have scared me." I grinned across the short distance between us. "But that was before I heard you yelp."

He shook his head and then rested it back against the wall. The action jostled the small statue on the table and it fell over the edge, hitting his leg.

He jumped again and without a sound, clutched his hand to his chest. He glared at me, his face braced for my reaction.

I was lost to another fit of laughter.

CHAPTER 20

You aren't alone.
Devlin

Kim's eyes had heavy shadows under them, and she could hardly hold up her head. Her skin was so pale it looked like it might shatter if kissed. The last few minutes had really taken it out of her.

"Why aren't you sleeping?" I asked.

She made a face where she scrunched up her nose and lips. Thunder crashed and her whole body tensed.

"Are you afraid of the storm?"

"I'm not afraid," she said. "I just couldn't sleep through it." She yawned. "Then you scared me."

"I scared you?" I asked in a flat, sarcastic tone. "I live here. You were the one wandering around setting off the security cameras."

Her eyebrows shot up. "Security cameras?"

"Yes. But don't worry, they're only set when we're sleeping or not home. They're motion activated."

Her eyes widened. "They weren't going during the SWS meeting, were they?"

I kept my face blank and watched her. No. They hadn't been recording, but now I sort of wished that they had been. What had those women been cackling about? At least the bathroom incident happened after that. I shuddered to think what they would have thought of the eyeful that Kim got.

Finally, after a minute of letting her sweat it out, I said. "No. Privacy and all that."

"Right. Of course." She let out a breath and looked so boneless she might need carrying up to her room.

The image of her asleep in my arms again tightened my chest with something like longing. I recalled holding her like that before, how trusting and innocent she'd been in her sleep. It was a far cry from her uncontrollable giggling a minute ago, or the Kim that challenged Wes at dinner.

"Hey, remember when you morphed into a praying mantis and yelled like one of those screaming goats?"

"I remember." I flared my nostrils.

"Good times." She yawned again.

"Praying mantis?" I asked.

"Yeah," she said. "When you jumped. Your arms sort of tucked up like this." She mimicked what I thought looked a lot more like a Tyrannosaurus Rex.

"It was a real hoot," I said flatly.

After a minute, she sighed and looked around. "I'd be scared all the time if I lived in this big house all alone."

"It's not so bad." My chest tightened. There were times, more recently, that the emptiness of this house got to me. I'd imagine what it might be like to sit by the fire with somebody. Or hear the soft hums of another person in the next room. But it was my choice to be here. I was happy being alone.

This time, her yawn was so big her jaw cracked.

"You need to go to bed," I said.

"I know." She didn't move from the wall. She scratched her nose, a stall tactic I was beginning to recognize when she debated whether or not to say something. "I just—I had some rough nights in rehab, where I was alone and I dunno …"

"You aren't alone," I said. "But neither of us are asleep."

"True. Can I ask a favor? And can you just agree to it without hearing it?"

"No," I said instantly.

"Pleeeease?" She dragged out the word.

"I'll never agree to anything without hearing it first. That's how people end up with a tattoo of a platypus on their ass."

"I feel like there's a story there. We'll circle back to that later." As she spoke, she thumbed the worn fabric on the knee of her sweatpants—my sweatpants. "I just don't want to sleep alone."

If she didn't want to sleep alone that meant … "Uh," was all I managed.

"It's not that I'm scared."

"You said that already," I said.

"I just don't want to be alone in my room. Don't read anything into it."

"Okay." I swallowed.

"I can sleep on your floor?"

"My floor?" my voice cracked.

"I'm sorry. I know this is weird."

"It's not weird. I just—" *Boundaries, boundaries, boundaries.* She was taking a blow torch to all the walls holding our roles in place. I had to tell her no. I had to be strong. Lightning flashed again and her whole body tensed. She was exhausted. I was exhausted. There was really only one way to ensure we both got sleep.

Five minutes later, Kim and I stood at the side of my bed, staring down at the king-size with equal looks of hesitation.

"Okay." Kim broke the tension first. "We could let this be awkward, but let's be honest, we're both so far past that point that it would serve no purpose. It's a sleepover and we're both so tired."

"And the bed is a king," I added. "I could build a wall of pillows."

"I'm about to pass out face-first on this bed. You could probably give me that platypus ass tattoo and I wouldn't even wake up. Let's not worry about pointless walls."

I cleared my throat, not thinking about her ass. Nope. I said, "Me too."

We both got under the sheets. What did she think of my room? It was unadorned. A giant bed in the middle of a giant room that I fell into every so often. More often, I slept on the couch downstairs in the studio. No personal touches decorated the walls or sat on the dresser. Just bare. But the bed, at least, had top-of-the-line, high thread count sheets that felt like butter. Before I turned off the light, I caught her nestling deeper into the sheets with a soft smile on her face. A rumble of thunder, farther off now, didn't even disturb her.

"Why do you hate being alone?" I asked in a low whisper.

"Why do you love being alone?" she murmured in a slurred voice.

Being alone wasn't something I actively chose. It just happened that way. Years of people showing their true natures. Not knowing who to trust. Traveling. New places. It was just easier that way.

"I don't," I finally said.

The soft sounds of her deep sleep were her only reply.

CHAPTER 21

I HEAR YOU PLAYING IN MY DREAMS.

KIM

*M*y body felt too hot. My skin was covered in a damp sweat. It was too soon to wake up. I was still too tired. Not all of my senses worked yet. My mind balanced on a thin line of consciousness. But something had woken me. Something I hadn't felt in a long time.

Lust, all muddled and confusing. It was like being drugged. I couldn't really tell what was happening, but I knew I wanted sex. My body craved weight pressing down on it, filling it. My hips rocked trying to find relief that wasn't there. My nipples were rock hard; my breasts ached to be teased.

I was on fire. I was pressed against a source of incredible heat igniting me from the inside out.

Desperate for relief, I turned on my side to rub my body closer to the source of heat. Had I ever felt this level of arousal? It was the type of horniness that came from watching something naughty. There was an over-arching sense of dread that I couldn't pinpoint. Dread wasn't the right word. A fear of being caught. Like a ticking clock warning time was running out. A thrill …

My back arched. This was wrong. I shouldn't be doing it. But why not? It felt so good. The sense of wrongness only fueled the lust burning through me.

But I couldn't stop.

Realization that I wasn't alone drifted into my still waking brain. I registered a massive muscular body beneath me. A thick thigh flexed between my legs. My fingers clenched on muscles. I dug my nails deep into hard flesh. Hands rubbed up my arms and down my body, squeezed my ass. Pulled me closer. I was sweating now. Panting. A rigid length rubbed against my hip. If I could just reach it, shift it closer so I could … my hand found its destination.

A moan escaped me as I continued to rock.

The form under me stiffened.

Then the rest settled in. The thunderstorm. The sleeping arrangement.

I froze, stock still.

The body under me shuffled, causing me to fall slightly off. The light clicked on. Devlin and I shot apart.

"Oh my God!" I clutched the sheet to my chest. Not that I knew why. I was fully dressed but my nipples were still hard, my breasts heavy with fading desire.

Devlin shook sleep from his head. "Shit," he mumbled. He glanced to me, still clutching the sheet. "Are you okay?"

"I don't know—"

His gaze followed mine to his lap and he quickly covered himself with a pillow. But not before I saw the massive hardness barely restrained by cotton boxers. I sucked in my lips.

"Sorry—I was sleeping," he said. His hair was ruffled, and his eyes were squinting.

"No. It's okay. I just woke up." My cheeks flamed red.

I was humiliated. But at the same time … unsettled. Restless. And I was still on fire.

Even in the dim light of the table lamp I could see color in his cheeks. His chest heaved. We were panting and our gazes met. We both looked away quickly.

"Shit," he repeated. He ran a hand over his face. "Kim. I'm so sorry. I don't—I was sleeping," he repeated.

I bit my cheek to keep from smiling. "I was too. It's okay. It was a dream. I was dreaming and then I wasn't."

I studied the bit of space on the bed between us. There was dampness in my underwear, and I recalled how I had been grinding against him. I was embarrassed but maybe not as embarrassed as I should be. Had he felt the dampness from my arousal on his leg? God, what was wrong with me?

He was taking deep breathes with his eyes closed.

"I was dreaming too," he said.

I would pay good money to know what he'd been dreaming.

"This was an accident," I said.

"Yes. I wouldn't have—"

"It's okay." I smoothed my hair before twisting it up into a quick bun. I slept with it down and could only imagine how it looked. He watched the action closely before looking to my lips and then eyes.

"We were both sleeping," he said almost in question.

"Yes. Definitely sleeping. It was just. I think—I mean, we're human. And I don't know about you, but it's been a while for me." I clamped shut. I really needed to stop talking.

He cleared his throat. "Yeah, I just—"

"Just what?" I asked too quickly.

"I mean yeah, it's been a while for me too."

"It has?"

He gave me a look.

"Sorry. Don't answer that. Boundaries," I mumbled.

"I knew this was a bad idea," he said softly, almost to himself.

"The storm ..." It had shaken me more than I had wanted to admit, but the second we'd climbed into bed together I'd fallen right asleep. I'd slept better than I had in ages. It was like our bodies had just made a decision in our sleep for us.

"I understand. I really am sorry. Did I " he cleared his throat. "Are you okay?"

"I'm fine. You have nothing to be sorry about. You didn't do anything. I mean I was the one on top of you. I was the one—"

"It's okay." He took another deep breath. He lifted the pillow to look and quickly put it back.

"You knew it was a bad idea?" I felt shame with that. A different sort of shame. I was the one who walked in on him in the shower. I was the one that was basically dry humping him in his sleep. I kept crossing the lines while he worked to keep them in place. How long until he'd want to stop working with me all together?

"You're a beautiful woman. I'm a man. I'm alone a lot—not that it excuses it. Our bodies must have just—" He was rambling, talking almost to himself.

"Totally. It was a subconscious thing." I situated the blankets to cover my smile.

For all of my talk about not caring for being called beautiful by men, when Devlin said it—as though it was just an obvious fact, as though he'd always felt that way, and it was just something he was used to—well, I was ashamed to say that it lit me up. I felt sexy. I hadn't felt sexy in a very long time. I'd kept myself muted. He only knew me as a muted shade of brown, and yet he thought I was beautiful.

He grabbed his phone from the nightstand.

"What time is it?" I asked.

"It's only 5:30."

"I usually get up at this time. I won't be going back to sleep," I said.

"Me neither."

Our gazes clashed again, and I smiled. He smiled back, but it was tensed. "This could have been very awkward."

"Thank goodness it's not awkward at all. We can just get up and have coffee. We should check the roads. No need to ever talk about it again." I shrugged. I played it off so he wouldn't get freaked out. I'd pushed too far.

"Good idea," he said.

"Right. So, I'll just go make some coffee?" I asked.

"Sounds good. I'll meet you in the kitchen."

"Okay." I blew out air from pursed lips.

The arousal had worn off and I was left with a wired restlessness. I rolled my head side to side and stretched my arms over my head.

He cleared his throat. "I'm just going to go take a quick shower."

"Okay." I nodded with an expectant look.

He shifted before scratching at his beard. He subtly tilted his head toward the pillow in his lap.

"Oh. Right. Well, I'll just go get that coffee going."

A smile crept on my face as I made my way down the hall.

CHAPTER 22

PRACTICE IS NOT AN OPTION.

KIM

Weeks passed. Spring melted into summer.

Devlin and I worked every available weekend. My courage increased. I spoke up more and more. He always listened to my suggestions. Our relationship matured. My attraction to him was ever present, yes, but I was beginning to long for more. My fingers itched to check in with him and ask about his day. We texted almost daily now. At first, it was about music or our schedule, but now we were just talking. Sharing stupid memes about platypuses and music jokes. I learned more about life with an older brother and a set of wonderfully typical parents. He knew my schedule and accommodated it. He snuck me snacks when my blood sugar dropped. I would give him coffee and a solid hour to fully wake.

We still didn't talk about the mask. We never referenced a time after the *Smokey Mountain Suite* would be complete.

I wanted so much more.

Now, June was passing in a blur. As I walked into the SOOK rehearsal on what I thought was just another Monday, I quickly realized something was up. Nobody was set up, and in fact, most of the musicians stood around whispering. Typically, strings would be plucked and tuned, horns would be tested, and drums thrummed.

I spotted Erin and made my way over. "What's going on?" I asked.

Erin widened her eyes but kept her voice neutral. "We're having guests."

"Oh, no." It was supposed to be a rehearsal. Nothing else was on the calendar. I purposely wore baggy boyfriend style jeans and a worn Death Cab for Cutie tee, hoping to avoid notice, per my usual plan.

I had been attracted to men before. It was easy to justify away pure physical attraction. But my feelings for Devlin were growing into something away from cotton candy closer to meat and potatoes.

"Where's Devlin?" I asked Erin.

She narrowed her eyes at me. "Devlin, huh?"

"Maestro. Shut up."

"I didn't say anything."

I glared. "Your tone said plenty."

"How are those practices going? Anything I should know—"

"Attention." Devlin chose that moment to walk in the room. Saved by the baller.

"Remind me to circle back to that," Erin whispered before running back to her chair.

"I will not," I responded under my breath.

I sat down and stared pointedly at back the of Barry's head, focusing on how his ears protruded much like Mr. Potato Head's. I continued to focus on my breathing even as Devlin brushed past me, squeezing through the rows of chairs so close that the back of his hand brushed against my arm. His scent filled my nose. His scent that night weeks ago still haunted me, thick with arousal … Chills prickled up my arm.

Ah, nuts, I had it bad.

"We aren't having the usual practice today," he said in a normal voice. The room was so quiet, I'm sure the percussion section heard just fine.

I risked a glance up at him. It always took me aback to see him with his mask and hat on again. I had forgotten what he looked like with them. Or rather, I'd gotten used to being able to openly study his face as I pleased. I was greedy to memorize the details of his face. The deep indent of his upper lip. The few strands of gray mixed in his black eyebrows. The flare of his nostrils when he was particularly into a piece of music, even if I was the one playing. Especially if I was the one playing. The deep black of those piercing eyes was somehow more arresting without the distraction of the mask. Now, all I could see were his eyes narrowed in focus.

They flicked to me. I looked away as though I'd been burned. Too late. I'm sure he'd caught me staring. Way to play it cool.

When the room grew loud with whispers, he clanged the baton against the podium. He cleared his throat. "I understand that a break is in order. You've all been pushing yourself with these constant rehearsals. We could use a change of pace."

Erin and I exchanged an intrigued look.

"We will be playing for a special group of visitors today."

There were more whispers, so when he spoke again his tone was sharp with warning. "But even though this wasn't planned, that doesn't mean we shouldn't give the best performance possible."

I couldn't identify a single person, but there seemed to be small groan of understanding that we would be playing for someone who could potentially give us money. Blah. A group of rich, old-money types were gonna come in and judge us, and here I was dressed like it was laundry day.

"I'm going to bring the guests in and then we'll play the 1812 Overture. I'll be back in ten minutes sharp. Be prepared to play immediately." Right before he left the room, he stopped and turned to add, "This may be one of the most important performances the SOOK plays. I know you're all more than capable. Make me proud today, but more importantly, make yourselves proud." He stepped out and the door clicked closed behind him.

The room stayed silent in disbelief for several beats.

All at once whisper broke out as instruments were lugged out and unpacked.

"Was that a compliment?" someone whispered to my right.

"Something is up with him," another added.

As instructed, we were all in position when Devlin returned. Violins lifted to chins, arms raised, we were ready.

I didn't look, but behind me were the softs sounds of shoes shuffling as bodies filled the room. Across from me, the violins—who faced the door—relaxed their arms and a few confused smiles crossed their faces. Devlin lifted his arms, commanding our attention, and before I could look, we were off.

We played the music as we had a hundred times, but this time it was immediately different. Softs gasps and shocked whispers from our audience filled the air as we began. Devlin looked to the still-unseen guests and gestured with his chin as if to say come in.

To my utter shock and delight, in my periphery, I could see children move into the space in the front of the room. They walked slowly, with wide eyes, in clumps, afraid to make too much noise. I couldn't help the smile that split my face. The children ranged in age, from maybe ten and up? Middle and high schoolers?

As soon as the horns and the drums started, they began to relax. Each child's eyes greedily jumped from one instrument to the other. Suzie's Ford, a cute guy in the back with salt and pepper hair, wore a Ford's Fosters shirt and grinned with ease as the music built and built.

The kids relaxed and moved their arms to mimic the musicians and one brave kid even stood behind Devlin in a showy move of silliness to impersonate conducting arms. Devlin spotted his shadow. I thought he'd been about to scowl, but the surprises kept coming. Devlin gestured him to come up and take the baton. He helped guide the teen's hand for a four-count then dropped it. Obviously, the kid couldn't keep the beat but at this point, we didn't really need it. Devlin didn't seem to care that it might mess with the performance.

Erin's eyebrows were high with shock, matching my own feelings. My chest swelled with pride, as though I'd had something to do with this.

As the music built and built, their gasps of delight grew wider. By the time the climax came, there wasn't a single one of them who didn't have look of shock and joy on their face.

My own smile couldn't be wiped off and my heart ran away with the tempo. I remembered all at once what it felt like to love music. To hear the power of it. To remember the pure unadulterated joy that came with hearing an entire room come to life with sound. Music from nothing. Sounds from brass and wood and metal, all from talented musicians. I remembered that feeling. How it ached in your chest and made you feel both tiny and infinite.

I got so into the music, I just played, hardly needing to glance at the music. The others did too. When I looked around the room, they were all moving, dancing in their chairs, sweating and smiling like they felt it too. This was what music was all about. It was exactly what we'd all needed to feel and see. Hokey or not, there was a reason this song was a crowd pleaser.

By the time he cut off the last note my eyes were glossy, because duh, and the kids burst out with whoops and clapped and jumped up and down. Some pumped their arms and a few even shared looks of awe.

If I had hoped to nip my feelings in the bud, I'd been terribly mistaken. My feelings for Devlin just bloomed like a flower garden after a spring storm. Admiration was a lot harder to ignore than desire.

CHAPTER 23

MUSIC CONTAINS LIFE.

DEVLIN

Kim might have been right. Maybe, just maybe, yelling wasn't always the best way to get results. The whole point of coming back to this place was to make it through one season. To play *my* music. In order to do that, my symphony would have to respect me. We all needed the reminder of the power of music. Seeing all the looks of joy from playing to the students awakened a feeling deep inside of me I'd long forgotten. People needed to respect me, or worse, trust me.

The booming crescendo of the piece made all the visiting students clap. Pride stirred me up instead of letting me down. They played with life and zeal yet unseen. It was exactly what I had been trying to force out of them, but this had coaxed it out so naturally.

The music ended and my arms lowered. Thankfully, my mask was firmly in place or they'd see the grin that matched theirs. It was one thing to try a different tactic; it was another thing to start smiling and palling around.

Once the group of observers behind me settled down, I said, "Thank you all for coming."

The students clapped with whoops of excitement. Some of the more outgoing ones bowed dramatically. "Everybody, these are Ford's Fosters, a local organization that specializes in showing the world to those who may not be able to see it otherwise. Let's welcome them."

The symphony stomped their feet in their own version of applause and it rolled like thunder in the room around us.

My gaze flicked to Kim. Her face was lit up with a huge grin and her eyes glistened. She wore her heart on her sleeve. Emotions shone out of her like sunshine even when she tried to diminish herself. She wasn't looking at me; instead, she examined the group that hovered behind me. Did she remember mentioning her friend Suzie and her fiancé who ran this organization? It was an offhand comment made in one of the many conversations we'd shared these past weeks. Would she notice how closely I hung on to every word she said? Would it give away too much, too soon?

Turning back to the students, I said, "Feel free to walk around and ask any questions you like. Maybe some of you will be lucky enough to try an instrument."

Before I finished, several had already made their way to the musicians. The drums were the most crowded, ever the crowd-pleaser, but almost all the musicians were soon matched to a student.

I paced the room like a surveyor. Small talk had never come naturally, but I fielded a few questions. I didn't love to do it, but it had its place. It felt like a few of the performers looked at me with something more than fear or resentment. Something like begrudging respect at worst, and maybe just a few of them saw me in a new light at best. Kim had been right.

A gaggle of young girls surrounded me, each of them twisting a foot or twirling their hair while they batted their eyelashes. I was familiar with this, at least.

"Why do you wear a mask?" one asked bluntly. Her head was shaved all the way around the bottom and the top was a bright purple color.

"Insider secrets," I answered, and they all giggled.

When I glanced up, Kim was talking to a young girl with long, thin braids, who hesitantly plucked at Kim's strings. Even Carla seemed to be enjoying showing off to a kid with several facial piercings. The gaggle moved on to try their luck with a stand-up bassist.

"Devlin?" the voice came from my side.

"Clifford?" I asked.

"You can call me Ford." The man I had only spoken to on the phone extended his hand.

"How are you?" I asked as we shook.

"I'm great. That was fantastic. I had chills. Thank you again for having us."

"I'd love to say my motives were purely altruistic, but the SOOK needed this more than I would have thought."

We both took in the scene around us.

"That's the great thing about doing good. Everybody wins. Happiness only gets stronger the more it's given out."

"Truer words," I said.

I studied the man at my side. He looked a bit like a stuffed shirt. I wouldn't have expected him to be with a woman like Suzie Samuels. Their pairing was like a sleek black panther hooking up with Garfield the cat. But you never knew with love. There was no logic.

"How do you know Suzie?" he asked.

"I don't actually. Not well. Her friend Kim from the SWS mentioned you."

I wasn't sure if Kim was hiding who she was, or who knew her only as Christine. When we looked to her, she waved with a happy smile at Ford. He smiled and waved back. So maybe she wasn't concerned about it. Then again, she'd probably smile like that at just about anybody she deemed worthy.

She smiled at me like that sometimes.

Ford said, "I've only met Kim a few times, but I'm glad you thought of us. These kids seem excited. I wouldn't have thought playing music would be so physical, but after that, I can see I was wrong."

"Music is a powerful thing. Maybe for the kids who seem interested, we could arrange some private lessons or instrument rentals. It can be an expensive hobby, but maybe the SOOK can work something out."

Ford's eyes lit up. "That would be fantastic. Suzie mentioned that Kim does private lessons for free. I wasn't sure how common that was."

I kept my face impassive to hide this startling new information. "Most charge an hourly rate. But there might be a way around that," I said.

"These kids are judged harshly sometimes." Ford spoke with quiet intensity. "But they have just as much to offer as anybody else given the opportunity."

"We all need someone to believe in us," I said. My eyes flicked to Kim and back again. "The SOOK is striving to be a bigger part of the community."

"Well, we appreciate it. Thanks again. Oh, Xander is getting a little aggressive with those big drums over there. I'll talk to you more later." He clapped me on the shoulder and shuffled over to the percussion section.

Warmth filled me. My mind struggled to recall the last time I'd acted in somebody else's interest. It came up short. For so long, I'd been so caught up in myself and my own needs. I'd been goal-driven, but with blinders: the next big composition, the next big symphony. The SOOK was small. Knoxville was small. But for the first time in a long time, my mind didn't recoil at the idea of sticking around a little while longer.

My gaze moved around the room and landed back on Kim. Just until the end of the season …

* * *

After the kids from Ford's Fosters left, I hovered around, waiting for an opportunity to talk to Kim. Several of the musicians seemed eager to speak with me. It was surprising, though I supposed I had always rushed to and from our rehearsals without much chitchat. Making conversation was an exercise in futility. Usually, people either wanted to talk about themselves or about my mask; I was interested in neither. Admittedly, the conversations today weren't too excruciating. My focus kept being pulled to Kim, who took her time packing up her cello. I kept trying to get her attention, but to no avail.

I was eager to know what she thought of today. She seemed to be avoiding me, though I wasn't sure why. I had hoped that the day would show that I was open to her suggestions. I was desperate to hear how she thought it went.

All that changed when the world's most punchable face stepped in front of me.

"Chagny," I said.

"Devlin. That's what you go by now, right?"

I was too stunned by the offhand comment to respond. I stood frozen in place. What had he meant by that? Nobody at the SOOK knew of my life before Devlin.

"Or would you prefer Maestro?" So that was what he meant. I took a breath in through flared nostrils.

"Yes," I said.

He went on, a smug smile plastered to his face. "You should call me Roderick." He adjusted the cuffs of the suit he wore. "We're going to see each other a lot more. I'm sure." He glanced to Kim, who'd just finish packing up. "If you'll excuse me." He bumped me as he passed.

I glared. I wouldn't excuse him. I was about to grab him by the collar and kick him the hell out of my rehearsal space.

"Ah, Maestro, might we have a word?"

I took a steadying breath before I turned around. I had been riding so high after our performance; now I crashed back to earth.

"I'm busy," I said.

"I understand. We'll only be a minute," Dick said it affably, but there was no choice in the matter.

"Let's go to your office," Andy suggested.

I glanced one last time to see that Kim had set her cello case down and stood to hug Chagny. My lip curled.

"Why is Chagny always here?" I asked as soon as my office door shut behind me.

"Mr. and Mrs. Chagny are proud donors. Their son is welcome anytime." This was from Andy.

"It was a private rehearsal," I said.

"About today's rehearsal ..." Andy said.

"You didn't have permission to bring those students in," Dick said.

"I didn't realize I needed permission."

"Of course you did." Dick sputtered. "There are waivers to sign. Instruments to secure. Had we known they were so ..."

"Urban?" the other offered.

"Right. We would have put the instruments away. To have them walking around, touching them. That's risking thousands of dollars. There's a liability there. The musicians should have been aware beforehand."

I ground my teeth before choosing my words carefully. "They wanted to hear real music. They get enough garbage blasted at them. Studies have shown that children who can read music and play instruments consistently do better in other areas of studies and life. In fact—"

"Sure." Dick held up a hand. "We're glad to have more community involvement. But there are certain ways of doing things. You can't just invite a busload of young people without asking."

"I thought the goal was to generate interest in the SOOK," I said. My blood pressure was rising. My intentions were good. The goal had been to make people happy, and it had worked. Now I was be chastised for it? It was only because they wanted me out. They'd find any excuse to fire me.

"Of course, perhaps we could—"

I stood. "If we are done here." I was sick of paperwork and bureaucracy. It was about the music. The room closed in around me. Heat burned my cheeks. I needed fresh air.

Neither of the men moved. The sweaty one refused to look at me. I was tempted to yell, "Boo!" just to see if he jumped.

"I'm afraid this is your second strike, Maestro," Andy said.

"Second?" I asked.

"The first was announcing the chair additions the way you did. You have to learn to communicate with your symphony and coordinate with the board," Andy explained.

I frowned, but had no excuse to speak to. I needed to talk to Kim. Was it possible that I had made the wrong choice? Should I have cleared this event with management before I did it? I felt helpless and embarrassed for screwing up even when I tried to be better. Maybe I'd never get things right.

Dick added, "There can be no more warnings."

I bit my tongue. If I didn't, I would prove them exactly right. I stormed out of my office. By the time I got back to the room, Kim was gone.

CHAPTER 24

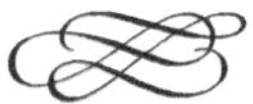

YOU'RE DISTRACTED. GET YOUR PRIORITIES IN ORDER.

KIM

My stomach was twisted with a dread I didn't understand. So when Roddy suggested we leave for lunch I accepted without hesitation. I needed some space away to work through some thoughts. Today had been a good day. Devlin had done a great thing. So why did I feel so sick and weird?

"Are you okay?" Roddy asked, opening the passenger door of his sports car for me.

It was fancy and fast and red. I dropped into the low bucket seat and plastered on a smile for him. "Of course. Just hungry."

He nodded and shut the door. When he was buckled in, he asked, "Anywhere in particular you want to go?"

This was a dreaded question. If I picked and the service was bad or the food was subpar, then I'd be the one at fault. I could eat anywhere. It didn't matter to me, but he needed a decision. Just this minor choice added to the quickening dread doubling inside me.

Still, I wanted to contribute and sound interesting, so I said, "There's this new French bistro with an appetizer that has six different types of cheese. Sounds interesting."

"Let's try it," he said affably.

At the restaurant, I regretted my decision almost immediately. The hostess was short in tone and pretentious. The ten minutes to even be sat felt too long.

"I should have just called up my friend. He owns the Waterfront Grille. We could be eating by now," Roddy said, glancing at his phone.

When we were finally sat, I spent the entire meal silently wishing the server would hurry. I had been looking forward to spending time with Roddy again, but now that I was here, I just wanted to leave.

"I'm sorry," I said. "You should have picked."

He laughed it off. "Not every place in Tennessee is fine dining."

I returned his smile but my food sat untouched.

"Quite a stunt he pulled today," Roddy said as I pushed a piece of bread around my plate.

"Stunt?" I asked. It hadn't felt like a stunt.

"Devlin. With the kids. He's trying to get people to like him and using children as a tool. It's sad. I feel bad for those kids."

"I think he was just trying to interest the next generation." I pushed my plate away. I didn't want to think or talk about Devlin or rehearsal.

"Why not bring in the kids that go to Camp Hickory? That's real talent. It's still around, you know. They've been upgrading a little, thankfully. But man, some of the best memories, right?"

"Well. Some of them," I said.

He searched my face. "Right. Well. Our time together, at least."

The napkin twisted in my fingers. "You know. After camp. I wasn't—I struggled with what happened with Ariana."

I hoped he'd sensed my need to talk about it. I hoped he wanted to talk about it too.

"Don't think about it. It was a tragic accident," he said.

"I—"

His frown quickly snapped into a smile. "I've missed you. I never stopped thinking about you."

I flushed. "I thought about you too." I thought about so much.

"Yo-Yo, I want to start new. As adults. We have a wonderful history together, and that's part of why I feel so at ease with you."

I smiled. I had thought I'd feel at ease with him, but I hadn't felt relaxed since we'd left.

"I want to be with you. We should give us another shot," he said abruptly.

"Oh." Shouldn't this be just what I wanted to hear? A cloud hung over my head from my complicated feelings for Devlin.

"I don't want to rush anything. Only if you're ready. I know we were away from each other for a long time. I'd like you to take your time and get to know me again."

"That sounds nice," I said. "Getting to know each other now."

"But the notes. The time at camp. You need to move on. I worry about you."

"Your notes saved me." If he could just understand what the notes meant for me, maybe he'd be open to talking more about everything. I didn't want him to regret sending them.

"I was just a kid back then. I'm a little embarrassed about it."

Was it possible that I did give the notes too much power? I was an adult who cherished a shoebox of old scribblings. It had never felt childish to me though. This wasn't the time to breech this topic. I had too much on my mind.

"You're right. Let's start over," I said. "I've been distracted."

"Devlin asks too much of this symphony. I mean, God, it's the SOOK, not New York or London."

I took a sip of water as I felt myself bristle.

Was I self-sabotaging? Pushing Roddy away because of my confused attraction for Devlin? A man, who, by the way, had not shown any returned interest but that I continued to fawn over like a helpless teenager. Was a school-girl obsession swaying my thoughts?

I wasn't being fair to Roddy. I was in a funk, but it wasn't his fault. He was genuinely trying. Maybe I was over-thinking an opportunity at a renewed relationship with an old friend.

"I think I could make you happy. You don't have to do anything." He put his hands on the table between us and gestured for me to take them. They were soft and warm. He offered so much simple security. He had always cared about me. I needed to remember that.

"You're a good friend." I smiled at him.

His smile faltered for a flash. "There's no rush. Just trust that I want what's best for you."

I nodded. "I trust you."

As he spoke the intense pressure that had been building all day began to melt away. There were no choices to be made. It had always been Roddy. He was back in my life for a reason.

"I see such big things for you. You're so beautiful and talented. I'm so incredibly proud to know you."

I flushed. "Thank you."

Roddy was safety. Devlin stirred up dark part of my soul and had me questioning myself. I couldn't trust my own judgment around Devlin and facts were facts. Roddy was here. Roddy straight up told me he wanted what's best for me.

"I just worry about the pressure Devlin is putting on you," he said. I must have had my thoughts clearly written all over my face. "Just because you inspire him, doesn't mean his work should come at cost to you."

"He thinks I'm talented."

"Of course you are. I have no doubt of that. You could do anything. That's one of the things I have always appreciated about you. I just want to make sure that working with him is what you want. That you weren't pressured into it. He may see you as a muse, but I know you're more than that."

"I don't think I'm his muse." But hadn't Devlin confessed something similar? Hadn't he said that he needed me to help him finish his composition?

"The fact is you're beautiful. I'm not saying there's any reason other than your talent, but there's talk around the SOOK, I'm sorry to say. People are questioning why he chose you for the solo. Obviously, I've told them it's because you're the most gifted."

"No, I'm not—"

"But there is talk, you know. Because he's a conductor. He wants you for something more."

"It's not like that." I hated that we were even having this discussion. It was making me angry for reasons I couldn't define in that moment. Something I would have to unpack later. I should be flattered, right? People thought I was beautiful. But it didn't feel like flattery.

I pushed the thoughts away.

"Let's not talk about work anymore," I said.

"Good idea. Let's have some wine to toast our new venture." He poured from a bottle he got for the table. I hadn't had any.

"What new venture?" I wouldn't drink, but I took the glass to not push the issue.

"You're amazing, Yo-Yo, and more important than that, you're gorgeous. I'm going to represent you."

"Represent me?" I managed to ask as I gripped the chair to keep from spinning.

"Yes. You need to go solo. You're bigger than this place."

"How so?"

"Touring. Albums. You have the look. You're sort of ethnically ambiguous but still gorgeous. You'll be huge. Just imagine being on stage." He held up his thumb and pointer finger from both hands to create a box around me he looked through. "Your hair down would be amazing—maybe streaks of wild colors, add some curl and volume. Your clothes could be updated, maybe some short skirts, hate to say it, but that's what sells. You could even get one of those chic electric cellos. I have ideas."

"Wow. Yes, you do."

I blinked and the world spun. I couldn't wear a skirt with a cello. I literally spread my legs and straddled wood. I didn't like the sound of an electric cello, not for my style. And I couldn't play with my hair down; it gets caught in the fingerboard and tugs.

He'd clearly put thought into this and he was so excited, but this was all a lot and very fast. Why was it so easy for me to share my feelings with Devlin, while I worried about offending Roddy?

"Maybe we can talk about it more later?" I settled on. Maybe I could talk things through with the SWS.

"Let me tell you what I'm thinking for your solo tour." He pulled out his phone and pulled up a map to show me.

"I don't know if I'm ready for a tour."

"When you're ready. But I've already talked to several concert hall managers. My parents have big connections, you know. I say we start there. Stops all around the southeast. Then we start promoting you on social media as we go. You could be huge on YouTube and Instagram. Really sell your image."

"Wow. This is a lot. I need to think about it," I said firmly.

"Of course, of course." He put his phone back in his pocket. "I will take care of you, Yo-Yo, forever. Let me take care of everything."

"That sounds nice." And it did.

CHAPTER 25

FIND YOUR INFLUENCES IN ALL THE GENRES.

KIM

"Yeah but why do the rumors make me so angry?" I asked the group of women around me.

The SWS was at Genie's for an unscheduled, emergency meeting at my request. The girls were happy to meet up. Country music blared all around us. My voice was hoarse from talking so much all at once. There was so much to tell them. Genie's was decently packed for a Thursday night. There weren't a ton of bars in Green Valley that weren't overrun by bikers. Genie's was the place to be. Their fried pickles and wings were fuhgeddaboutit.

"It makes you angry because it's bullshit," Gretchen shouted back. "Women are told that they only have value if they're screwable and then when people want to screw them, they get judged for it and labeled things like whore. GAH!" She threw up her arms.

Blithe nodded. "It's true. Damn if you do, damned if you don't."

"Damned if you do *it*, damned if you don't do *it*," Gretchen said.

"Beauty is totally subjective and superfluous anyway," Roxy added. Her eyeliner was extra dark tonight, even for her. I made a mental note to make sure she was okay. "Everything is a construct of the patriarchy."

"True that," I said.

"And I won't feel guilty for wanting to be sexy either!" Suzie said with emotion. "I can wear sweatpants, or I can hooch it up. But it's for me ... okay, sometimes for Ford ... but anyway."

Just being here with my girls and venting had already improved my mood.

"Also, it's a creepy double standard. If it was Barry chosen for the solo, nobody would bat an eye. But because I'm young and objectively not ugly, they assume I've used sex to get ahead," I said, feeling empowered around my girls.

"Not ugly?" Gretchen dramatically clutched a hand to her chest. "Watch out now, Kim's getting a big head."

I stuck out my tongue at her. "It just sucks because there's nothing I can do."

"So cluck 'em," Suzie chimed in. "Listen, as a stripper, I've been on both sides. People hate no matter what. Who cares? The people who really care about you won't judge you."

"Cheers to that," Blithe held up her glass and we toasted for at least tenth time that night. Mine was just water, but the feeling was there.

"I know it's easier said than done though. When you're the one living it and hearing it," Suzie added, "it just plain sucks."

I nodded with a pout. "It doesn't help that I'm really, really attracted to Devlin."

I lowered my voice, but the music must have stopped at that exact moment because I swore it echoed across the bar.

"What?" This was from Roxy, who had been glaring at a rugged looking biker in the corner. "When did this happen? I thought we were team Roddy."

Gretchen said, "It's okay to be attracted to multiple people at the same time."

"I'm undecided on Roddy. It's the attraction to Devlin that's confusing. I feel weird about it. Especially if he only sees me as musical inspiration."

Once Roddy had pointed it out, I couldn't stop thinking about it. I had feelings for Devlin but what did he think about me? I didn't know. We'd never talked about that.

"You think Devlin is using you?" Roxy asked. "Actually, he does remind me of another devilishly handsome biker we all know."

"He who shall not be named," Blithe said.

Gretchen waved her hand, waving away her comment. "Don't forget Jethro had great taste. Look around you."

We all nodded in agreement.

"He just wasn't our person," Suzie said shrugging.

"Right. Our person. Cause that's a thing." Roxy rolled her eyes. "Also, Devlin is the conductor of a symphony and a composer of music—he isn't exactly riding with the Iron Wraiths and hocking drugs and women."

"But he's angry and …" I started.

"Challenging?" Gretchen asked sipping her drink.

"Yes. I dunno how it would even work between us." I shook my head, clearing thoughts of Devlin. "Roddy says he wants the best for me. He puts everything out there."

"How nice," Gretchen said.

"Don't do that," I said. "Don't rain on my parade. Not all men are evil."

She held my gaze. "If you're really happy and this is really what you want I, of course, support you."

"Thank you," I said.

"It just feels like you are trying to sell yourself as much as you're selling us," she added.

I frowned. I wasn't explaining myself well if that was how I came across. "Roddy and I have so much history. He calls me Yo-Yo. It's sweet."

"He calls you Yo-Yo? That doesn't sound fun," Blithe said.

"After the famous cellist, Yo-Yo Ma," I clarified. "He always has. It's our thing."

"He couldn't think of any famous female cellists?" Gretchen asked.

I glared at her. "Can you name a famous female cellist?"

"I'm not in that industry," she shot back.

"Also, am I allowed to ask something?" Blithe said. "Isn't that vaguely racist? I know you have some Korean heritage and Yo-Yo Ma is Chinese-American but … you don't think that's why he calls you that, do you?"

"No. That would be …" I paused to think. "No. He wouldn't. It's only because he's literally the only cello player most people know."

But truthfully, now that she'd said it, the seed had been planted. I shook my head to find my previous convictions. "I just needed to talk through things with y'all. I'm still processing a lot of stuff. It's all good." I grinned widely to prove my point.

I looked at each of them and they smiled back. Except Gretchen —she stabbed at a cherry in her glass.

"I don't want to sound crass," Blithe said, "but can we back up a little? I feel like we grazed over the details of the shower incident too quickly. I need specifics. A rough sketch would be fine too."

"You saw his dick?" Gretchen asked before sucking very suggestively on a straw.

"Yes," I said.

"And all the things?" Roxy asked.

"Like balls? I mean, not in great detail. I was distracted, but I saw *everything*." I took a deliberate amount of time to eat a fried pickle to avoid eye contact.

"What did it look like?" Roxy said.

"His penis?" Blithe blurted. Like she sneezed.

"Yes, his penis." Roxy twisted her mouth to the side. "I didn't want to say it, but now you've made it weird."

Heat flamed my cheek. "Yes. It is weird. But I said it too. Repeatedly. An unhealthy amount actually."

I waited for the other shoe to drop. I wouldn't spill Devlin's secret. It wasn't mine to share, and I had no way to know how'd they react. What if they wanted me to get an autograph? I could only imagine the irritated expression on his face if I were to ask him such a thing.

Blithe frowned at a cheese stick. "I didn't think anybody really liked to look at those things."

"I'm neutral," Gretchen said. "Some are nice."

"Are we still talking about the penis?" I asked.

"I want to know about his body too." Roxy's eyes lit up.

"For the record, I feel weird objectifying him," I said.

They all groaned and rolled their eyes.

"Yeah, totally, me too. We are all woke AF, blah blah. So what was his butt like?" Roxy asked.

"That being said," I continued as though I hadn't been interrupted. "He's a swimmer and ..." I made a swoony sigh. "To be honest, it's more than that. It's the fact that he can completely command a room of a hundred musicians. It's that when he plays the piano, he moves his fingers like a magician. It's that he can come up with an entire symphonic movement in his brain from nothing. It's almost like sorcery. I mean, that's incredible." I shook my head with a laugh. "And he can be really funny, too. It always surprises me when he makes me laugh because he tries to be so stern. Gosh, and you should hear him talk about his family. He has these two nieces—"

Four sets of eyes blinked at me.

"But it's obviously just physical attraction," Suzie said, a perfectly arched eyebrow judging me.

"I don't really know him. He hides himself. There's a lot that's off limits. I'm not gonna go telling Devlin I have this huge embarrassing crush only for him to look at me like I'm something he stepped in."

Devlin's intentions toward me were so unclear. Sometimes it seemed like he maybe he was ... I dunno, looking at me like a man looked at a woman. Other times we felt like no more than two business partners working toward the same goal.

"Can we talk about anything else?" I asked. "Suzie, how's the studio?"

"Crazy busy. It's amazing," Suzie said. We talked about Ford's Fosters and their fantastic visit. Suzie was in the middle of a story about Ford and Jack fighting over the proper way to load the dishwasher when her face completely changed and she cut herself off. "OH MY GOD!"

I looked to the door. I thought maybe Nico Manganiello had walked in. Stranger things had happened in Green Valley. A girl could dream.

When I brought my focus back to her, Suzie was looking at me like she'd just figured out crypto-currency. "You saw it."

"Yes. Penis. We get it. Can we move on? I'm feeling weird about it." Blithe threw a limp cheese-stick back in the plastic basket.

"Nooo. No, no, no …" Suzie shook her head. "That's not what I mean."

Adrenaline spiked my heart rate. Thankfully our waitress came to check on us. She was a cute brunette named Patty, about our age, maybe a little younger.

"Can I get y'all another round?" she asked.

Everybody nodded or said yes. "Anything else for you?" she asked me.

"Just water," I said. She was about to leave, but I didn't want to have to get back to Suzie's discovery. I desperately wracked my brains for small talk. "Patty, how's your momma?" I asked.

Patty placed a hand on her hip and cocked an eyebrow. "She's good."

Ugh, I was being so awkward. "And your cousin, Willa? How's she?"

"She's good too." Patty glanced quickly around the packed bar. "Haven't seen you out in a while. How are you?"

"Been busy. Oh, can you tell me about softball? You play softball right?" I asked with sudden inspiration. Suzie looked like she was about to burst with her discovery. I wouldn't be able to lie if they out right asked me who Devlin was. My face was an open book. I could only stall.

Patty smiled but it was strained. Her gaze flicked to several people trying to get her attention. She said, "I'd love to sometime, but I got about ten tables needing something. Open mic night is crazy. We'll catch up later. I'll get all y'all's round."

When she was gone, Suzie said, "Enough's enough. Spill it. What did you see when that mask came off?"

The others gasped and leaned closer, catching on. They threw out guesses of disfigurement and scarring. They were so wrong.

"You can't freak out," I warned.

They're eyes widened but they nodded with mouths clamped shut tightly. But then, the quick happy notes of a familiar melody cut through the air and the bar went quiet. It was as though someone made an announcement.

"I love this song," Roxy whispered.

We all nodded. *Tiny Dancer* by Elton John was one of those songs that brought everybody together no matter their age or background.

Chills traveled down my body as a familiar voice broke through the air. My eyes shot to the piano player on stage. Devlin was here. Excitement shuddered through me.

Devlin's rich guttural voice broke through the air. He sat at the piano with his back to the bar. His mask was pulled off his face so he could sing into the microphone, he couldn't be fully seen with his hat on. But I would know that profile anywhere.

I glanced to the other girls to see if they figured it all out. Their shocked expressions told me they did. That voice revealed all. He was a ragged mix of Eddie Vedder and Hozier. His rich voice burned like Tennessee honey whiskey showing his roots, but his range and technique came from years of practice combined with his own virtuoso talent. The man was captivating. It wasn't just me who noticed. All the women and dang, most of the men, were just as entranced as I was. Pure, raw talent like that was hypnotic.

He had the skill of a classically trained musician with the cool casualness of a busker. The muscles of his neck, shoulders, and back were prominent under his thin shirt. They strained as he sang with every note. He poured everything into it.

My stomach flip-flopped. I hadn't been prepared to see him. Been prepared to have this reaction.

A guitarist went up on stage and asked to join in. Devlin nodded to him with a smile in his voice. The guitar strummed along so perfectly it could have been staged. A tall woman with a shaved head joined on the steel guitar.

As the chorus built, people went to the dance floor. I couldn't move. The things happening in my body were more than the music and more than the attraction. The things happening in my body were infinite. I had serious feelings for this man. Hearing him sing transported me back in time. Heat pooled deep inside me when he groaned out a particularly intense line.

A drummer got on stage and softly kept time. His grin spoke to the magic of the moment. It *was* magic. There was no other way to describe it. The lyrics were about holding a woman close, laying with her, softly, slowly—how she was always with him. My heart raced. I wouldn't read into it.

As the famous chorus broke out, the whole bar sang along. Even busy Patty stopped to listen to the impromptu band on stage. Without talking, the five of us moved to the floor, rocking slowly at first, smiling and swaying.

Everything felt so perfectly coordinated that anything planned could never possibly top it.

This moment. Right here, with my closest friends, singing with unencumbered passion, I felt fully alive. It was more than I could ever ask for. I wanted to scream along at the top of my lungs. I wanted to cry. I was happy. I was loved. I wasn't alone. I wished I could hold on to this feeling even when the doubt settled in.

Gretchen, Roxy, Suzie, and Blithe laughed and sang. But when Gretchen caught my eye, she shook her head with a laugh. "Oh, girl, you're in big trouble," she yelled over the music.

I shook my head looking to the ceiling. "I know."

Blithe grabbed my hand and twirled me.

I wished I had my cello so I could run up on stage too. Then I allowed myself just for a moment, to imagine what it might be like playing with him without any expectations or a deadline. Just to play together. To hear him sing so beautifully, to play any instrument he wanted, while I joined on the cello. We would make beautiful music together.

The whole bar sang along loudly. Devlin's hands danced happily up and down the keyboard, but he still kept his face from the crowd. The girls and I belted out the lyrics at the top of our lungs and yes, I had tears in my eyes. How could I not? This was the power of music.

There was no going back from here. I could no longer delude myself that my feelings for Devlin were anything less than epic.

CHAPTER 26

YOU ALREADY KNOW WHO I AM.

DEVLIN

It was Wes's stupid idea to go out. I was perfectly fine staying at home, working on my current composition and brooding. Just another Thursday night for me.

We were at Genie's, not because the SWS was having a meeting there, but because Kim had technically invited me. I'd finally caught her after rehearsal with the SOOK today, after her previous clear avoidance of me. I still hadn't heard what she'd thought of the Ford's Fosters rehearsal. She brushed me off quickly, saying she had plans before rushing off. Maybe she'd felt obliged, but she *had* technically invited me. When Wes had wanted to go out for drinks, I suggested the only decent bar in town. It wasn't anything more than that.

The bar was packed. Wes snagged us a small standing table near the dance floor, hidden from the rest of the room. I could push my cover down to drink without drawing attention in the darkness. My gaze very casually scanned the room. A brunette waitress came to take our order.

I said, "Two of whatever draft is on special."

She winked and said, "You got it. Anything to eat?"

"Just the drinks," Wes said with his usual charm.

She politely smiled back and went on her way.

"What's Kelly up to?" I asked dryly.

"She's putting the kids down," Wes said. "I can only stay for one drink. I was promised some 'Netflix and chill' later." He wiggled his eyebrows.

We chatted for a while and I positioned myself so that I could see Kim as she spoke with her friends. Whatever she talked about had her going. Her cheeks were bright red and her delicate hands mimicked catching a large bass. What I wouldn't give to be a fly on the wall of that conversation.

"Remember that time you peed your bed in third grade?" Wes said loudly.

I blinked my attention back to him. "What?"

"You are listening. Just checking."

"I didn't pee my bed. That was you, dumbass."

He shrugged. "I see your Kim is here. That's a strange coincidence."

I frowned. "Not mine. Don't talk like that, or I will have her come over and lecture you on people being treated as property."

He shuddered. "I learned my lesson the first time. Still. I can't help but think maybe you aren't being honest about your feelings for her."

The label of my beer sat in a pile of strips. "She isn't what I expected."

"In a good way?"

"I'm not sure. She seems to be two different people. Christine at work and then Kim at my house. Christine is the ideal musician; prompt and dedicated. But Kim is funny. So funny. And she's just so open. And talented. I knew she was. But I had forgotten how much power there was in her playing."

Wes raised his eyebrows and took a long pull from his beer. "Have you told her any of that?"

"God, no."

"Why?"

I just shook my head. My feelings for Kim were complicated. I settled on. "I'm her conductor."

He nodded. "I get it. You want to make it through the season without being fired. Still … You could show her that there is more to you than the masked-man schtick."

I glared up at him.

"You obviously like her but don't want to screw up. I get it. So let it be her choice. I'm not trying to make you cross any lines, but don't forget the ultimate secret weapon at your disposal."

"Secret weapon?"

"For wooing!" he said and slapped the table. "Come on man, you know you have a super-power."

"With great power comes great responsibility," I grumbled into my glass before I gulped down the rest of my beer. My hands started to shake. A very bad idea was settling in.

"Talents are wasted on nerds. One song," he said. "It'll be fun."

My heart started hammering. Going on stage … people watching …

"Lay off me," I snapped.

"Don't do that," Wes said, completely unfazed. "Don't get pissy with me because you don't like what I'm saying."

I crossed my arms tight and my foot tapped wildly.

He shook his head at me. "I forget how shy you are."

"I'm not shy." Shy wasn't the right word. It was more than that. "Not everybody can charm a salesman out of his wallet."

"I can't turn it off," he said. "Do what you want, but don't be an idiot."

"Rich, coming from you."

He hadn't been trying to piss me off. Well, he never tried. That also came naturally for him. But in his defense, I sometimes got ticked off if I felt myself being pushed into something I didn't want.

"Ha. Look, I gotta go." He stood up, pulled out a twenty and threw it on the table. He came around to hug me goodbye. "I'm glad you're back in town."

"You said that last time."

"That's cause I mean it."

"It's not all bad being back here," I admitted.

"Don't screw up and leave us all again." He gripped my shoulder and looked seriously into my eyes. "It nearly broke Ma when you stayed away so long. Stay here. With your nieces and family. Do what it takes to make it permanent."

"Why do you think I'm working so hard?"

He shook me lightly. "Then keep at it. And don't be a chicken-shit," he said nodding at the open mic flyer on the wall.

"Goodbye, brother," I said.

"Goodbye, brother," he mimicked me.

After he left, I flagged down the server for a shot of tequila and asked about the line-up for tonight.

"Now or never," she said as she set down the shot. "There's an opening, but you gotta go up now."

"Thanks." I pulled down my mask to take the shot quickly before pulling it back up. Her eyes squinted like she was trying to place me. I wiped my mouth and walked away as she opened her mouth to speak.

"Okay." I took a deep breath and stepped on the stage.

I got behind the piano and felt the room take notice behind me. I hadn't played for an audience in a very long time. A familiar thrill of nerves energized me. My back was to the audience because it was an accompanist piano, off to the side of the stage. I tugged my mask down. My hands shook as I played a few chords to warm up. I launched into the opening stanza, hoping the jitters would wear off as my voice warmed up. At least Elton John was an almost-guaranteed crowd pleaser. My fingers found the notes easily.

I was desperate to turn around and gauge Kim's reaction to the song. God, if only I could play like this for her all the time. But I felt it—I felt the bar's energy coursing through me, felt the transformative power of a great fucking song. My body came alive as I played. My voice belted out the words. I was raw with explosive energy. I'd missed this—playing for people. I thought I'd shut this part of my life away. But here I was, loving every second of it.

* * *

As the whoops and applause broke out, I pulled my mask back into place and stood to bow.

Kim and her friends had made their way to the front and were clapping and pumping their arms. I jumped off the short stage and pulled Kim into a hug. When we pulled apart, she looked as dazed as I felt. I hadn't thought about doing that. I was just buzzing with adrenaline and my body moved without thinking.

Gretchen smacked my shoulder with the back of her hand. "Erik Jones in the flesh."

My eyes widened. Nobody seemed to hear it in the cacophony of the bar.

"Gretchen!" Kim punched her in the arm.

"Ouch! What the fuck?"

"Language," Suzie warned.

"It's not like anybody could hear me." Gretchen rubbed her arm with a frown.

"Still," Kim eyes were wide imploring. "This was exactly why I didn't want to tell you."

"How many people would connect that random guy in Genie's with the pop star?"

"Okay, you have got to stop talking." Kim grabbed my hand and pulled me away from her group of chattering friends.

The ones who weren't talking were staring at me with wide, shell-shocked eyes. The blonde whispered to the brunette and I swear I heard her ask about an autograph as I was tugged to a quiet corner near an old cigarette machine.

This was exactly what I was afraid of. In any other circumstance, I would have just been a guy. I wanted to, God, I dunno, impress her? I'm such a tool. This was what I got for listening to Wes about anything. I wanted to show her something more than my instructor side without giving away too much of what I felt for her. But it back-fired. I didn't think they'd all recognize me. This was why I wore the mask. How differently would I be treated now? Because now I was only some former celebrity with a crap career.

"Hey." Her finger poked my cheek and I cursed the mask for the distance between our skin. "I can't tell, but I'm pretty sure you're frowning under there. Don't worry about them. They won't say anything. They're just surprised. They are of that generation that was a little, uh, obsessed with you. Not me. I wasn't. I definitely didn't have posters of you all over my room ..."

"I'm not worried about it." I was bothered though.

She shifted from foot to foot, studying the scuffed-up wooden floor. "That was an awesome performance."

"Thanks." I studied her, desperate to see any signs of her feel-ings. "It's a classic song."

Her hair was down tonight in a straight, dark style that fell almost all the way down her back. It had been in a tight twist today at rehearsals. Had she come straight here? I imagined her shaking her hair loose. Pulling her fingers through it, back arched ... slow motion.

Jesus Christ, I needed another drink.

"Sure. But your singing ..." Her cheeks flushed too. She was half a breath from twirling hair around her finger.

And there it was. She looked at me with hearts in her eyes. We had been making such strides with my composition. But all at once, I was a teen pop star again. A crappy one, at that. It was one thing to see my face these last months, but it was different to hear me play this kind of music. I triggered a fangirl crush she'd kept hidden. I wanted to be more than that to her. Would I ever just be Erik to her? I wanted to be more than a Maestro, more than a popstar. The rest of the world be damned, what did *she* think of the real me?

"Well, anyway. I promise that they won't bother you about it. And they won't say anything, okay?"

I nodded and tucked my hands deep in my pockets.

"I'm going to go back to my, uh, meeting. I'm glad I got to see you here tonight." She spoke seriously enough that I forced myself to meet her gaze. "It was nice to see you outside of practice or rehearsals. Sometimes, it's nice to just feel the music and be reminded. You know? Yeah, you know." She licked her lips.

"Yeah."

"You could probably come hang out for a drink but I wasn't technically allowed to invite boys. It's against the code …"

"Don't worry about it." I waved away her offer.

"Okay, well, bye." She stepped up on her toes to kiss my cheek. The one little sliver of exposed skin between the mask. Her lips were warm and soft. Her head bumped the bill of my hat. She giggled and rubbed her forehead. "Sorry."

She walked away quickly with fists balled and a little shake of her head.

It was time to leave. Coming here and performing like that had been a lapse in judgement. I went to the bar to square up my bill. I was glaring at the bar top when someone sidled up next to me. I wasn't in the mood.

"I feel bad." It was the redhead, Gretchen. "I shouldn't have spilled your secret identity to the whole bar."

I shrugged but didn't face her.

"Nobody heard me," she said.

"It's fine," I grumbled.

"I'm easily excitable and sometimes words just blah," she said, motioning words coming out of her mouth with her hand. "But it isn't my jam to spill people's secrets. I'm usually like a vault."

I tilted my head to convey my disbelief.

"It's true." She blew out a long breath making a show of it. "Like I wouldn't tell you, an almost total stranger, that Kim was a big fan of you back in the day. She tried to hide it, but your song was always playing. It was her go-to bad mood song. You know the song that makes you get up and shake your tail feather no matter how dark the day is?"

I sighed and turned toward her. "Like a vault, huh?"

"It's true. I wouldn't tell you that. Because that was forever ago.

She's hardly the same person now. Definitely not the same person that used to keep a shoebox full of old notes."

I cleared my throat. Despite the cold dread her other news brought me, this had me taking notice. "Notes?"

"Yeah, from some band camp. I definitely wouldn't tell you what those meant to her."

Heat burned down the back of my neck. It took all my strength not to run to Kim ask her about it.

"And I absolutely would not tell you that Roderick Chagny has been taking credit for them her whole life."

My whole body jolted. "What? That pea-brained, coattail-riding little shit? He wouldn't know how to compose a grocery list, let alone a note."

Gretchen shrugged like I had a minute ago. "Not my business. Things locked inside." She acted out locking her mouth with a key.

"Why are you telling me this? I thought you didn't trust me." The last time I was around her, she had given me a definite look. In fact, I think she'd even whispered a not-so-thinly-veiled threat.

"I don't trust you, but I trust Roderick Chagny less."

"Something tells me you don't trust men," I said.

She pulled from her beer bottle. "What have you done to deserve it? As a species, men are wholly disappointing."

This was a woman scorned for sure.

"Men have done some good things," I said. "We helped make the population."

"Barely."

I shook my head with a laugh. Then remembered. "Fucking Chagny." I gripped the edge of the bar, wishing I could rip it off and throw it out the window.

"He says he wants to take care of my girl." Gretchen rolled her eyes.

"He wants what she can get him and that's money. That's all anybody in the industry cares about." My voice was low, mostly to myself, but I was sure she heard.

"It's weird, isn't it? Him showing up right now? Right when

she's getting attention." She shook her head and lowered her voice. "Deep down, she has to know he isn't the author of those notes. Kim is smart, but she's also fragile. She clings to them so desperately. I'm not here to take something away from her that brings her comfort. My only concern is that she'll listen to anything Roddy says because he represents safety to her."

We both drifted our focus to Kim. She danced with the other girls, her hair flowing around her as she line-danced across the floor. Happiness was written all over her face.

"You're going to have to tell her one day," Gretchen finished.

I licked my dry lips. My Adam's apple sat too high in my throat. "Why's that?"

"It's written all over your face, how much you feel for her."

"You can't see my face," I said.

"You should know I'm wise beyond my years. All us girls in the SWS have experienced things that aged us too young. We can see right through the bullshit. Actually, most women can." She took another drink. "Unless we aren't ready to."

"That's my fear." My heart hammered into my throat admitting this. "I don't think Kim is ready to hear the things I have to tell her. I don't want her to be swayed for the wrong reasons. She should come to her own conclusions, in her own time." I couldn't look at her friend while I spoke but couldn't stop the words from coming out either.

She nodded. "She isn't ready. She's living with too much fear. But she can't do anything without all the facts."

My heart sunk. I knew that Kim was attracted to me. I was ravenous for her. If we gave into those surface feelings, the intensity of what I really felt for her might push her away. Her feelings would never deepen. I realized that now, talking to her best friend.

I needed to gather myself and double down on the music. Let us get to the showcase. Let her see what she was completely capable of and then tell her everything. For now, I had to be patient.

"You need to be honest with her," Gretchen said. "Or I will introduce you to my collection of bats."

"Noted," I said.

Even if I could never have Kim in my life at the level I wanted, at least I knew she'd be taken care of.

"Just so you know. It's totally obvious when you're smiling," she said before pushing off the bar and rejoining her friends.

CHAPTER 27

STOP WHEN YOU ARE DONE, NOT WHEN YOU ARE TIRED.

KIM

Something had changed, because the next few weeks of practice with Devlin were off. Really off. The chair announcements were delayed yet again, for the reason that the committee couldn't decide on a few chair positions, like a hung jury. And tangible tension was ratcheting up in the Symphony. My feelings for Devlin had bloomed to a point where the mere sight of him sent a bolt of adrenaline through me. I remained professional, but wondered if my feelings were transparent. There was still the issue of Roddy, too. He seemed to offer so much, but my heart was not interested.

All the while, Devlin seemed to have retreated. He reset those strict boundaries after the performance at the bar. I had been given a glimpse at an alternate reality, a life I found myself daydreaming about. One where we were a couple that went to bars and sang and danced and everything was out there. There were no dark secrets, no shame from our pasts. I longed to peel back his layers and learn everything about him. Yet he pulled away.

We were more than halfway toward his showcase performance.

Pressure sat like invisible bags of sand on our slumped shoulders. Technically, the composition was written and complete. At the end of each practice he would return to scribbling notes in the pages with a furrowed brow, a hand tangled in his hair.

"That spark isn't there. I can feel it," he'd say. And no matter how I encouraged him that it was wonderful, he would reply, "Wonderful isn't good enough. It needs to be perfect."

There was no such thing as perfect. I understood that better than most.

Now, it was our last weekend practice before the Fourth of July, and I was at his house. I skipped the pretense and packed an overnight bag. Not for any lusty reasons but because this was going to be a long weekend and going home was a waste of time. Better to at least be prepared and sleep in my own clothes. My parents had been relatively quiet on the issue and that too added to my anxious thoughts.

"Before we start today you should know something." He stood towering over me as I gripped the neck of my cello. He was all business, with dark brooding eyes and full delicious lips. The ring finger of his left hand tapped lightly on the knee of his jeans. It was the only indication of nerves in an otherwise smooth demeanor.

Whatever he was about to say was important.

"Yeah?" My gentle tone reflected an attempt to stay cool.

"The delay with the chair decision is because I'm sampling the cello solo from the *Smokey Mountain Concerto*. As a sort of teaser for the September showcase."

Small tendrils of dread swirled my thoughts like early morning fog on a lake. I nodded once, urging him on.

"As you may assume, the first chair cellist will have that solo at the Fourth of July performance."

My stomach filled with fiery heat like I'd taken five shots too fast. Was he telling me I got first chair? It felt like a warning.

"That makes sense."

"I don't decide the chair ranking alone. The whole point of an unbiased third party is to ensure there was no favoritism or nepotism in the decision making. I won't even know who is sat where until the positions are officially decided."

"First chair is a huge decision," I said cautiously.

He held my focus and I searched those dark eyes for answers.

"Whatever they decide, let me assure you that these last few weeks have shown me without a doubt that your talent is astounding. *You* are astounding."

"Thank you." I swallowed a lump in my throat. Neither one of us looked away. We sat watching each other in the silent room not saying a hundred things on the tips of our tongues. "Devlin, I—"

He broke our trance first with a small shake of his head. "Let's rehearse."

We played through the same piece we'd played a thousand times. Today there was no focusing. If he was telling me I got first chair and the solo, that would change everything. My breathes were quick and shallow, matching the tempo of my heart. My mind raced with too many distractions. Mechanically, I was fine. Most people wouldn't even think there was anything wrong, but instinct told me this performance was subpar. Every passing measure the temper that gave the Devil of the Symphony his name seemed to grow.

I needed to tell him the truth about how I felt. I was so tired of pretending. How could I when he'd just told me I was astounding? It might ruin how far we've come together.

He stood up from the piano so abruptly the bench toppled over. "You aren't trying."

"I am." My insides shook. I needed to tell him.

"No, you aren't. You're holding on to something. Just play. Hear the notes between the music. Listen to the message."

"What message?" I asked. He always talked about this, some hidden meaning or feeling. I tasted that power he spoke of—at the bar and for Ford's Fosters—but I couldn't just make it happen.

He shoved the bench farther out of his way, standing so he had to hunch to play the accompaniment on the piano. "Listen, Kim. *Feel* it."

I played as my frustration grew. I matched him note for note. If he used anger as a weapon, I would give it right back to him. It was immature, but I was so tired of trying and falling flat. That anger fueled my fingers despite every muscle in my body burning with fatigue.

"Better!" he shouted.

I played harder.

"More!"

My fingertips went numb.

"Faster!"

I screamed out a growl. "Why don't you just play it!" I snapped. "If you're so fricking sure of how it should sound."

He glared at me, and at that moment, I had no idea why I was even here. Why I had even been chosen. I wanted to attack him with punches and scream until my throat went raw.

"It's your piece," he said.

He'd said that time and time again, but I didn't understand. Any cellist could play this. I needed to understand why. He wanted me to listen. I was listening. I screamed out with a growl of rage as my hands flew.

"You aren't trying!" he yelled over the music.

"I am!" I yelled back but my fingers missed a slide into their position. Tears threatened.

I collapsed into my cello. Pressed my cheek against the hard wood. Inhaled the smell of resin and polish. I hated this version of him so much. We'd reverted so far back to the beginning. He'd pushed me too far. This was what he had wanted, wasn't it? Maybe he felt my feelings shift at the bar when he sang to me. Maybe he was scared of the feelings I couldn't hide. Of another fangirl falling over themselves for him. He wanted this reaction. He wanted to push me away.

He was selfish. I was nothing to him but another instrument in his beautiful room. A tool for his own purposes. Maybe Roddy was right, and I was his muse. And a disappointing one, at that.

I laid my cello down on its side carefully despite my shaking hands. "I'm done here."

"We aren't done for the day." He turned to face me, wiping his hands on his pants.

"Devlin." I stood and held his gaze. "I'm done."

"You promised. You committed. You can't just go."

"You don't want me. You're mad about something, and you're pushing me away. So fine. I'll leave. I'm done."

His nostrils flared and his chest rose and fell when he stood to match my stance. "You can't just leave."

"I'm tired," I shrugged with effort and made my way to the door.

"Don't put this on me. You're the one who's holding back," he said calmly.

I turned around, my voice cracking with emotion as tears balanced on my eyelids. "I've given you everything. It will never be enough for you."

"Liar."

"What?" I threw out my arms.

"You keep saying that, but you aren't. Something is stopping you. It's the reason you hide yourself. It's the reason you only really open up when you're alone."

I couldn't help it. I stepped toward him. I was shaking with anger and exhaustion. A tear spilled over, so I swiped it away. "I have given everything to this, but it will never be enough. And don't you ever talk to me about hiding yourself away. You wear a flipping mask."

"That's not real. You know that. You know more about me than anybody else. You can tell yourself it's my fault, but you know the truth. You *are* holding something back. Until you let go of your demons, you'll never move forward."

* * *

I stomped out of the room. Just the stubborn set of his jaw caused another wave of anger. How could he possibly put this on me? What a self-centered egomaniac. Sure, he was a genius musician in the body of a sex god. Yes, he had more talent in his pinky than most people could have after years of practice. But I was a strong, independent woman, and I was sick of his childish temper.

"Kim."

I had made it about four steps down the hallway when he stopped me by grabbing my hand.

I tugged it free from his grasp.

"Please, don't cry. I didn't mean to hurt you. I'm sorry." His thumb brushed a tear from my cheek. "When I get … when I can't find the words … sometimes I get so angry … the yelling." He took a deep breath. "I'm sorry."

"You can be so mean," I snapped, as the tremble of my chin belayed my ferocity.

"Please, don't cry because of me. I'm not worth it."

"I'm not crying because of you. I'm crying because I'm mad. I do this. I won't be ashamed." I took a deep breath in. "Displaying emotion is a healthy way of dealing with things." I sniffed.

"You're right." He ducked down a little trying to get me to look at him. I was finding it very difficult to do that. Then he did that look-up smolder-frown thing, looking exactly like the Erik Jones of my adolescence and my heart just about threw in the towel. "I envy that about you. You're so good at feeling things. At communicating them."

His words softened my anger. His brow crinkled with sincerity as his gaze moved over my face.

"I really am trying, Devlin. This whole time. Since I started. I—I'm just not who you think I am."

He shook his head. I could feel him grow angry and then swallow it back down. He took a deep breath to steady himself. "God, Kim. If you could only see yourself as I do." I shook my head as he kept talking. "But you are holding a part of you back and I don't understand why."

"I don't want to. Not anymore. I'm so tired." The exhaustion of it all weighted my words.

"When your guard is down you play beautifully, full of passion. You are grace and light."

I opened my mouth but had to swallow instead. With him standing so close and his man smell encompassing me, I couldn't focus. Could I tell him the truth? No matter how ridiculous it seemed? I'd tried talking to Roddy about it, or with others over the years, but it made them uncomfortable.

"You're keeping something at bay. I can't understand why when you have so much life in you, bubbling right here." He placed a hand on my chest above my heart. The warmth and weight of his palm radiated through me. He had to feel my heart slamming against his hand. "You're magic when you let go and really play. That's why I chose you. That's what you are capable of. I know this."

I closed my eyes and dropped my head back against the wall.

"Why did learning about the solo upset you so much?" he asked. "I thought you might be happy."

How did I explain it to him when I hardly understood it myself?

"It's not that I don't feel like I have earned it. I know that when I really try, I have potential."

He waited patiently for me to go on.

"It's that potential that scares me," I said.

We stayed in this safe space of the hall. It felt like if we moved, I'd lose any courage to speak.

"You don't feel like you deserve it?"

I shook my head but met his gaze. "When I go after things, people get hurt."

"Explain," he said.

"It sounds ridiculous."

"Just talk. It doesn't have to be perfect or make sense. Just share. Is it just because of Jethro? Did he do something? Because that's where you went on hold as far as I can tell. You were vibrant at camp. I went away on my first tour and when I came back everything had changed. You had changed. You went from this bright, ambitious cello player to this grayed-out shape of a person."

"No." I pressed icy fingertips to my burning cheeks. "Jethro was more of a symptom, I think."

"People don't just shut down. They don't just mute their lives for almost ten years without something to cause it. Talk to me."

He wouldn't stop staring at me. I knew he wouldn't relent. "That last summer at camp, before senior year. You were already gone. Something happened."

His nostrils flared. "Roddy?"

"No, it's not like that. Roddy and I were sort of dating by then." My heart was pounding. I wrapped my arms tight around my middle. I didn't want to share this. It made me feel sick. He'd know what an ugly person I was. People loved to tell me I was beautiful, but if they only knew how ugly I was on the inside …

"I've never told anybody this. You're going to think the worst of me, and I deserve it. I was this poor little rich girl through and through. And I just fucked up. I just fucked up so big." My voice cracked.

"Tell me," his face was open and listening.

"The stuff with Jethro. All that that came after. That was me freaking out. The rehab helped bring me back to a middle place, but I was never okay again."

He nodded like he understood.

"Remember how the camp voted for the soloists at the year-end talent show?" I asked.

"It was a pointless popularity contest."

"Yes. But I wanted it. I wanted it so bad. I had something to prove. I wasn't first chair—Ariana was."

His face softened to pity. He remembered her.

I went on. "She was perfect. I was so intimidated by her. She was everything I wanted to be. I wanted that solo. I had to prove to my parents, to myself, to everyone that I was worth it and that I was going places."

"Kim," he said softly.

"Let me get it all out." This was the part that changed everything. "I asked Roddy to fix the votes. To make sure that I got everything I wanted. I didn't care who I hurt in the process."

"Okay." He moved to leaned against the wall, facing me.

I stayed facing forward. It would be easier not looking at him.

"I got it. I played the solo. That night Ariana went to the lake and drowned. She left a note. She was miserable."

"Kim—"

"I know what you're going to say. I didn't kill her. She took her own life. It was just one solo. I understand that rationally—I do. But I was the straw that broke the camel's back. My ambition. My cold hard ambition. For what? Just to play a freaking solo at a summer camp? Ridiculous."

He reached out to rest a hand on my arm. "You can't know why somebody takes their own life. It's tragic and confounding, but it's unknowable. You are not responsible."

"She was me. I knew the stress she was under. I knew what it felt like to go after everything with blind ambition. I could have shown her kindness. I could have been her."

He pushed my shoulder to turn me toward him. "You were a kid. Everybody at that age is completely stuck in their own head."

"But ..."

"And now you think your success will ultimately come at the cost of someone else?" he asked.

"It's not sound reasoning."

"We can't help how our minds handle trauma." He squeezed my shoulder. "We can't help how we view things through our own lens of experience. We manufacture truths to keep ourselves safe. You fear doing well, making choices, because of one mistake. But you're more than that one misjudgment. You're so much more."

"I feel so scared all the time. One wrong move and who will pay the price?" I squeezed my eyes close. I was so tired and lonely and scared.

"I can't believe you've carried this around for so long. I understand now. About Carla and the solos. Why you've held yourself back." He let out a low breath. He rubbed up and down my arm. I didn't feel like I deserved comfort when I was the one that was here.

"I remember when that happened," he said, referencing Ariana.

"You do?"

"I was already gone, but I'd heard all about it. Everybody saw how much pressure she was under. Her parents put so much on her shoulders. She was miserable. They found her journals after. Apparently, she'd been struggling for a long time. Nobody knew how bad it was."

More pain tightened my chest. "I wish I'd offered her support. My parents never pushed me. I always pushed myself. The pressure she must have felt if she couldn't imagine living ..."

"She needed help. All of us felt partly responsible. Had we known, or asked, maybe things would have ended up differently."

"Nobody knew," I whispered to myself. Digesting all this terrible new information. "It's so sad."

"It is sad. But it is not your fault." His voice was firm.

I would tell somebody the same thing. But it was because of me. I was that final straw. I pushed and pushed. I thought I was so totally untouchable. I was not a good person.

"How am I ever supposed to trust myself?"

"You aren't malicious. Plenty of people go after their dreams without hurting people."

"It was my ambition that drove it. I was going to be big. No matter what."

"It was more than that. I know what greed looks like. I know when somebody takes at any costs for themselves. That's not you. If you've been feeling this way for so long, it may be hard to hear all this. But it wasn't your fault. She wasn't happy. She took her life. You're a good person. Playing well and with purpose won't change that. You think you will want to be eighty years old knowing you were given a second chance at life and you wasted it?"

I winced but knew he was right. I wasn't living. Rehab had been my wake-up call, but I wasn't out of the woods yet.

"I'm sorry you've been feeling this way for so long. I'm sorry your guilt has marred reality. You're kind and good. Embracing your talent won't hurt anybody and hiding it sure as hell won't change the past. Come here."

He hugged me tightly. I squeezed him back.

"Thank you," I said. It was though somebody had stopped standing on my chest and I could take a full breath again.

"Thank you for sharing with me." He held me for a long moment before speaking again. His voice rumbled in my ear. "When people hear you play it brings them joy. That's the light you give."

I looked up into his eyes. "I've never thought of it like that."

"That's the only mark we leave on this world." He cupped my face. "The only lasting thing, is how we leave people feeling."

"That's a lovely way of looking at it."

I'd been making myself small. I didn't feel like I deserved a legacy.

"Thank you," I said.

"I wish I could take the years of pain away." His face was inches from mine. His eyes burned with such intensity that I had to break the hug, but I didn't leave his arms completely. It was too much to be this close to him.

And then ... then I thought about this position we were in. This physical position. How my body was trapped back against this wall. How his arm was around my waist. He held me to him like I was an instrument made of glass. Sturdy but delicately. I was trapped but not at risk of breaking.

I wanted to break. I wanted to shatter into a million pieces. I felt excitement and potential brimming right under the shell I'd been wearing.

His head was bowed and apologetic, like a mourning saint in a Renaissance painting. His face was so close to mine that if he just leaned lower he could graze my neck. He could rub his nose up the column and inhale deeply. And I would let him. God, how I wanted him to. I wanted his body pressed hard with the same pent up energy I was feeling. I wanted him shaking for me as I shook for him.

But I wouldn't be out on this ledge alone. It was like holding on to a single branch with an abyss underneath me. I couldn't let go unless I was absolutely sure he was there to catch me.

And then,

The tiniest shift in the air. A feminine awareness. I swallowed.

Too afraid to lift my gaze to see what he was doing. But he watched me. Not watched—memorized me. I felt his gaze moving over my skin as though he dragged a feather against it. Goosebumps prickled down my chest.

"Kim." My name was a pained whisper.

His was closer than ever. Heat permeated me. Please, just touch me. Kiss me. Do anything.

CHAPTER 28

I WISH YOU COULD SEE YOURSELF AS
I DO.

DEVLIN

Kim had been suffering for so long. I knew that something had been holding her back. How could nobody else in her life see it? Why hadn't anybody stepped in sooner? I wanted to put her back together.

Kim was loose and languid as she leaned back against the wall, barely held up by my arm wrapped around her waist. She didn't blush or pull away. She waited. Almost patiently, as though she'd wait all night if needed. But the heat would consume us long before then. My want for her was a real presence between us. The closer I inched, the more it saturated into my skin.

Her face was tipped toward the ceiling, hiding her expression from me as a flush spread over the tops of her breasts. The sweet, long column of her throat was exposed to me. Her pulse fluttered there, gentle compared to my own thrumming heart. Her chest heaved up and down.

She felt it. That shift when we went from talking to *other*. The other was the thing between us that had the most power. It always had.

"Kim," I said.

It was all that I could manage. I was going to cross a line that we would never come back from and I couldn't form any other sound beside her name.

She was beautiful. She was more than that. She was everything. I couldn't wait a moment more.

I stepped closer, moving with slow decisiveness. If this wasn't what she wanted, there would be plenty of time to stop me. I leaned forward until every part of her was pressed against me. Every bit of me, against her. Let her feel my want for her.

She gasped so lightly I wouldn't have heard it if not for her mouth being just below my ear.

Her neck called out to me. I bent and inhaled deeply there, tracing the flushed skin. So soft. The tip of my nose tracked up her neck as I moved up to take in her sweet essence. She smelled so damn good. Like woman and desire. My mouth watered to taste her.

Her body shuddered as I moved, perfectly responsive in every way, in learning and listening, and talking, and I knew this, what we were about to do, would be no different. My left arm had her pulled close, my right arm began to dance up the skin. Slowly, delicately, like she was a new piece of music for studying.

My lips lingered just under her ear where the small soft hairs grew in under the dark length. I brushed the long strands behind her shoulder, and she tilted her head, opening to me, gifting me with room to explore.

I sucked gently at that delicate transition.

Another soft gasp escaped her. Both our bodies thrummed to the same fast melody. She drove me to movement. I moved to kiss her jaw where it met her neck. I moved to her cheek and kissed it softly too. I kissed her closed eyes. I gently tilted her head and showed similar attention to the other side of her neck and shoulder. All the while, my left hand moved from her lower back to caress and squeeze her full ass. I cupped it and pulled it harder to me.

She melted into me. My right hand continued to trace up and down her arm until I made a choice.

I leaned back to put distance between us.

"No," she gasped out, her eyes shot open.

"I just need … I need more." I pulled my shirt off over my head. I wasn't thinking clearly but I needed to feel her cool skin against my burning body.

"Oh," she said. "Good idea." Without another second passing, her own shirt was off and tossed aside. She pulled off a lace bra and threw it down as well. Not a moment's hesitation. An unexpected bonus that spoke of trust and desire.

We stood naked from the waist up. I tried to memorize the shape of her. Her breasts were … perfect. My mouth watered for them. I needed hours to study them.

She threw her arms around my neck. I wrapped my arms around her. I felt bulky against her lithe frame. Her skin was soft, but not cool as I'd expected. It blazed as hot as mine. She was so soft. She tasted so good. I knew it would be like this. I knew she would feel this good to me.

We held each other, in awe of how amazing it was to have our skin bare and blazing like this. She loosened her tight hold and I used the opportunity to slide my hand up between our bodies and around her neck. My thumb pushed up her chin. Her eyes were closed again, like she was too afraid to watch.

"Kim," I whispered.

"Hmm?"

"Open your eyes."

She needed to watch this. She needed to know it was me when I brought her pleasure. She needed to associate this person with happiness for once. Nobody else.

She blinked her eyes softly open. "Hi," she said.

"Hi."

My thumb grazed over her lips as we stood staring into each other's eyes.

"What is even happening?" she asked with a dazed smile.

"I have no idea."

"Should we stop?"

"We haven't even started," I said.

I took her mouth and kissed her, craving more of her taste. I needed to taste her tongue and devour her from the inside out. We moaned in unison as our heads tilted to accommodate tongues and lips, delving deep with exploration. One hand moved through her luscious, thick hair. The other one traced up her side, feeling every little response.

I pressed a leg in between hers. She groaned and broke the kiss as my thigh pressed against her core. Even through two pairs of jeans, her heat burned my thigh. Fuck. She was so hot and responsive.

Her pleasure was all that mattered now.

Something shifted. What was once a languid, exploratory kiss inflamed into a wanton mouth fuck. Our tongues collided. Our fast, hot breaths filled the hall. Her hands scratched down the expanse of my back. They pulled and rubbed all over the muscles of my arms and shoulders. Her hips rocked against my leg. I hoped the seam of her jeans was in just the right spot. I wouldn't stop until she came.

I found her nipple and gently squeezed. That caused her to break our kiss and gasp out for air. "Devlin," she gasped out.

"Yes," I growled.

I loved her calling out my name like that. Fuck, I could flip a car.

Since my mouth was no longer engaged, I lowered it to the nipple I'd been teasing. I sucked it into my mouth as both hands were filled with her breasts. I crouched a little to reach her and pulled her up harder onto my thigh. I nuzzled my face into her breasts, squeezing them together. All the while I flexed my leg muscles harder against her. She ground down against me, with abandon.

"Erik, if you don't stop I'm going to—"

"I need you to come."

She gasped. "I—I feel so out of control. This is …"

She was thinking too much.

I stepped between her spread legs. I hefted her up on to me so that her ankles were forced to link to stay wrapped around me. It was nothing; she was weightless, and I was pure adrenaline. I had one goal. I pressed myself against her. I ground hard against her wanting center. She was so hot. We rocked in tandem.

I groaned, dropping my forehead to hers and she grated out, "Devlin."

"Come. I need you to, Kim."

All at once, I kissed her mouth hard, cupped her breasts as I tugged her nipples, and rocked myself against her core.

She tensed up and broke our kiss to gasp for air.

Her fingernails dug into my shoulders. Her face twisted up with concentration and flushed cheeks. Jesus, she was so beautiful as she came apart.

As she came back to me, I slowly moved myself away. I kissed her softly wherever my eyes found skin. Her fingers unclenched from my shoulders. I bet she left a mark. I wanted to take a picture and frame it to hang in my office to always remember the fierce pride I felt in this moment.

CHAPTER 29

YOUR TALENT IS BREATHTAKING.

KIM

I came back to my body slowly. That was … transformative. It sounded hokey, but even as I lived it, experienced it, I had changed and there was no going back. Deep down, a part of me worried about the shame that might come later. Against a wall. In the hall. Grinding against his erection like some hard-up teenager.

But right now I didn't worry about that. Devlin was kissing me softly.

I sighed into him. "Thank you," I said.

He groaned and kissed me more but not greedily. He lavished me with tender love. I ran my hands down his tensed body and palmed his hardness, the hardness that helped me reach the peak.

He stiffened when I cupped him.

"You don't have to." He pulled on my wrist gently, but I was a girl on a mission.

"I want to." I'd had a peek of what was under there, but I needed more. I was greedy for it. I wanted to see all of him. Would I ever be satisfied with this man, my curiosity quelled?

I unzipped him and slid my hand down between our bodies. He was dangerously hot and hard. I stroked down once just to feel the full length. We gasped in unison. My pace increased as his eye went even darker.

"Another second of that and—" He thrust into my hand.

There was no time to find the rhythm he needed. My grip tightened as he thrust again.

"Shi—" He groaned out as he came into my hand.

I grinned against his shoulder as he caught his breath. I was the cat that got the cream.

"Sorry." He panted. "I hadn't planned on it."

"I liked it," I said.

And I did. I didn't know what it said about me that I loved that we'd just made each other come like this. That desire was already tingling through me again, feeling his mess on me. The smell of our fooling around in the air was potent and heady. I loved every dirty second of it. I couldn't think about what that said about me. Not now.

I gently bit his shoulder.

"No biting," he chided.

We both straightened to clean up. He handed me his shirt to wipe my hands and then used it to clean my stomach. God, I was a wreck for this man.

"Probably need to wash this now." He balled up the shirt and reached with his free hand to tuck some hair behind my ear. The look in his eyes caused my heart to flutter. Nobody had ever looked at me with such fierce softness. "I've been working you too hard."

He picked up my hands one at a time to kiss each palm softly.

"Thank you," I said again. "For everything. I feel …"

He hugged me again. "Come on. It's been a long day, let's go to bed."

"Your bed?" I asked and wiggled my eyebrows.

He growled again. "That's not a good idea. I want you to sleep."

Heat flushed over my skin at the implication. He held my hand as he walked me upstairs to what I had come to think of as my room. I was ready to get out of the jeans that rubbed too tight on my tender flesh and put on fresh underwear. The naughty part of me loved feeling the signs of his effect on me. I couldn't believe I had come that way. I couldn't believe how he'd inflamed me. Even now, just thinking about it, holding his hand innocently as we walked, his thumb rubbing the tender skin of my wrist, caused new heat to bloom in me.

At my door, he dropped his head to kiss me again. Chastely. Probably a good idea at this point. Apparently, it didn't take much to get me going.

"Get some sleep. When you're ready, if you're ready, we'll start back up tomorrow," he said. "With practice," he added with a grin.

"Sure." I had been going for flirty, but a big yawn came out instead. Sleepiness hit me hard. Never underestimate the power of a great orgasm. But it was so much more than that.

"I want to be good for you Devlin," I said. "That's all I want. To be good enough."

He closed his eyes as though pained. "You've always been good enough. I didn't mean to make things worse. I was just trying to dig out the Kim that I remembered from camp." He shook his head with a frown.

"I'm trying to find her too," I said.

He smiled. "Well, good night. And thanks for that," he blushed, and was so sweet I could die.

"Are you kidding me? You just moved to the top of my Christmas card list," I said.

He coughed out a laugh. Moving into my space, his face fell serious again. "Watching you come was a gift." He bit my bottom lip gently before kissing me.

He walked away, and with him went my heart.

* * *

Sleep had hit me so hard, I woke up in the same exact position I'd fallen asleep in, wondering what year it was. My phone illuminated the dark room telling me it was still very early the following morning. Devlin would still be sleeping.

I dropped my head back to the pillow and sighed. I felt lighter than I had in years. I hadn't realized how much I needed to talk to somebody about my past. I would still need time to heal, but fear didn't grip me as it had.

To my immense relief, when I replayed the night before, shame didn't come crashing down on me. Only drowsy pleasure. But a niggling something else tickled the back of my mind. Like remembering that you left your curling iron half a day later. No, that wasn't it. A bigger something. It had been years since I had experienced this. I sat up in bed.

There was no time to wait. When the feeling struck, you didn't wait. I slid a robe over my nightgown and into some slippers. Do not pass go. Do not collect two hundred dollars. Just move.

It was inspiration. I was desperate to play my cello. It had been such a habit for so many years, I didn't have time to miss it. Now, I felt it. An excitement to play. I wasn't afraid of the dark anymore, knowing Devlin was nearby. I shuffled through the dark house and down to basement where my cello waited for me. It glinted in the soft light, winking, like it knew I'd coming crawling back. It was ready. I was ready.

Time to play. I didn't bother with turning on the brighter overhead lights. I wouldn't be reading music and the soft glow from the recessed bulbs was enough. The scratch of the rosin along the hair of my bow instantly soothed. The cello tuned perfectly in the climate-controlled room. It nuzzled into my body and I warmed up my fingers with scales and arpeggios. When I was ready, I didn't even have to decide what to play. His piece had been welded into my brain. I knew every note.

But as it was currently written, it didn't fit my current state. My mood was a slow gondola-ride through an underground lagoon with swirling mist and stacked candles all around. His piece was written as a roller coaster ride on a sunny summer day.

I took his composition and wrapped my emotions around the

music, slowing the tempo to suit my mood. And just like that, the notes flowed out. I was connected to my instrument and the music felt transcendent. For the first time in what felt like forever, I was able to let go of my regret and fear and just focus on Devil's words. What would be the message I left behind? How did I want people to feel when they heard me play? The message was love. It was the feeling of being cherished. It was pure and unadulterated. It was everything that was good in life.

Heat travelled across my arms and torso as the robe began to rub against my movements, interfering. I forced myself to place the bow down and ripped my robe off, freeing my arms.

My hair fell loose, sticking to my skin, and tugging as my fingers blurred and my arms pushed and dipped and pulled and floated. There was only this moment. This understanding.

This was what I'd been missing these last few years. I'd been missing a reminder of everything I loved about playing the cello. Why I loved music. I was at home. This wasn't ugly ambition. This was love. As my feelings expanded and ignited, the tempo naturally increased and my body moved to keep up. My eyes were shut tight and all I could do was feel. It was magical. This was what it should feel like. This was what playing was all about. Transcendence. I was the instrument for the message being conveyed. We were one.

CHAPTER 30

PRACTICE WHEN IT'S EASY; PRACTICE MORE WHEN IT'S HARD.

DEVLIN

*S*leep never came easy with her in the house to begin with. My body was on constant edge. Her energy vibrated and disturbed me to my very core. After making her come with only my touches and kisses, there was a risk I'd never rest again. Inspiration had struck. New bits of symphonies and tunes haunted me as I tried to sleep. I gave up the ghost hours ago and came down to get it all out of my head and onto sheet music. My head was filled with her scent. Her softs sounds rang through my ears. Her taste still hung on my tongue.

I scribbled a new piece at my desk when the first notes came to me. My pencil stopped moving. I lifted my head from my hunched position, desperate to hear more.

Kim.

It was the same passion I'd heard all those weeks before when I'd listened from my secret office. The music tightened my body, quickened my breaths. As though being summoned, I stood to find the source. The music carried me toward her, stalking like an apparition.

She was back in the rehearsal room practicing.

I gripped the wall to keep from gasping and breaking her trance. She played in the dark but there was enough light to see her eyes were closed. Her entire body and mind were wrapped in the music— as it should be. This was what I had been trying to draw from her these past months. She played as all music should be played. Not how the composer wrote it but as her body guided her. As her instinct drove her. It was perfection.

My eyes drifted shut to listen better. Chills spread over my skin. How were these the same notes I'd thrown together? It didn't even feel like my music anymore. I didn't want or deserve the credit. The music sped up—moved from a dream-like state to something more sensual.

In between the notes, her inhales of breath sounded like the gasps she made when I touched her. It was the most erotic sound imaginable.

As much as I told myself to only listen to the music, my eyes opened. They were greedy to absorb every flash of skin. Her hair was down and pushed over her right shoulder. Straight strands stuck to her damp skin. The sheer fabric of her nightgown was barely held up by one hard nipple. Every sway of her body tested the ability of the material to hold on. My body hardened at the sight. Her creamy thigh was fully exposed with her legs spread so wide to accommo- date the instrument. What I wouldn't give to run my hand up that skin. I would give up everything.

I panted along with her. Her head fell back. That neck had taunted me before. I wanted my tongue running up that expanse of skin. I wanted to test the weight of her peaked breasts. I wanted to stand in place of her cello with her legs open. I wanted to sink myself into her. I wanted to lose myself inside her. I wanted.

Her bow pulled across the string playing one last, slow note. Her body heaved as did mine. When I lifted my eyes to hers, her gaze was intent on me.

If that instrument wasn't blocking her, I'd be able to see every- thing. Had my music undone her?

"Something like that?" she asked breathlessly.

My gaze returned to her face. I swallowed with difficulty. How long had she known I was standing there?

I walked until I was in front of her. I took the cello and gently lay it on its side. I took the bow and set that down as well. I took my time. Every movement was careful and deliberate. Then I knelt before her.

Her eyes followed my every action. Her eyelids were heavy with what I now recognized as desire. She didn't shift her position, her legs remained splayed, the nightgown bunched up revealing her. I swallowed.

"Perfection," I said with a raspy voice.

I rested one hand on each knee and slowly slid them to the top of her thighs. My thumbs met at her core, finding it hot and soaking wet.

"Did you get wet from playing?" I asked.

She shook her head. Her skin flushed from her chest to her cheeks. "From you watching me."

As she spoke the thin silk strap of her nightgown finally fell down and her breast was exposed. She sucked in her bottom lip. I leaned forward and blew gently on her nipple until it pebbled. My tongue flicked out to caress it once, while my thumbs continued to rub in soft circles.

"You like when I watch you?" I asked in a deep rumbling voice, already knowing everything.

I let one of my thumbs slide under the fabric of her underwear, meeting the slickness and swirling it around.

"Yes," she gasped out.

"I like watching you. I liked making you come too."

She didn't speak, only ground against my thumb until I slipped inside her, just enough to tease. She inhaled sharply.

"I liked it when you were in my bed too," I said. "How we woke up with each other."

Her eyes shot open with shock as I pushed my thumb fully into her. As she gasped, I felt her flex around me.

"I was so embarrassed." Her cheeks burned bright, and her hands gripped the chair at her sides.

"Our bodies knew what we wanted before we did. I haven't stopped thinking about it since that night."

"Me too. I felt guilty, though. Dirty," she whispered.

With that word, *dirty,* heat flashed through me. I was on fire. I needed more from her. Her skin was flushed as she writhed again, unable to keep still.

"There was nothing to feel guilty about," I said.

I lowered my mouth back to her breast and sucked on her.

"God, the things I have thought about since that night." I broke away to say, "Since you saw me naked. How many times I've thought about ..."

I shifted to suck on her other breast. I was so turned on I was about to fucking burst. The dirty talk was obviously working for her, but I didn't want her to hear the truth behind it. I still didn't think she was ready.

"Tell me," she gasped out. "Tell me what you've thought about."

I looked up at her as her breast popped out of my mouth. "Curiosity killed the cat." As I said it, I moved my thumb up and down, every so often teasing her with a quick tap. Every time, a tiny tremor shook her.

"Oh God." She grabbed my head, digging her nails into my scalp. "Magic fingers Devlin," she mumbled.

I chuckled as I nuzzled the area between her breasts, inhaling her scent. "I've thought about this. Touching you. Seeing you. All of you." I leaned back and took in her whole figure. Disheveled, flushed, panting, wet. "You are magnificent."

"Wh-what else?" she asked.

I grinned up at her. "I thought about rolling over in bed that night and sinking into you. I knew you were ready for me. I think about that a lot."

"Erik," she groaned.

Yes. It was just her and me. Nobody else. No memories, no pasts, no associations. Just this moment.

I lowered my mouth to her core, underwear still pushed to the side, and flicked her once with my tongue.

Her legs tried to squeeze shut. I could have stayed like that forever, but my knees were starting to ache and we both needed more. I was deciding what to do next when Kim made the decision for me.

Kim said, "Ah, screw it," and pushed my shoulders until I stumbled back on to the floor rather clumsily. A second later she stood up, letting the other strap of her nightgown fall. The whole thing slid right off her body. She pulled her panties all the way off, shimmying out of them.

Her naked body was more perfect than I could have ever imagined. Smooth slopes and sensual dips. Every freckle, every inch of skin, was a new area to be memorized and explored. I propped onto my elbows. "Kim," I said awestruck. "You're amazing."

"Shh," she said and straddled me right there on the floor. The Turkish rug scratched the damp skin of my back and legs but it could have been a bed of nails and I wouldn't have moved from this spot.

She went to remove my boxers—all I wore—and I stopped her. "Kim."

"I know. It's too fast." She sat back on my thighs.

"We should slow down."

"Probably." But she reached into my boxers and pulled me out, stroking down the length of me. A tongue dipped out to lick her bottom lip. "But where's the fun in that?"

I groaned and threw my head back at the same time she said, "Oh my God."

"Kim, we don't have any protection. We shouldn't—"

I hated my stupid, responsible self so much. My head was clouded. My balls were pulled up so tight, I dug my heels into the carpet to keep from coming.

"We won't. Not tonight. But I need you—and you definitely need me." She stroked faster.

I gripped her thighs to keep from losing control.

"Just this," she gasped. "Because I wanted to see this that morning. In your bed."

I propped back up on to my elbows to a sight I wouldn't forget as long as I lived. Kim straddling me, touching herself furiously, as she stroked me. Her breasts bounced with the effort, and her skin shone with sweat. I wasn't going to last a minute.

"Kim, I'm gonna—"

My hands squeezed up her thighs and she gasped.

"Yes. Please. Me too."

And so we did.

CHAPTER 31

YOU ARE ALWAYS IN MY THOUGHTS.

DEVLIN

*L*ater, after some clean up and redressing, Kim lay on top of me on the couch in the music room. I wanted to go back in time and fucking high five myself for deciding to put a couch in here. We could have used it earlier, but the rug burn on her knees was like the scratches on my shoulders. Battle scars. Frameable art.

"Turns out, I'm a bit of a horn dog," Kim said. "Sorry I launched myself on you."

"Never be sorry for that." I looked down to where her chin rested on her balled fist on my chest. Her face was soft with happy sleepiness.

"Part of me feels like I should be a lot more embarrassed about the things I did and said … and admitted. And yet I feel so good I don't even care."

I kissed her forehead. "Never feel ashamed about what you feel with me. I loved every second of it."

She buried her face into my chest and her cheeks were hot with blushing.

"I don't know how I'm ever going to look at you again when we're at the SOOK," she said.

My chest tightened at the idea of the real world. When it was just the two of us, the rest of the world disappeared. I didn't want to think about all that just yet.

"The mask will help." I had meant it as a joke, but it came out ominous.

"So, that's the plan then? Wear the mask for forever?" she asked.

"Pretty much."

"Can I just say something?" she asked.

"Has anybody ever asked that question and not just said what they wanted to say anyway?" I tweaked her chin as I grinned.

She ignored me and pressed up on to her arm. There wasn't a ton of room to maneuver so she sat up a bit awkwardly. Regardless, with her dark hair flowing around her and the satisfied glow to her cheeks, she was breathtaking.

"What's the worst that could happen? So you were a teen pop star? So what?"

"Let's not talk about this right now." I tugged at the end of her hair.

"I'm not trying to ruin the moment. I'm just saying I bet nobody would really care. You don't have to scare people to get respect. If anything, they'd think your background was cool."

"Nothing about my time as a pop star was cool. I was thrust into a world I hated. I was used up by people who couldn't have cared less about me and after about a year of undeserved fame, I fell off the map. I was dropped like that." I snapped. I heard the tension amping up in my voice. "All my years of musical training, all my credentials and supposed gifts for instruments and composing, all forgotten. I was and will only ever be Erik Jones, one-hit wonder. That person is gone. Evaporated into anonymity. Devlin, at least, is known for musical composition and talent."

"I just think—"

"I appreciate what you're saying, but please drop it," I said.

My hand itched to push her off me and leave the room. The anger was bubbling up. Why would she take this amazing moment we'd shared and ruin it?

She looked like she was about to spit venom but then she closed her mouth. A little crease formed between her brows. "Earlier. You said that sometimes you get angry when you can't find the right words. Is that what you're doing now? Getting mad at me because it's easier than talking to me?"

My heart hammered against my chest. Her face was soft but determined. Sleepy but focused. "I don't like to talk about this."

"Clearly. You wear a mask to avoid connection with people. I just thought after we—after we shared so much, you'd maybe loosen the reins a little."

I let out a breath and studied the ceiling. "There isn't anything to talk about. People find out who I am, and they freak out."

"Is that what happened with the other symphonies? You got fired when they found out who you were?"

Her gaze pierced mine as I held it. I chewed my lip before saying, "Yeah. Pretty much." I was so close to telling her the truth. I hadn't been fired—I'd quit. Because every time they'd found out who I was, they'd wanted to exploit me. They'd wanted me to sing *Can't Look Back* as though they had any right to it.

"I'm sorry that happened. You're so good. You are so, so good. It blows my mind a little. It's hard not to put you on this pedestal because of your accomplishments."

"I'm just a man." My thumb tugged at her bottom lip.

"Oh, I know." A slow smile spread on her face. Her hand moved up and down my chest. "Trust me." She let out a breath and it tickled my nipple. "Still. It must be really frustrating to be judged by one thing you did a long time ago," she said.

"Yes."

"I wouldn't know anything about that." She smiled so big at me I couldn't help but return it.

My God, if the symphony could see me now. If they knew what a sap I was for this woman, how she destroyed all my defenses with a single smile, I'd have no career left.

"Let's not talk about our pasts anymore." I pulled her back to my chest to kiss her lightly.

"You're right. Let's just be here now."

I wrapped the blanket around us. We would have to face the real world tomorrow, but for now, we were here.

CHAPTER 32

GET OUT OF YOUR HEAD.

KIM

Sunday evening when I returned home, I was surprised to find the house quiet. Usually there were a few stragglers leftover from my parents' Saturday night festivities that often merged into Sunday brunch. I was glad to be alone for once. I floated on a cloud of ecstasy from the weekend and didn't want to have to explain my good mood to anyone. Or worse yet, explain my relationship with Devlin. Which would be really difficult, because we'd never really gotten to that point. I wasn't about to bring it up.

I just wanted to lay in bed with my few hours of free time and replay the highlight reel from the past few days. I'd had a breakthrough, I'd had some sexual experiences that rivaled walking on the moon, and I had found a sense of yearning to play my instrument again that I hadn't felt in over a decade. Things were coming up Kim.

I had just passed the dining room when my mom called out, "Sweetie, can you come in here?"

Mom and Dad sat on a leather sofa with a small stack of papers, magazines, and books between them. My mother had her legs tucked under her—looking more elegant at close to seventy-five than I had in all my years on this planet. She had an arm around Dad. He took off his "readers" and placed them on the stack.

"Hey," I said.

My mother wore a large loose-necked cowl sweater dress and black leather leggings. My father was wearing brown loafers with fancy little tassels. I noticed all this because I couldn't quite bring myself to make eye contact with them. Could parents sense when their child had had mind-blowing orgasms? Lord, I hoped not. Why did it feel like suddenly a sign flashed above my head saying, "Your daughter got freaky this weekend!"

"Sit down, sweetie," Dad said. "Let's have a chat. Catch up. What's going on with you?"

I sat in the armchair across from them, sliding in the leather as I tried to find a position to get comfortable. I ended up tucking my knees under my chin which made me feel even more like a child under interrogation. Nothing good ever followed a forced attempt to have a casual conversation. I was reminded of the ease I witnessed between Devlin and his family, of how they laughed and shared and spoke with the familiarity of long-time friends.

"Sure." I settled on a vague, less was more response. "I'm good. How are y'all?"

My mother hummed a sigh and shot a look at my father.

"Best to just put it out there, Meredith. You know these things are worse if we build them up."

An icy dread had me squeezing my legs tighter to my body.

She patted his head before picking up the glasses he had just laid down. They perched on her nose as she picked up one of the papers and began to read. "'Devil of the Symphony makes more outlandish requests.' Are chair auditions really that bizarre? It goes on. Yellow journalism, for sure, but here: 'His muse and prized pupil, Christine Day, has moved quickly up the ranks as the new conductor seems to have taken a liking to her. Rumors of walkouts abound over the perceived favoritism.'" My mother put the paper back down, carefully folded up the glasses, and set them on top.

People were going to walk out over this? Devlin was supposed to be working toward bringing us together as a symphony. I was distracting him. I was causing this. I tried to clamp down on the wayward thoughts, but they ran wild with my heart rate.

"This is rubbish, obviously. You're extremely talented and that's why the Maestro chose you."

"That being said …" my father started.

"That being said, we've heard unsettling rumors," Mom finished.

"What sort of rumors?" I asked, knowing I was not pulling off casually unaffected.

"We've heard he's been following you places?" Dad asked. "Then there are those ridiculous rumors of kidnapping."

"Of course we know the truth of that first night at his place. He talked to us first." My mother laid her arm on his shoulder. He squeezed her hand back.

"People are sensationalizing things for the sake of drama."

"I'm sure those two that run the symphony are feeding off it."

"They're probably the ones who started the rumors."

"No doubt."

My parents volleyed back and forth, forgetting that I was in the room. As they spoke, my worst fears began to stack in my mind. I had lost control. I had let myself give in to deep desires and take what was not mine. Would all of Devlin's work be destroyed because of this reputation? Would the SOOK really revolt?

"Honey?" My mom cut through my thoughts. "I'm sure it's small town minds and all that. Richard has said that Carla is going to quit. Change like this is bound to happen when a new person takes over. We just want to make sure you're being careful. If you're feeling any unscrupulous pressure from Devlin …"

"He wouldn't do that. He's not like that," I quickly said.

"We didn't think so either. But you let us know, ok? If anything starts to feel like too much or …"

"Or any of those old worries and anxieties start to creep up again?" Dad finished.

Of course. They were worried I was backsliding. I'd been going out more, staying away from home. They'd never known the truth about camp. I'd been so scared to tell them, and even now, I was too gripped by growing anxieties to get the words out. In their minds, they probably saw old habits returning.

"Okay, well, we were concerned. Lots of buzz about the moody conductor and his current cellist muse." Mom said.

"Muse?" I asked. Roddy had said that too. Was that what I was? It didn't feel like that when I was with him. It didn't feel temporary or fleeting. But what if that was how all muses felt?

"You know how artists are. He must have taken one look at you and felt inspired," Dad said.

"Right," I said focusing on the paisley pattern in the thick rug I squished my toes into.

"She attracts the wild ones, doesn't she?"

"Oh, don't you dare put the blame on her," my mother said.

"You know I didn't mean that, Meredith."

"Well it's not her fault people find her attractive, Lindsay. That added nothing to the value of this conversation."

"I'm sorry. I didn't mean it that way …"

Their voices faded away. I couldn't take any more. I couldn't hear any more. This. This was why I couldn't be trusted. One moment's bad choice, and everything got derailed. People got hurt.

I got up and left the room without another word. They had slid into a full-on debate and wouldn't notice. I had to clear my head. I had to think. I climbed the stairs and locked myself in my room.

After I got back from camp, after Ariana's suicide, I took on the blame for everything. I came home in search of freedom and distraction in the form of charming Jethro Winston. Juilliard turned into rehab instead. Returning to Green Valley, I was convinced that every person I passed in the street was gossiping about me. Every service-goer at church, every donut-eater at Daisy's, all of them pointing at the girl who ruined lives, including her own. The girl who had been given everything and threw it away.

Changing my name to Christine Day and living primarily in Knoxville had stopped most of the gossip. I grayed out until I faded into the background. I toned down and tuned out. That was fine. I was fine. I was existing. Until now.

All that had changed with Devlin. While he wasn't the charmer Jethro had been, he was definitely a distraction. And people were getting hurt.

* * *

I walked into rehearsal the week before the big Fourth of July show. My head hurt from all the thinking I'd been doing. No answers had come to me, but then I'd felt the silence and I knew. Like all the other times. All the whispering stopped when I walked in. All the eyes shot to me. Then to Devlin. Then they sucked their teeth or snuck glances to their neighbor with eyebrows raised, implying "the nerve."

Somehow, they knew there was something going on between us. Or at the very least, they guessed. And the worst part was their guesses were probably close to the truth. He was another man I shouldn't have.

Devlin was at the front of the room. He tapped the podium and the room silenced. "Chairs are posted."

Energy burst around the room in a quiet wave. People were desperate to jump out of their seats to go look at the postings, but kept themselves locked down as he continued in his authoritative tone.

"You will go up to front one section at a time to avoid chaos. These will be your positions for the performance. The first chair cellist will have the opportunity to play a solo from my upcoming concerto, *Smokey Mountain Suite*, debuting in the fall."

The room grew louder and people squirmed in their seats, arching their necks to try and read the papers posted at the front of the room. Carla lifted her chin and smirked at Barry. Maybe she knew something I didn't. Maybe she had earned first chair after all.

Delvin held up his arms again. I couldn't look directly at him. All the lascivious things I had said. All the things I'd admitted. The way he'd touched me. If I looked right at him, I worried explicit details might blurt out of me. I might beg him to tell me what I meant to him. I dug my nails into my palms. I sat stock still and kept my face neutral. I could feel Erin trying to get my attention, but my muddled emotions would be written all over my face.

"I did not choose these chairs alone. I worked with a committee, the same committee as we've discussed before. We came to an agreement together. I can do nothing without the committee's approval. Once you see where you now sit, calmly go back to your chairs, and move as necessary. This is our last rehearsal before the performance. We will make it a good one."

He cleared his throat. "You have all exceeded my expectations these last few months. I'm honored to play with all of you tonight. Your commitment to the SOOK has been noticed." Faces of equal parts surprise and pride swept across the room. "Percussion, you're up first. You have ten minutes until the next group will be called up."

And so it went, for the next hour. One group at a time. Every time they went up, I swore after they checked their own name, they glanced to the cellos to see where Christine Day had been placed. I was the fourth chair who went from obscurity to being Devlin's pet. I couldn't keep the fear from my eyes when Erin passed. My lip bled where I'd been gnawing on it. She gave me a very quick and very subtle thumbs up as she passed. God, I wished I could text her, but no phones were allowed in rehearsal, ever. Of course. I kept trying to get her attention, but she was distracted as she moved her stuff up to first chair. I smiled so big. I had been so caught up in my own drama it hadn't even occurred to me that she may be changing seats.

When she eventually looked my way, I gave her the biggest smile and double thumbs up despite the dread somersaulting through my gut.

Finally, it was our turn, the cellos. I let Carla and the others go first and kept myself firmly in the middle.

If Carla's swearing under her breath was any indication, I knew what was coming.

"Third chair. *Third*? Are you kidding me?" she was growling at

Barry. When I got close enough to look, she didn't move. I had to bend around her to see.

It read: First chair - Christine Day.

My heart plummeted when it should have rejoiced. Now the rumors would have even more fuel.

I was first. Barry was second, Carla third, and Joe had slid from third to fourth but he just nodded like it was the result he'd expected.

"This is bull," Carla said. "My father promised—" She cut herself short and crossed her arms.

My heart slammed against my chest. She shot me a look of pure hatred. I had no excuses. She waved away Barry's comfort. I had done this. I had caused her reaction. What if—

"Carla, I'm sorry," I said.

She looked at me and frowned. "Isn't this exactly what you wanted?"

My head was shaking. "No."

"You should be happy," she said. "After all you sure did earn it." She wiped away a quick tear.

Had I earned it? What if … what if Devlin thought …

I couldn't think. That pressing weight sat firmly on my chest again. I needed out of that room. I didn't want the solo. I didn't want first chair. Not like this.

"Ms. Day, where are you going?" I was almost out of the room when I stopped at Devlin's question.

"I just need to—"

His brows drew together. "Rehearsal isn't over."

"Teacher's pet," Carla mumbled.

I couldn't speak. The room started to spin. I didn't ask for this. I wanted to scream it.

Carla was glaring at me with red-rimmed eyes. I'd made a huge mistake. I had gone too far. My whole body shook with tremors.

"I don't feel well. I need to go."

CHAPTER 33

PLAY LIKE THERE IS NO ONE TO OFFEND.

KIM

*R*oddy was waiting right outside the room holding a giant bundle of flowers.

His smile was huge as he said, "Congratulations."

I ran right up to him and threw my arms around his neck. I squeezed so tight. A friendly face was so desperately needed. I drew up all the good things his smell and memories did for me. I brought up all the happy and pushed away all the negativity.

"Yo-Yo?"

I squeezed him harder but then let go. "I need a break. Get me away from here."

"Okay. What's wrong? I thought you'd be happy to get first chair. My parents told me. They were pleased. So am I. Why aren't you?"

"Please, let's talk somewhere else."

I tugged him toward the exit. If I could just take a minute to right my thoughts, talk through some things. A big part of me wanted to go to Devlin for this, but I couldn't now. Not with all those faces watching.

Roddy stopped me before we got outside and put his hands on my shoulders. "Talk to me, Yo-yo."

"It's just too much." I gestured back to the performance space. "I appreciate it, I really do. I know that means the committee saw some talent in me, but people are talking about me like I did this or did something … unprofessional to get it."

I focused on his Adam's apple as I spoke. His skin was fair, more fair than mine. There were little red bumps where he shaved.

"I heard the rumors too. Absolutely absurd. Trust me, I've talked to Richard and Andrew about it. My parents too. Nobody will stand for this."

"You have?" I asked.

"Yes. Can you imagine? You and Devlin? Like he has anything to offer you." His face was contorted with disgust. "Even if he does want you as his little pet, I won't let him use you up like that. You'd be wasted as some moody artist's plaything."

"Roddy, I didn't do anything. I didn't want the solo."

"I know. It's okay. Don't worry about anything." He pulled me in for another hug. "The only reason these rumors are even going is because they're trying to sell seats. It's abhorrent and selfish. But don't worry. I have a plan. I'll take care of everything."

Relief settled into my bones. "Thank you."

I stepped forward to rest my head on his chest. He smelled nice, sort of clean like baby powder. He was shorter than I remembered. And bonier. I adjusted my cheek to find a more comfortable spot.

"Don't worry about the gossips. You earned that chair. You did earn it. You work so hard."

I squeezed my eyes shut against the worry.

"If it's really upsetting you though, you don't have to do it, you know?" he said cautiously.

"What do you mean?"

He tugged me to the side. "Listen. There's interest in a tour. If you wanted to leave today, I could have everything set up with a few phone calls. This could be your chance to get away from this place. Away from the gossips and Green Valley."

"Leave Green Valley?" I asked.

Could I escape my past? Would it be that easy? I had always hoped Roddy would be the reason things changed. I didn't want to upset the symphony. I didn't want to ruin Devlin's chances at success. If I went on that stage in this state, if I tried to play the solo, I'd hurt too many people to count.

"Carla would be happy to take your place. The people who think you didn't earn this would be happy. Not that that matters. But I'd be happy too. I've always wanted more for you. I want to keep you safe. You decide, and I'll take you away from all of this."

My heart was beating so hard my body shook. I couldn't take a full breath, and the hallway blurred.

I didn't know if I wanted to do that. But I also couldn't face the thought of stepping on that stage and playing Carla's solo. I thought of the hurt and sadness on Carla's face. I thought of Devlin and my confession in the hallway. I know he'd said it wasn't my fault. I know he wanted me to play for me, but he didn't understand that it was happening again. My success was hurting people. I couldn't do that again. I couldn't stay and hurt people.

I could take myself out of the equation though. I could go away. Changing my name had been step one but I needed to leave Green Valley to truly become Christine Day. I would just explain that it was all happening too fast.

"Come on. Let's go. We will go to my folk's place and figure this out." Roddy pushed open the back exit. He tugged me along after.

"Wait. I need to—"

"Where are you going?" Devlin yelled.

I spun to see him eating up ground in only a few steps. His fists were balled and his face was furious.

"I need some time to talk, Maestro," I said.

His focus was on me, brows furrowed and chest heaving. "You can't just leave. You're first chair."

"She doesn't want to be here. You can't make her stay." Roddy put himself between us.

"I wasn't speaking to you," Devlin growled.

Roddy crossed his arms.

"Move or I'll move you."

"Roddy, it's okay—" I started.

"It's not okay," Roddy said. "You are scared. Look at you, you're shaking and pale. And he's done this. All of this. He's pushed you to this point."

"I didn't do anything. You are the one scaring her. Now move, let me talk to her."

"Why don't you back off?" Roddy puffed up his chest and stepped up to Devlin.

I tried to pull Roddy back. "It's okay. I can explain."

"No." Roddy brushed me off, causing him to bump into Devlin.

Roddy wasn't small by any means. He was almost six foot easily, but Devlin had mass and height over him.

"She's had enough of you and your scare tactics. She wants to leave."

"I'm not scared. Let me speak, both of you!" Nerves made my voice shrill.

Both men looked at me.

"I just need to think," I said more calmly. I pressed my fingertips to my temple. I couldn't bring myself to see Devlin's face. Would there be hurt or disappointment?

"Can't you see what you're doing to her, man?" Roddy asked.

Devlin's fists clenched and unclenched. His anger was barely restrained.

"Why don't you take your temper and go? Stop making her pay for your piss-poor attitude." Roddy got right up in Devlin's face. "Not so tough now? Now that you know I'm right."

A shadow passed over Devlin's face. He looked to me. "What's going on?" He spoke low and directly to me.

Before I could answer, Roddy shoved Devlin's shoulder and said, "You know what? No. I'm tired of him playing you, Yo-Yo. I've had enough."

"Please, stop," I said.

"No. He's hurting you." He shoved again.

Devlin crossed his arms. His jaw flexed as he ground his teeth to stay quiet. He didn't look at the other man at all. His gaze burned into mine.

Roddy gave up and turned to me. "I knew he would do this. Since the moment I came back. I knew he would find a way to hurt you. He takes too much. Pushes you too hard."

Roddy lowered his voice and grabbed my hands. "All I have ever wanted was to help you. In camp. Even now. I want to help you. He wants to take from you."

With every word that Roddy spoke, Devlin grew more tense, though he tried to pretend he wasn't listening. He kept his focus locked on me as though trying to convey something.

"What's this about?" Richard came out from his office with Andy at his side.

A few others from the symphony had leaked into the hall to watch the commotion. With every added witness my anxiety grew. I needed to calm everybody down. I needed to make things better. More people spilled out into the hall. I knew what they'd think. Roddy and Devlin fighting over me. This could break Devlin's career. This could ruin his reputation if I didn't calm things down.

"I wrote those notes for you. I took care of you," Roddy dropped his head and spoke low. "Agree to leave with me and start your new life."

I looked into his ice blue eyes, searching for the man who could make all this better. He lowered his head as though he was about to kiss me. I reared back to explain that it wasn't like that for me, but I didn't have a chance.

Devlin gripped Roddy's shoulder, spun him around, and punched him right in the face.

Chaos erupted.

CHAPTER 34

YOUR COMMITMENT TO WORK SETS YOU APART FROM THE REST.

DEVLIN

People moved all around. Some to Chagny. Some pulling me away. My fist throbbed. But the pain had been worth it to see blood streaming down his face.

I didn't give a shit that I'd lost control. I was only human. My control had been thinly tethered since rehearsal had started and Kim was visibly distant from me. It had frayed further still by his arrival and the flowers. Further again with his attempt at taking her victories and making them his. Then he'd lied to her face and my last thread snapped. And I couldn't care less.

When he lied to the world, he took what was mine. Was he insane or did he really think she would never know? How could she not see through his bullshit? Kim was frightened by something, maybe the depth of our connection or her own future, but she wasn't an idiot. She was brilliant and it boggled my mind that he could even garner any of her attention, let alone affection.

My thoughts were incoherent. Kim crouched at his side. I stood there shaking out my throbbing fist until I was forcibly dragged into Andy-Dick's office. I wasn't sure by whom. I just knew that one second I was watching her try to staunch that asshole's bleeding, the next we were all in the office together.

"We will deal with you later." Dick dabbed sweat off his face as he spoke to me. "First I have to go calm everyone down."

"It's unfortunate," the other half said to me. He touched his nose when he looked at Chagny sprawled out in a chair with his head held back. "You had been warned."

The two left. Apparently, no one thought that leaving Kim, Roddy, and me alone in the room was a bad idea. Kim was whispering apologies to him.

"I knew he liked you, but I never thought he'd be so immature," Chagny said as though he didn't know I stood only a few feet away.

"I should hit you again," I spat.

"Maestro, please," Kim said from his side.

Maestro? Was she kidding me? "Are you serious?"

"Please, let me handle him. One thing at a time," she pleaded with me.

Her face was so pale, more so than when the chair positions were posted. I knew she'd been holding herself back, avoiding the limelight. I understood her fears now, but she would never change if she held on to them. I had tried to warn her. Ethically, I couldn't say too much.

"So that's it? You were just going to leave? With a show coming up?" I snapped. I should have waited until I was calmed down, but I needed answers. I couldn't stomach the sight of her babying him. How could she so easily push me aside? This wasn't the Kim I knew.

"You're out of control," Chagny lifted his head to spit the words at me with a congested sniff. To Kim he said, "I knew he was dangerous. To think all that time you were alone with him. God, the worst could have happened."

Kim glanced at me and back to him. "Roddy. Listen. We need to talk. You really shouldn't have pushed so hard either. This has nothing to do with either of you."

"It has everything to do with me and you know that." I heard the crack in my voice. I was giving my hurt away. She saw too much. I steeled my voice. "How long have you two been together?"

At this her head started to shake. "No. It wasn't like that—"

"But it is now?" I asked.

"Of course." Roddy sniffed checking for blood with his hand. "Since I've been back in town."

Kim shot a look to him. "Wait, what? No. Roddy, I think you and I need to talk separately."

"What has all this been Kim?" I hit a hand to my chest. "Am I just your fun distraction waiting for the real thing?"

She held my gaze. "Is that what you really think of me?"

"I don't think you're a liar. I would never think that. But you can't speak your truth and that's just as dangerous. You let people live your life for you. I won't do that or be that way. I don't know what to think anymore. I certainly had no idea you were about to go on tour. This is all news to me. You made promises."

"I did commit to help with the concerto. You've finished it now. I'm trying to do what's best here. Be patient with me while I figure this out." Her eyes pleaded with me. I had to look away. "If I take that solo, if I stay here, you know how it would go over."

Roddy added sheepishly, "I was going to surprise you after the show. Everything has come through perfectly. People are dying to see Christine Day already."

"This is bullshit. You committed to me!" I yelled and kicked the desk.

She flinched back. I knew I was only making things worse, but we couldn't end like this. She couldn't be pressured into leaving. She'd promised me.

Roddy remained quiet as his gaze flicked between us. It was calculating. I didn't like it.

"I'm sorry." Kim brought my attention back to her. Her face was creased with a frown.

"Why don't you want her to go?" Roddy asked me. "Are you worried about her or your September showcase? Did you tell her you'd always intended for her to have the solo? How you fought for her on the committee?"

Kim's head shot to me. More color seemed to drain from her face. "Devlin. I was so worried you would push me into this." Her voice was a hurt whisper. "I told you everything. You knew what that solo would cost me."

"I was going to make sure you were ready." Of course I had wanted her to play it. That's why we'd been rehearsing so much together, but I would never force her.

I couldn't lose her. I'd just gotten her. Fear seized my chest. I couldn't take a full breath.

"You can play it. Nobody else can," I growled. I didn't have to explain to them. She'd been there too. She felt the connection, the music, the … love. Fuck, it was love. We both felt it, but she was too chicken to admit it.

"But did you ever consider if it was what I really wanted?" she asked.

Fear stacked behind her eyes. I knew she couldn't be pushed too soon. I wasn't trying to, but she had to at least stay and try. I couldn't lose her.

"You deserve it. You need to stop hiding yourself." How could I convey this to her? We had talked, she was right. That only convinced me she was ready to move forward. I thought now more than ever she could let go of her past. But she was retreating again. She was pulling away from me.

Fear of losing her, of losing everything we had surged panic through me. I couldn't stop the words from coming.

"You have to choose. Right now." Desperation made my words sharp and defiant.

"Don't make her choose to save your ego," Roddy said in soft condescension. "Yo-Yo, you don't have to listen to him. He's upset because he thinks he's lost his muse. But you need to tell him what you told me. Be honest. Tell him that you want to go home."

My heart slammed against my chest. If they weren't here, I'd grip the wall to keep from collapsing. Had she talked about me to him? How often where they talking? After I had made her come? When we spent hours sharing and playing with each other? I felt like I was growing a new life with this woman and now I was finding out she was a total stranger. Everything had been for her. This tool knew nothing about what made her amazing.

Kim turned to me, her eyes mournful. "It's not that I don't want to help you. I do—"

"Can you take off that ridiculous mask? We all know you're Erik Jones. Erik Devlin Jones." He rolled his eyes.

Kim's eyes widened and she covered her mouth. *No.*

"You told him?" I asked feeling like the ground under my feet crumbled with every passing second.

"No. How could you even think that?" She stood and her gaze was restless with worry.

"I don't know anything anymore." I shook my head. I couldn't trust anything. My own feelings for her must have colored every happy memory we had together. Now all I saw was her laughing with Chagny about me. Every time she left my house, did she go to him? I imagined it—the two of them with bent heads, whispering about my past.

"She didn't tell me." Roddy stood too. "You think I'd let somebody I love spend all that time with you without knowing who you really are? I thought it was harmless. I didn't know you were obsessed with her."

"I don't give a fuck what you think." I went to Kim. When I tried to grab her hands, she pulled them away and wrapped them tightly around her middle. "Kim, I know you're scared. It's just you and me, remember?"

She shook her head, no tears. She looked checked out. "I need time to process."

Roddy stood and came to Kim's side. "I'm sure if you really want to stay, we could explain everything to the orchestra. Carla and the others think the worst, especially now. But we could make it work, if that's what you really want. You know I could make that happen for you."

Kim closed her eyes tightly as his words hit the mark. He knew exactly what he was doing. I couldn't compete against that. I *wouldn't.* I wouldn't use her weaknesses to emotionally manipulate her.

"Kim." I stepped closer to her. Not too close to crowd her. I didn't touch her, but I let her remember the heat of our bodies close together. "Please look at me. Tell me what you want."

"She goes by Christine now. It's time to let the past go," Chagny said.

"I swear to God, if you don't put a muzzle on him …" I shook.

"I need time to think." She didn't open her eyes, just brought her balled fists to her temples.

"You need to choose," I said.

"I can't."

"Are you staying or going?" With every second of pressure she was closer to breaking. She was a drum I was tuning too tight, but I couldn't stop. She needed to say it. She was in charge of her life. Not either of us.

"Roddy," she said, and my heart fell to the floor. "Can you give us five minutes?"

He nodded and headed for the door, he stopped to kiss her temple on the way out. "I'm here for you. If you need anything, I'll be right outside."

By the time he was out of the room my joints hurt from the rigid tension my whole body held.

"If you are going to break it to me gently, don't bother. Just do it. I'll find another cellist."

I shouldn't have said that. It was a stupid thing to say, but I couldn't let her see how deeply she'd cut me. How much she'd hurt me. That was her song. That was my soul on paper again for her and she wouldn't accept it.

She stepped closer. She grabbed my hands.

"Things are happening too fast. I never would have … with you if … Roddy and I are just friends."

"But you're leaving with him, aren't you?" I pulled my hand

away. "You're taking his little tour and you're going to do whatever he says."

"Tell me to stay." She grabbed me tighter, with both hands. "Give me a reason. I cannot destroy someone else's life. I need to know why you wanted me this whole time."

She held my gaze, imploring. I knew what she needed to hear. My chest seized. The words wouldn't come. Hadn't I been transparent this whole time? Hadn't she always seen the core of me? I'd shown her my love in the lessons. In the music. I could tell her everything. I could tell her the truth of my love for her, but then what? It would still be me choosing for her. She needed to make a choice about her own life. I wouldn't be another person telling her what to do. I wouldn't hamper her growth. I loved her too much.

I memorized her face as I spoke, knowing it would be one of the last times I ever saw it this close. "You want somebody to tell you exactly what you want and need so that if anything ever goes wrong, it's not your fault. I would never make it that easy on you and you know that. Everything you feel in your heart, everything you know to be true, you're willing to ignore just because you don't want to make the wrong choice." As I said the words, the world faded out of focus around me.

This would be last time I held her hand. I knew it as sure as I knew anything. She closed her eyes and a tear dropped onto our clasped hands.

"You don't want to have to choose. You want someone to make the choices. You think because you can argue about big ideas and theories, that you are assertive and know what you want, but I have never seen somebody who knows less about themselves."

She looked up, her beautiful eyes glistening. "You're right then, I guess."

My fingertips went numb.

"You think he's offering you security, but you couldn't be further from the truth. He's taking away any chance you had to find yourself again."

She shook her head slowly. "It's never been about me." Her voice was soft as she spoke. She still wouldn't look at me. "It's always been about you proving something. About showing the world they were wrong about you."

Her accusation unnerved me. Rage built up inside me. She had no clue how people took and took and only wanted to be in your life for what you could provide to them.

"You have no idea how it feels to be me. Even you. You changed when you saw my face. I never know if you are Kim or Christine. If you want Devlin for his talent or Erik Jones because of some childhood crush."

She cringed. "It has never been about your fame. You can't see that. Your soul just sees darkness and corruption. You're pushing me away before you even give it a chance."

"You chose him," I spat. "You chose him and the tour over your commitments to me."

"This was never about me," she said almost to herself. "You told me once that my past was a lesson and not a life sentence. You should have been talking to yourself. If anybody is in the prison of the past, it's you. You're missing everything because you hold onto anger so tightly."

I covered my ears with my hands. She lied. I couldn't take another word. "Just leave. Go with him. Let yourself forget all that we shared. How you tapped into the truest part of yourself for the music. Forget you were ever here. Forget you ever saw the real me."

With that, I left the room. There was nothing else to say. The choice was made.

CHAPTER 35

WITHOUT THE LOVE, MUSIC HAS NO POINT.

DEVLIN

"Let's get this over with." I slammed the door into Andy-Dick's office.

As soon as this was finished, I was going home. She'd taken everything from me. She'd taken my music and my pride. I'd given her everything.

"Ah, Maestro. Have a seat," Andy said.

"Just fire me. I'm not sitting down for that," I said.

My palms itched. My stomach was twisted with anxious energy. I hated being in this position. Why I'd ever thought coming back to this place was a good idea, I would never know.

"Please. Sit."

There was nothing left in me to care about this place or any other place. Screw this town. Screw the SOOK. I could move on.

But could I? I had burned every bridge I'd ever built. Coming to the SOOK was supposed to be the easiest thing I ever did for my career. I couldn't even make it work. I really was a loser. Had it ever really been about the SOOK, or had it been about Kim?

"It's an interesting thing that happened," Dick said. "You were on thin ice, but in the interest of full disclosure, the drama between you and Miss Day has been great for our sales."

"Tickets sales are up. Google searches. Instagram, hashtags. I don't really get it, but our PR intern tells us these are all good things," Andy finished.

"Great." I was so thrilled that the pain that crippled my chest was entertainment.

"Gossip sells tickets. Now, I obviously don't want to run a business on sensationalism, but right now, leaving wouldn't be the wisest thing to do," Dick said.

"And we don't want it to look like we are condoning this sort of behavior. There would have to be a probational period. A slap on the hand. A few weeks off to cool down a little, after the Fourth of July show, of course. But we still have the September showcase." Andy pointed to a calendar hanging on the wall.

"I'm not fired?" I asked not believing.

"You are absolutely fired. Unless …"

Dick said, "We still need tickets sold. Something else interesting has been brought to our attention."

"Turns out you're a bit of a celebrity. Not sure why you would hide such a past from us. That's fantastic!" Andy said.

"Perhaps we can come to an arrangement for the September showcase. In addition to your *Smokey Mountain Suite*, we'll advertise your famous background. You could play your most famous song, *Don't Look Back*," Dick said.

"A rock concert and a concerto in one." The other smiled broadly at his own idea.

"I will conduct for the Fourth of July concert. I won't leave the community hanging like that, but you're out of your minds if you think I'll …" I reached for the door. The last thing I would ever do was bring that life into this one. Not a chance in hell I'd play that garbage song. It was bad enough I was even back here.

"Of course we'll continue the Fourth of July as planned," Andy simpered.

"The choice is yours for September," Dick said.

"Take a couple weeks to think about it. It's summer break anyway. You have the choice. You can come back or you can ruin your career."

"Great options," I mumbled. "You know what? Consider my fist to Chagny's face my official resignation."

CHAPTER 36

IT'S OKAY TO PUT YOURSELF FIRST.

KIM

September

It had been seven weeks since I'd talked to Devlin. Seven weeks since I'd left home. Seven weeks since I'd remembered what it felt like to be Kim Dae. I wasn't even sure I knew who Christine Day was, either.

The reflection that stared back at me in the mirror was a caricature of a person. A caricature that got a lot of likes, and re-posts, and compliments. Empty clicks from faceless people.

After the Fourth of July concert, which had gone as rehearsed, sans one cellist, Devlin had gone MIA and his concerto had been put on hold indefinitely. There was no bonus cello solo performance. I wasn't going back to the SOOK if there was no show. I'd committed to help with the showcase, but with Devlin gone, my commitment was voided.

Devlin had made it clear what I was to him. I all but asked him to love me and he had told me he'd replace me with another cellist. I couldn't let myself think about it or sickness would eat away at me.

The numbness of tour was the way to go. Never had I itched more for those days of Jethro, for the drugged-out haze of life.

Roddy had already booked several stops throughout the Southeast playing local theaters that seated around three hundred. Tonight was the last show of the summer tour, and I was grateful. I was numb and empty. When asked if that was what I wanted, I simply nodded. I had no opinion. I didn't care. I just didn't want to hurt anybody else.

Roddy assured me that he was working on more bookings for the fall and soon we would be filling stadiums. Stadiums of people wanting to see Christine Day. What a life. The crowds were pretty decent even now. He'd done a good job of taking care of my social media presence. When I flipped through the pictures on Instagram, I didn't recognize myself. There weren't any traces of Kim Dae. It was Christine Day. Long flowing hair, fancy electric cello, false lashes, and heavy makeup. She was beautiful, but she was a different person.

It wasn't an easy life. I worked nonstop. The distraction helped push aside the constant ache in my heart. The countryside blurred into hotel rooms and stages. I was grateful though, and thanked the venues and the fans. Many people dreamed of this life. And Roddy, bless his heart, he took care of everything. The fans grew with every show. It was all happening very fast, but he wasn't surprised.

"That's how it happens nowadays. That's why you have to keep up with it. You're doing great," he'd said.

A few times he'd tried to kiss me. I told him I wasn't interested in him that way. I made it clear before ever leaving on tour, we'd be in separate rooms and I was not his girlfriend. I was a business partner. His only response was that he was happy to go slow. He'd wait for me. The truth was, I felt nothing. This was how I felt before Devlin. Before he turned up in my life and turned everything upside down. Now, every sporadic memory of happiness was linked with a man I fought to forget.

I missed my parents and their weird ways. I missed my girls in the SWS and Erin. I missed swimming. I even missed the symphony. I didn't miss Carla—I wasn't that out of it. I felt myself getting stir-crazy even with all the moving around we were doing. It was the same routine even if it was different every two or three days.

We were at a hotel in—I wasn't even sure what city we were in. I was tired already. I loved playing and meeting people, but this was draining. I was set to go on stage again in another hour for the last show of this tour. I was too tired to even lift my head from my bed.

"Knock, knock," Roddy said as he peeked in his head through our shared door. Hadn't that been locked? "Hope you're decent."

I waved from the bed. "Hey."

"What are you doing? We gotta get going soon." His gaze moved over my prone form. "Your hair isn't done."

"I thought I could put it up tonight. I keep pulling it when I play."

"Oh, that's frustrating. Man, I totally understand why you'd want it up. But—" He made this face like he was going for pained? Concerned? "But you have your brand now. When you're a household name, we can play around with your style, but for now we have to keep a real consistent look. Plus, it looks so beautiful when it's down and flowing."

I sat up and dragged my feet to the bathroom. I began the hour-long routine of doing my hair. Roddy stood in the doorway, smiling as he leaned against the frame.

"What?" I asked.

He was watching me in the mirror as I pinned up different sections of hair. "You're just so beautiful."

I smiled back, but my reflection showed it didn't reach my eyes. "Thank you."

He said it a lot, especially, and almost pointedly, more often when I was done up.

Every time he did, it spurred the image of me tired and undone with Devlin smiling down at me. Had Devlin ever told me I was beautiful? I couldn't recall. And yet I'd never felt more beautiful than I had when he smiled at me with soft eyes, or fire in them as I stretched over him. That was when I'd felt most perfect.

My stomach soured and I pushed the thoughts away. Over these last few weeks there were so many times my mind pulled up memories from our brief time together. Each time, I examined the scene in a different light. I forced myself to see it through the lens of reality, not the rosy hue of sentimentality. I knew that I was a muse. He would offer me no more.

Roddy stayed in the room while I got ready. I felt like I was being checked up on. I got dressed and suddenly felt like I couldn't take a moment more of this life. I knew I should be grateful but …

I couldn't do this. I shook with the nerves that came with voicing my opinion. My outfit was tight and revealing. My breasts were pushed up and my hair was long and loose around my shoulders. My eyelashes were as fake as all the makeup covering my face. Who was this person? Could I just go home and curl up in a ball?

"I don't think I can do this," I said to Roddy. My voice must have sounded as panicked as I felt because he immediately came to my side.

"Hey, hey. What's wrong?" He brushed my cheeks. "Don't cry. You'll ruin your pretty face."

"I can't do this. This isn't—" Panic crushed in on me all at once.

This wasn't what? The words were so close to the surface.

"I don't want this life. After this tour is done, after tonight's show, I'm going home." I said on a rush. I couldn't believe it. I said it and I knew it. I knew in that moment that while this was a wonderful life and so many people would be happy to have it, it wasn't what I wanted.

Roddy wrapped his arms tight around me. "No, shh. You're tired. It's too much too soon."

"No, I don't want—"

"Listen. You need to relax. I put too much on you too soon. Try this."

Out of his pocket, he pulled a small, unmarked prescription bottle. My heart raced at the sight of it.

"What is that?" I asked.

"It's all natural. An herbal supplement. My doctor told me about it when I wasn't sleeping. It'll calm your nerves."

My hands reached for the bottle as my mind screamed no. But a little part of me wanted it. I'd taken a lot of pills before I'd detoxed, all sorts of shapes and sizes and colors. I couldn't remember what any of them were or what they did besides bring oblivion. This pill could bring freedom. I could let go. I'd been holding on so tightly to a life I didn't want. I'd worked so hard to make it fit. If I took this pill maybe I could just exist.

"I don't think this is a good idea," I said.

"It's over the counter. It may be a placebo for all I know. No pressure. But it will help you relax." He cupped a hand around my head and pulled me in to place a soft kiss on my forehead.

I grew antsy. I wanted to push him away. I felt a scream trying to tear its way out of my throat. Why? I had no right to be angry or restless. I chose this. Or rather, I let myself be led into this life by my lack of choice.

"I wouldn't let anything happen to you. You know that. I just want to help you relax."

My mouth watered as I opened the bottle. I would just take a glance at them. "All natural?"

He scratched his chin. "Of course."

I hid my response as I dumped out a pill into my hand. It was small and blue with a fancy "V" stamped on one side and "2531" on the other. Herbal supplement, my ass. I spent months in rehab. I knew prescription drugs. Just not this one.

I closed my hand around a pill and made to throw it in my mouth. Instead, I pocketed it. It was the most deceitful thing I'd done around Roddy. I had always been my genuine self and made the naïve assumption that he did as well. I thought with our shared history, there was no reason to be anyone but his real self. He was a shiny veneer but what about the content inside? What did I really know? We talked every day, a lot actually, but it was always about the schedule or memories or things that felt as substantive as marshmallow cereal.

I took a deep breath and relaxed. Inside I fumed. I didn't want to assume the worst. I had gone off on Devlin, and I'd seen how well that worked out. I needed to handle this rationally.

"I'll meet you out in the car. I've got your cello loaded already." He hugged me again and made for the door. "You'll feel better in no time. I've got you. I won't let anything happen to you."

"Sounds good," I smiled at him.

As soon as he was out of the room, I took a couple detailed pictures of the pill and sent it to the group chat for the SWS.

"First person to tell me what this pill is gets my undying love for eternity."

"No pressure," I added with a winky face. Damn, I missed my girls. And my home. My mind didn't pop up the image of my bed though. It took me to Devlin's bed. To the room I'd slept in. To the couch in the studio. To his bed. That was where my confused brain associated with home.

I closed my eyes tight. My phone was already blowing up with texts. They missed me too and promised to find out. One more show. One day at a time. I could do this.

I gripped the pill in my hand. I studied it for a long moment. It would be so easy to go back to being checked out. All I would have to do is swallow and live this life.

But no. I'd felt alive again. I had found joy in my playing without the help of drugs. I didn't need a man to have that power over me. I didn't need anybody to have that power over me. I was done letting others live my life. I would do this last show tonight and then I'd go home. From now on, I decided what I wanted.

I dropped the pill into the toilet and flushed.

* * *

In the car ride back from the show I shook with anxious rage.

Fucking Klonopin. Pardon my swearing. But was he clucking kidding me?

I knew the power of prescription drugs. They saved a lot of people's lives when prescribed correctly and controlled by professionals. They weren't candies to be thrown around at the first sign of stress. What he did was selfish and dangerous.

"Can cause paranoid or suicidal ideation and impair memory, judgment, and coordination. Combining with other substances, particularly alcohol, can slow breathing and possibly lead to death," Blithe's text read.

Suzie followed up with, "Often used to treat panic attacks and numb the brain."

"Highly habit forming," Gretchen added. And then right after "Read: STAY THE FUCK AWAY FROM."

These lovely women had responded within minutes of me sending that first text. I've said it before and I would say it again: they could easily rule the world. Their messages waited on my phone after my performance. I sent a very short text back letting them know I hadn't taken it and that I was fine. Because apparently sending that text and then disappearing for a few hours was on the "not cool" list of things to do to your girlfriends.

I had performed like the subservient little cellist I was. What was I even doing? Was this living? Because, I had to say, it didn't feel like it. I'd been such an idiot. Letting myself see what I wanted to see rather than face something that felt too big. Devlin had made me feel so much that I'd become overwhelmed by the possibilities. I was so afraid of making the wrong choice. Well, here I was quickly understanding I had made the absolute worst choice.

We drove in silence. At least, I was silent. Roddy jabbered on about likes and reposts and all the interest in a fall tour. My head was back against the seat. It would have been bad enough if he'd offered the pill to anyone, but he knew I'd been to rehab. The nagging suspicion I'd carried the last few weeks fully formed in my mind.

I narrowed my gaze toward him and spoke over whatever he was saying. "What did the note you sent me in rehab say?"

He stilled. "Let's not talk about that. It was a dark time in your past. You don't like talking about it." His words sounded like a mantra. Like if he repeated them to me enough, I'd believe them.

"Actually, I don't mind talking about it," I said. "It helps me move past it. Tell me what the note said."

"I've asked you not to bring up those notes. It embarrasses me."

How had I never seen through his facade? I was a willfully blind participant in the hostile takeover of my life. The truth burned through the fog of my mind, shining light on everything.

"It was only three words. Of course you can remember," I kept my voice light.

"I can't remember. That was a hundred years ago. Let's not discuss such an awful time." His complexion grew ruddy.

"No. It wasn't awful. It made me the person I am. I'm tired of pretending it never happened."

"You're all worked up. When we get back to the hotel, we'll go to the bar and have a drink." He loosened his tie to undo the top two buttons.

"Tell me what it said." I knew I sounded crazy, persistent, mad. I couldn't care less.

"That was over ten years ago. I can't remember."

"Three words?" I persisted.

He grabbed my hand, while the other held the steering wheel. He smiled at me in the most charming way as he glanced from me to the road. That smile had probably gotten him out of a hundred sticky scenarios throughout the course of his life.

"'I love you,' of course. That's what I said. And it's still true to this day." He squeezed my hand.

I squeezed back before lifting it off mine. I leaned back with a sigh and smiled. It was as though I could take a full breath again. All the fear and worry about making the wrong choice melted away.

I felt weightless with relief.

"It was never you," I said.

His coolness burned away in an instant. "Oh, for fucks sake!"

I jolted back at the sudden outburst. He'd never shown anything other than sweet insistence in my presence.

"Roddy," I chided.

"It will never be enough, will it?"

"What are you talking about?" I asked.

"I gave you everything. I do everything for you and you always go back to those fucking notes."

"It's not about the notes. I'm not happy here. I want to go home." I could make this choice with no hesitation.

"The SOOK won't have you. And nobody knows where Devlin ran off to this time. That's what this is about isn't it? You think he wants you still? You were a fleeting muse." He punched the cushion of the car seat.

With Devlin, the rage always felt hollow, an empty bolster to hide his clear insecurities. Roddy felt dangerous, spitting poison before he might attack.

"This isn't about Devlin either. I'm going home."

I decided my own fate. No more putting my life in other people's hands.

"This is about him. It always is," he grumbled. Louder he said, "After everything I did for you? Carla's sudden absence? Come on. I got you that solo."

I blinked totally in shock. Was he really this ugly inside?

"Roddy. What did you do?"

"I did what needed to be done. Just like I always have. Since camp. Yet you refuse to see the better man. The man right in front of you. I'm a man of action. That was what you wanted. You wanted me to take the lead. Do you know how much work all this took? And now what? You're backing out because of some notes?"

"Roddy, please." My heart beat so erratically, I thought I might slide into a panic attack.

He didn't stop. "I tried to protect you. I tried to put the past away. But you have to keep bringing it up, don't you? You think I don't remember what happened with Ariana at camp? I haven't forgotten what you made me do. Don't pretend you aren't just like me."

My entire body went icy. I closed my eyes against the accusation. Everything he said was my deepest fear.

"No," my voice was a whisper.

"You're exactly like me. You do what it takes to be the best."

I thought of what Devlin told me. I had the potential to be better. I could give back now. I could stop living in fear and I would be better.

"No!" I yelled out. I balled my fists against my knees. I glared at his profile. "I'm not like you. I don't want to hurt people."

He shot a look to me. "You're hurting me. I set this all up for you, but you don't like it so you're quitting."

I lifted my chin. "I finished the tour. I never signed on for anything more."

"Christine, please." He pulled onto the shoulder of the road and put the car in park. Immediately he grabbed my hands. "Look, I'm sorry, okay? We are a good team." He took a deep breath and laughed a smile back into place. "Let's just calm down. Trust me, you need this tour more than I do."

"Do I?" He had been pushing it from the first day. What exactly did he benefit?

"Where will you go?" he asked. "What will you do?"

"I'm not sure. But I'll figure it out. *I* will decide."

"You need someone to take care of you." He squeezed my hand in his clammy one. "I will always take care of you."

I pulled my hand free. Lightness I hadn't felt in years filled me.

"I can take care of myself."

CHAPTER 37

FIRST OF ALL, I'VE BEEN A FOOL.

DEVLIN

If people had thought I'd go around moping or pitying myself they were damned wrong. I left the auditorium after the Fourth of July concert, I went home, and I continued on with my life as a composer. Cut my losses and moved on. I didn't need the SOOK. I certainly wasn't about to go crawling back to them. I didn't need Kim. She'd chosen Chagny.

I was fine.

But ...

Being home, seeing all the places I'd shared with her ... I couldn't always muster the anger. I remembered everything about her; the gut-cramping laughter when she'd scared the crap out of me and then laughed at me for my perfectly legitimate response. In the bathroom, the way her eyes had burned with lust when she found me naked. I remembered her devotion to the music, to me, and I couldn't think anymore. Nights were the worst. I didn't sleep. I smelled her, tasted her, felt her, longed for her as though she was still a possibility. I thought of all the times she'd been so close and I didn't just tell her my feelings. I should have held her more. I should have put it all out there. It was like feeling deathbed-sick and cursing myself for all the times I took my health for granted.

No matter how I lied to myself, her absence was a physical, constant ache.

No texts. No calls.

No notes.

I was lonely. The further from that last night I got, the more ashamed I grew. I hadn't handled things very well. My shame kept me in solitude. It took almost two months until Wes managed to guilt me into another family dinner.

"We know you aren't working. It's all over the news that you were fired again. We're all coming over tonight. Make sure you're dressed."

They arrived at their usual time. Rose and Ellie wore matching Wonder Woman dresses and hugged each of my legs.

"Uncle Erik!"

"Daddy said that we could watch your fancy TV and eat on the couch," Rose said looking up from where she gripped me.

I took three-wide legged steps with them attached like barnacles, as they screamed in delight. "Oh, he did? Well, that's fine, but you tell Daddy he can replace the couches if anything happens to them."

They laughed and ran into the kitchen, and when they passed again on the way to the TV room, their arms were laden with snacks. Wes passed with Kelly. I hugged her and flicked his ear.

"Ouch," he winced.

"Oh, Erik, you're too skinny," Kelly said squeezing my waist.

My mom hugged me next. "I'm watching you tonight. You're eating two helpings."

"Okay, Ma."

Dad hugged me with a hearty back slap. "You were too good for that place anyway. They didn't know what they had in you."

"Right," I said. "I wasn't fired. I quit," I said but they all looked at me with faces of pity that said they weren't buying it for a second.

"About that." Ma shot glances at the rest of my family.

"Care to explain this?" Wes handed me his phone with an article pulled up.

"The Devil of the Symphony walks again …" I shoved the phone back at him after reading.

"What is this? You told us you were fired. This article says you quit the last three places," Ma said. "I don't understand."

I shook my head. Cold dread weighted down my shoulders. I didn't want them to find out the truth this way.

"Let's forget it and just eat."

My mom and dad had picked up pizza and salad from a place in town on their way up the mountain. Conversation was polite enough, but it wasn't long before my mom spoke her mind.

"Ellie, can you go take Rose to watch TV?" Ma asked.

My older niece grinned. "Sure, Grammy."

The little girls giggled and ran out of the room and I waited for her to lay into me.

"Mom, what is it?" I asked. Her heavy stares had been boring into the side of my face in a way that only moms knew how to do.

"Why have you been telling us you were fired? Why did you let everybody spread those rumors about you?"

"It's complicated." I pushed away the half-eaten slice. "They didn't understand me. Once they found out I was Erik Jones, that's all they cared about. They asked me to play the song at performances for the symphony."

"So, play the song," Wes said. "What's the big deal?"

"It's not theirs." I slammed my fist down. Wes's eyebrows shot up. "And I'm tired of that being all people care about. All the work I've done kept getting pushed to the back burner."

"You quit to prove a point?" Wes asked.

I lowered my voice. "I knew you wouldn't understand."

Wes raised his eyebrows like I was crazy. He looked to Ma for support and she shook her head as though to tell him to stop. "I'm sorry, sweetie." But she held something back. "Where will you go?"

"Ma, you know I can't stay here. Not now. I was only supposed to be here for the season anyway."

Wes and Kelly exchanged a look. The same look my parents gave each other.

"It's just such a shame when you leave this big house empty while you're gone," Ma said.

"We will move in," Wes jumped in.

"I just don't understand what happened. We've seen what the news said. But we know there has to be more to it than that," Dad said.

"Not really. I have a temper. I punched Roderick Chagny in his rat-face and I was fired. Well, I quit before that. Technically." More or less.

"Is this because of Kim?" Dad asked. "I was hoping she might still come around. I watched that documentary she suggested."

"Kim is gone. She's on tour with Chagny," I said.

"She's doing really well. I follow her on Instagram," Kelly added. "I never got to meet her, but she seems … lovely."

"That's not her. That's a doll being dressed up to get downloads. That's Christine Day."

The table went silent as I brooded.

"I'm sorry. You seem very upset about her being gone," Ma said.

"I'm fine. She's the one that left. She chose that guy who is clearly using her. It's the life she picked."

Wes sat back and sighed. "You can't put it all on her, man."

"What?" I glared at him.

Ma flicked a glance to me. Dad and Kelly stayed quiet.

"You're playing the victim in all this," Wes continued.

"I am not. I just don't care."

"You clearly do."

I might as well put it all out there. Everybody else was going to take Chagny and Kim's side in all this. I wanted somebody on my side.

"I gave her a choice. She chose him. She walked away after committing to me—to the solo."

"You gave her a choice?" my mom asked. "How? What does that mean?"

I explained about the notes. About how close we'd grown. About how that asshole had pretended they were his. How I punched him, and how he'd fully deserved it.

"She could never make a choice. Never. She wanted somebody like him to take all that pressure off her shoulders," I finished.

"So," Dad started. "Knowing that she finds decision making difficult, you put her on the spot with Chagny. The man who she's spent her whole life thinking was the author of those notes. Then made her choose, and risk hurting somebody no matter what? All the while not telling her the truth."

I blinked. Well, when he put it that way, of course it sounded bad.

"She had no qualms about hurting me. She chose him. I was only ever the fun-time guy before Chagny." My fork flew as I slammed the table with my fist. "And come on, she should have known about the notes. Chagny? Really?"

"Do you honestly believe that?" Ma pushed her plate back too and crossed her arms. "Because we all met her and don't believe for a second that she uses people. And were you two close back at camp? If she didn't know the notes were from you, then how would she have ever guessed you'd sent them? Especially if he'd claimed to be writing them. Why would she doubt that?"

I frowned at the table, scratching my beard. "She asked me to give her a reason to stay. She asked me to tell her that I would choose her long term."

Three blank faces glared back at me. I wished I hadn't said that last part out loud. Out of context it sounded bad on me.

I pressed on, trying to explain my point of view. "But that was her making me do the work again, don't you see? I needed her to decide. I wouldn't force her hand only to face her resentment as the years went on."

My dad at least nodded once as though he could see my point of view.

"Yeah, but what did you do?" Wes asked. He drained his bottle of beer and set it back down loudly before going on. "Did you tell her how you felt? Did you explain that you sent the notes and Chagny is a lying bastard? Did you fight for her even a little?"

"Language," Ma scolded.

"Why should I?" I asked. I sounded petulant. Dammit.

"Because that is what you do when you love someone," Wes said with vehemence I'd never seen in him. "You don't just give up before it begins. I'm really starting to see a pattern with you now. This quitting. Your talent, as always, comes so easily. You work so hard, but you quit before you can ever fail."

Kelly grabbed her husband's hand and made a face. "What you and Wes have told me about Kim, she has had some trouble in her past right? Well, Kim is chasing her life now. She is trying to do the best thing for *her*. She has made bad choices before. Maybe she's just trying to do the smart thing now. For her. He offered her everything she wanted."

"She doesn't want any of it," I spat. "She only thinks she does."

"Yeah, there you go. Deciding what she wants," Ma said. "She *thinks* that's what she wants. Love is about wanting what the other person wants and trying to make it happen for them. Supporting their dreams. And Chagny tells her all the right things. I'm not saying I like him, but he lays it out for her. He makes it an obvious choice. You just said that Kim struggles with making the right choices."

"Yeah."

"She's trying to be smart." Wes slammed his fist on the table. "You're broody and moody. You run around the world leaving any time things get hard. She doesn't know where she stands with you. Did you talk about any sort of life outside her playing? About what her performance means to *you*? Chagny says, hey, I'll do everything for you."

"He won't challenge her."

"No. He won't and that's exactly why she picked him. But you have to make it clear to her that you are worth the fear and the uncertainty. You're the real deal," Wes said. Kelly reached out and grabbed his hand to squeeze it.

"What do I have to offer her?" My question came out low and pathetic.

The whole table groaned.

"What?" I asked.

"Don't make me say it, man. Tell me you aren't that dumb," Wes shook his head.

"What?"

"Would you ever let anything harm her?" Ma asked.

"Will you ever stop wanting her? Caring for her?" Dad asked.

"Will you always want to talk to her? Hear from her? Do you want her to be that person that knows all the little things about you? And have her be the one that knows everything about you?" Kelly asked.

Wes said, "Is she the one who can make you laugh and hold your hand? That will push you in return? Will you always put her first? Make her dreams, your dreams?"

My throat tightened. I felt queasy. "Yes," I rasped.

"Well that's love, man. That's what you offer her. Real Love. Capital R, capital L. Chagny talks the talk but the second Kim doesn't make him money anymore ..." Wes shrugged.

"Chagny doesn't love her." Kelly gestured to her phone. "Not if these costumes and performances are for him and not her. She looks miserable in those pictures. She's trying, but her eyes are dead."

"It sounds to me like Kim made the best decision she could in that moment. That's all you can expect from people," Dad said.

"Well, she needs to do better." I sounded like an asshole, even to my own ears.

"Gosh, you've always held people to such a high standard." My mom turned to Dad. "Is that because of something we did? Did we put pressure on him?"

"No. That was stardom. It fucked with his head."

"Wesley."

"Sorry, Ma. But it did. He sets unrealistic expectations for people. Meanwhile he won't take off that fricking mask and just hides."

"I'm right here," I said. "And she could change. If she really wanted to."

Wes rolled his eyes. "Oh sure, because it's that easy. Step one: be better. Step two: happiness."

"You know what I mean."

"Okay. So then take off your mask. Not just here with us. Out in the world. Own your past and who you are."

"That is not the same," I growled.

"No? Okay, well, I thought you wanted to be better."

"Again. Not the same."

"It's something from your past making you cling to an idea that you won't let go of."

"When did you become a philosopher?"

"Wes is just trying to say people are a complicated set of rules based on their pasts. Kim can't suddenly make a rational decision under pressure any more than you can walk into a room as Erik Jones and feel like a competent composer," Kelly said.

"I know how people will react. I've seen how they are."

"And she hasn't? Kim was treated like a pariah. She's Jethro Winston's ex that went missing. She ruined her whole future because she was a kid that made a dumb choice. 'The girl that hung out with a motorcycle gang and ended up in rehab,'" Dad said.

"You were a kid when you were thrust into fame. We shouldn't have let you go." Ma shook her head.

"You couldn't have stopped me Ma, I was eighteen. That's not on you." I looked down and brushed my knuckles across the table. "I just wanted to be enough for her to stay."

"You are enough. She just didn't have all the facts," she said. "And here's the real kicker—it isn't about if she loves you. It's about if you love her, and what that love means to you."

* * *

This wasn't about whether or not she loved me. That was an excuse that I'd used to keep myself hidden from her. To push her away. God,

278

it seemed so obvious after talking to my family. Of course they knew me better than anybody else. I thought they didn't understand me, that they couldn't handle me if they knew I'd been quitting. I'd been quitting because I was afraid of things when they got too hard.

That would all change.

It wasn't about whether or not she loved me for me. It was about what my love for her meant. I'd been egotistical. I'd been proud. I'd locked love down inside me for so long that I had lost what it meant.

My loving her was what mattered. Her needs, wants, desires—those were what mattered. Those were the priority. Whether or not she loved me didn't matter as much as how I loved her. But only if she knew. To think that she might have thought, even for a minute, that it was about the music and my career and not her … I'd been such a fool. But not anymore.

After my family left, I replayed everything they'd said. When I truly replayed the last time we'd spoken from her point of view …

I felt sick.

She needed to know all the facts. They were right. She needed to know I'd sent the letters. She couldn't read minds.

I needed to tell her everything, and what better way than a letter?

I took out a piece of paper and a pen.

Dear Kim,

First of all, I've been a fool.

I've never been able to say words the way I've wanted to, which was why I wrote you all those notes so long ago. Here's the truth: you asked me why I chose you. And I never answered. I had convinced myself the lessons with you were about proving I could stick to something. I told myself that if I had someone from my past who could help me hold it together, I would make it through. I wouldn't quit. But that was me lying to myself. It was a poor excuse to spend time with someone I love. I love you.

I think I've loved you since I was seventeen and I first saw you at summer camp. My feelings felt too big back then. I needed time to grow into them. The notes were my immature way of getting you to notice me. You had Chagny. But I noticed you. I will never forget the first time I heard you play. You gave me chills. Your playing inspired me like no one else ever has. I've never stopped thinking about it.

Can't Look Back was for you too. About you. It's always been about you. I've wasted so much time not telling you everything. I have so many regrets. But not anymore.

Here's another truth. I came back to Green Valley to prove that I could commit to something. I came back to re-center and see my family. And then I saw you at the first rehearsal. You didn't recognize me. Why would you? But I knew it was you, name change or no. Whenever you play, you take my breath away. You tried to hide yourself, but I saw through it. You were still the most beautiful and talented woman I'd ever seen.

I'm tired of being alone and pretending like that's what I want. I pushed you and everyone else away because I couldn't chance not having you feel the same way back. I understand now that isn't how love works. I understand so much now that you're gone, and I can't see you smile and laugh every day. I miss just talking to you, catching up. All the little things.

I love you. I want everything for you. Please make sure that toolbag—sorry, Chagny—is taking care of you. All I want is for you to be happy.

Anyway. I'm sorry I pushed you away because I felt too much. I've been letting my past ruin my future. But I'm done. I'm no longer a prisoner to my life.

You've inspired that in me.

You made everything better. The months we played together are some of my best memories.

I love you. I always have.

I think I already said that. Anyway, I do. It's okay if you don't love me back. Well, it's not okay. I feel like I can't take a full breath thinking about it. But I get it. I did such a stupid thing. I'm sorry for that night. Not for punching Chagny; I'd probably do that again. But I am sorry I hurt you. So sorry. I only ever want to make you feel good. God, I've wasted so much time.

Like I said, not anymore.

I'm done.

I hope this letter finds you happy. I hope you are living the life you want to live. I hope you are spreading that light inside you now. That's all I've ever wanted.

Yours always,

Erik

I shoved the letter in an envelope and sealed it before I could change my mind. I'd send it to her house; her parents would ensure she got it. Writing it was crucial. My handwriting would prove my words.

Now for the part I dreaded. As the phone rang, regret had my anger boiling. But I didn't want to indulge my anger; I was ready for apologies.

"Hello?" the voice answered.

"Andrew, it's Devlin. I have a proposition for you."

CHAPTER 38

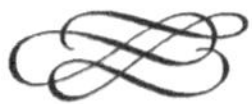

YOU'RE AN ANGEL WHEN YOU PLAY.

KIM

*I*t was hard to know what to do or who to be when you couldn't be trusted to make your own choices. I wasn't the same person I was before I met Devlin, before I knew him and spent time with him and learned what it meant to feel alive again. I'd tried to go back to that. I'd tried to let Roddy lead me to what I thought was the safe choice, but that had been a failure.

I was back home now. Floating. Back to waiting for my life to start. Or something. I wasn't even sure what I wanted at this point. But I knew the life Roddy had planned for me wasn't it. I was proud of myself for moving past that and owning that choice. But still, there was a hole in my soul, and I didn't know what to do.

"Kim?" my mom said from behind me. She was wrapped in an oversized pashmina despite it being the beginning of September.

"Hey." I sat on the back porch swing looking out at the fireflies. My legs were tucked up under my chin and I rocked slowly in the breeze.

"Do you have a minute? Your Dad and I would like to talk to you."

"Sure." I got up and followed her into the kitchen where my dad sat with three mugs of steaming tea and a plate of cookies.

"How are you?" he asked. My dad looked old, tired. Maybe my bad mood had permeated the house.

"I'm—" How did I answer that? Did they really want the truth? I wasn't bad, but I was far from great. Mom and Dad stared back at me with matching expressions. Their shared pair of squared-framed glasses were currently perched on dad's nose. He took them off and placed them on the paper.

"I'm neutral," I finally answered honestly.

They shared a look. It was one of their looks that always made me feel a million miles away. They were such a unit—twin planets rotating around each other's axes—and what was I? A satellite? A cold dark moon a thousand miles away?

I grasped the mug and studied the swirling steam.

"That's what we were afraid of," Dad said. "I think we owe you an explanation."

Mom took a deep breath. "As you know, when your father and I met, our lives were turned upside down. We always talk about how we left our partners and started a new life. It wasn't always easy as that. There was actually a bit of drama in the beginning."

"I was married," Dad added. "To a very nice woman. Divorcing her was hard. I felt terrible. But when I met your mom, I knew I could no longer live that life."

I'd heard all this before, but I didn't know that it had been hard. It was a piece of history, but I realized now how complicated it all could be.

"We never thought we would be good parents. We were from a time where children were an expectation, the next step in the life plan, not a product of love. We never wanted that," my mother explained. "We always said that if the universe wanted us to have a child it would be because we loved each other fully. And for more than a decade, it didn't happen. Until it did. We were quite old and set in our ways, but we wanted that child to have everything, for you to have everything."

"We were so set on being different from our parents and letting you be your own person and … well, we did our best," Dad said sadly.

"That's all anybody can do," I said automatically. Were they saying this because they knew I had messed everything up?

They shook their heads in unison. "You don't understand. We wanted you to have everything. We love you so much it terrified us."

My head shot up. They'd never seemed afraid of anything.

My dad's eyes watered. "When I met your mother, I felt an earth-shifting love. Literally, turned-my-life-upside-down sort of love. I would have done anything to be with her."

My heart constricted in my chest. I knew this. I couldn't quite breathe because I'd had a taste of that, and I'd lost it.

My dad gripped my mom's hand and reached across the table and gestured for mine. I placed it in his. "Listen. When you were born, the love your mother and I felt for you made our love feel like …"

"Suddenly, after all these years of having a printed postcard of a Degas or Monet, suddenly we had the actually original art hanging on the wall," my mom tried. "We loved you on a level that we never imagined possible. It was literally terrifying. We knew the stakes. Every choice and action, everything we said to you. You were this little wide-eyed miracle that came into our lives that made us feel wholly inadequate for the first time."

"What?" I said.

"You cannot understand how terrifying it was. I swear. At age five you carried your tiny cello around everywhere with you. You were always wanting to be with the adults, and you were so wise for your age. We were in awe of you. You knew who you were and what you wanted from the beginning. It was awesome in the truest sense of the word. We were filled with awe of you."

"I had no idea." My throat constricted. "I'd always thought, I dunno, like you didn't want to be around me."

Dad squeezed my hand. "Sweetie, no. You were a miracle, but we were terrified of screwing you up, and then you seemed so perfect. Juilliard acceptance at seventeen. We were the proudest parents.”

Were.

“But we never felt like we had anything to do with it.” Mom shrugged.

“It was surreal,” Dad added.

“You came out of me as this perfect, fully-formed adult, I swear. We joked about it all the time. We were always so set on letting you be you and not pushing ourselves on you. We knew we would be oddball parents, so much older and more eccentric than the rest. We wanted you to be whoever you were going to be. We can see now that you put so much pressure on yourself to be perfect.”

Dad frowned and said, “Let me be clear about something. We never, ever, stopped being proud of you. Even now. I’m thinking we need to communicate better.”

Mom nodded. “I love you. We are so proud of you. You’re amazing to be around. But sometimes it feels like *you* feel the need to be something you’re not around us and that’s heartbreaking.”

“After you came back from camp, we could tell that poor girl’s death changed you. You were so distant,” Dad said.

I swallowed down a lump that formed. They had seen the change in me but hadn’t understood why. I couldn’t talk about it. I was so ashamed.

Mom said, “When you fell in with that bad boy, in a weird way, we were relieved. At least at first. We were like, ‘Okay, she’s living a little, getting some world experience.’ But we couldn’t have seen what happened coming. As soon as we saw you go too far, we freaked out.”

“It’s possible we overreacted,” Dad said.

Mom rocked her head back and forth as though weighing his words. “I don’t think so. Well, regardless, you were changed. You were so afraid to do anything. You had scared yourself straight. You didn’t go back to being the girl with big dreams, you became some-body else entirely. When you first got out of rehab, you seemed so ashamed. We should have emphasized that none of that mattered. We should have made sure you knew you were still loved. But you checked out," Mom said. "It was so hard to see. We wanted you happy and protected and so we saw how much it was easier for you if we made some decisions for you. At least at first, until you found your feet. So we did. We put you on a routine and we made you comfortable. And when we suggested a stage name, like you father's pen name, you latched onto the idea. The separation helped. But then it went on like that for years. You leaned on us for protection and decision making."

"And selfishly, we were glad to have you here with us still." Dad smiled. "The three of us at home. You seemed to enjoy the restrictions, and your anxiety got better. The less choices you made, the better you got."

"Because here's the hard part of where we are going with all this," Mom said.

"Okay." I swallowed.

"We know now that we aren't here to make your life comfortable. You weren't living. You've become crippled by the fear of making the wrong choice."

"And it's understandable." Dad smiled sadly.

"But listen, honey, we were young once and did some really crazy and stupid shit. The only difference was we didn't have parents there to step in with money and concern. Does that make sense? What I'm saying?" Mom asked.

"But … the only good choice I made was to come home." My voice cracked as I spoke. "Now what? What if I keep choosing wrong?"

"So? That's life. You make choices and you move forward. No matter if they're good or bad. Make them and commit to them. Because that's how you grow and change."

I shook my head. "It's more than that. You don't understand."

I took a deep breath in. It was time to tell them everything. About camp and what I did to get that solo knowing they'd be ashamed of me.

After I'd finished, they shared a look. "I had no idea." Mom looked to Dad who shook his head too. "We knew her death hit you hard. It makes sense, why you'd blame yourself. I probably would too," my mom said.

"You would?" I asked.

"Of course. But it wasn't your fault. You know that. I wish you had come to us sooner, but I understand why you were afraid."

They squeezed my hands in tandem. I let out a long, slow breath. Sharing it with people who cared was like having more hands to help carry the emotional baggage that had weighed down my shoulders for so long.

"You were never a disappointment. Nothing has changed. If anything, it makes sense. In fact, it might be a good idea to make an appointment to talk to someone."

I nodded because I had been thinking about that myself. "I will."

"Good. We have always been proud of you. We have always loved the person you are. Please don't think anything else. But you have to try. This half state of being, crippled by fear. That's not living. That's killing time."

Dad glanced at Mom before saying, "Nothing great ever happens when you're comfortable. I'm not trying to sound trite, it's just a fact."

"Why are y'all telling me all this now?"

"Because we see you living out of fear. You think safety is the most important thing but safety doesn't always work. Fear isn't always a good indication of risk. And failure isn't always bad. We need fear to keep us from doing stupid things, but it's hard to know when to trust it when it is the same fear that keeps us from making choices that could ultimately help us."

"Well how will I know? How can I keep from making the wrong choice?" I asked desperate to know the secrets.

"Trust your heart. But more than that, trust that if and when you make a mistake or fail, the world will still turn. You will be okay. We will still love you. That will never change."

"I love you guys," I said as a tear spilled over.

"We love you so much."

My dad released my hand. He pulled a letter with familiar handwriting from his jacket. "This is for you. Take it and read it. Decide what to do from there. Let it lead to action or put it away with the others and move on with your life."

"But *you* make a choice," Mom said. "And own it."

* * *

I left the kitchen feeling lighter. The little girl in me had needed to hear everything they'd said. Unconditional love was always nice to be reminded of.

I took the letter and went to my room.

In my closet, I moved aside the rolled-up posters of Death Cab for Cutie, Weezer, and Erik Jones (oh, the irony) and grabbed out my box of notes from the top shelf.

Years of notes, worn from folding and rereading time and time again. These notes had been everything. Holding them transported me to my childhood.

I took the box and dumped them out. The new letter sat untouched to the side.

I opened random notes and read them, the critiques and the meaning behind them. That handwriting. Of course. Of course it was Erik. My eyes burned as I madly sifted through one after the other. All those years Roddy lied to me. So much time spent trusting him. I wouldn't be mad at myself for trusting him, but I was sad about the time wasted. Why hadn't Erik just told me?

Then again, it seems so obvious now. How could I think anything else? The handwriting was the same as it was now. I had been lying to myself. Holding back in fear. But something happened as I read the notes. I understood something more. It was never the notes. It was what they represented. The innocence. My youth was over as quickly as it began. I took that from myself.

With each note I understood that more and more. These notes represented a life lost. They represented that warm, hopeful thrill that only being young and having the whole future ahead of you could give. It was that bubbling sensation in my chest that dreamed big. It was the hope and love of the future.

It wasn't really about the person who wrote them.

These notes represented a future full of hope and I'd held on to them like they could change my past. But I couldn't change my past. I owned it. I was still me. I was still loved. I was still a person with a life ahead of her.

I mourned the girl that got these notes, but I had to let her go. She was gone. I needed to live the life I had now. I had held on, hoping they would help me feel that zest for life again, thinking, "if I just met the right person ..." But she was right here all along. *I* was here all along.

It was time to move on.

I started a fire in the fireplace. Once it burned bright and hot, I held the notes above them. They were holding me back and I was done being afraid.

I pulled my hand back.

Okay, I wasn't going to burn them. I was still sentimental at heart. The message had sunk in. No point in burning them.

I put the shoebox away and took out the new letter.

Dear Kim...

I closed my eyes and gripped it to my chest. I had made a choice before I finished reading the letter. I was done choosing fear. I was going out on a limb. I was choosing possible rejection. I was ready to lean into the fear and jump anyway.

"What exactly am I seeing here?" Gretchen's voice came from the doorway.

I dropped the letter I'd been sniffing. "I'm checking for structural integrity."

"Because it looks like you're snorting that piece of paper."

"She was definitely sniffing it." Suzie appeared behind her.

"What are y'all doing here?" I scooted the letter under my leg.

"We came to check on you," Suzie said in a soothing voice.

"You've been real weird since you've been back," Gretchen said.

"I'm coping. Actually, I'm okay. I really am. Just a little sad is all."

Gretch nodded. Suzie squeezed my hand.

"I understand that I have been hiding in life. I get that now. But how does someone just change that?" I asked, glancing between the two of them.

"You take it one day at a time. Think about what you want."

"I want to move forward," I said. "I want to know how to do that. I've been afraid of hurting people for so long. How do I act just for me without taking from others?"

"Maybe try thinking about things this way: It's not what you are taking away from others, but what you have to offer," Suzie said. "I never thought I was anything more than a stripper. Then I realized that my dancing and showing people how to feel good in their bodies was something I could give. Happiness is one of those things that only gets bigger the more you give out."

I smiled at her because she really was amazing when she danced. And Gretchen was so full of life she turned heads wherever she went. She lit up rooms. My smile fell. "I'm not like you two. I'm flat."

Gretchen guffawed. "No, you are not. Get out of here with that nonsense."

"You have fire in you," Suzie said. "We've seen it and heard it."

"Me?" I'd worked so hard to make myself small.

"When you play, you bring people joy. You give your lessons for free to kids who can't afford it. Don't pretend that you aren't spreading light," Gretchen said.

"Imagine if instead of worrying about taking, you put all that energy into giving," Suzie said. "You really put your soul into everything you say and do."

"Devlin said something similar. He said that's what you leave with people. How they felt, not what you did," I smiled.

"Ah, dammit," Gretchen said. "I hate when a man is right."

Suzie and I shared a smile. A bubbling sensation filled my chest. It felt like hope. It was that feeling after my breakthrough with Devlin. It came back after talking with my parents. Now it was here again. What if I could make a difference? What if I could be a person that brought other people joy through my playing?

Even if the SOOK wouldn't have me, I would find a way to play. I was alive when I really let myself go and played fully with my heart. I missed that. I could still do the lessons for the kids in town. Maybe I'd find another symphony to play with.

"I think I would like that," I said.

"I know what I want. I want to go to this awesome concert." Gretchen turned her phone to me.

"'The Devil Unmasked? With special guest Erik Jones.' What's this?" I asked.

"Not sure." She shrugged not so innocently. "Guess we should go and find out."

"Oh my God. Is he going to take off his mask?"

Suzie raised her eyebrows. "Sounds like it."

"So hypothetically speaking, if you were going to start playing again. Is there maybe a song you'd play? Maybe one you've spent months perfecting?" Gretchen asked with a wry smile.

A new thrill crossed my mind. I glanced at my phone. What day was it even? I had a plan. I could make things right and start living again.

"I have an idea," I said. "But I need your help."

"Yeah, yeah. I'm a step ahead of you. The bats are in my car."

Suzie shook her head. "Oh, for crying out loud …"

CHAPTER 39

I LOVE YOU. I ALWAYS HAVE.

DEVLIN

I sent Kim the letter four days ago. I hadn't heard back, but I wasn't dwelling. I had a plan.

I'd begged, groveled, and sold myself out. As part of being reinstated the Board had insisted I talk to each and every member of the symphony. I begged for one more chance. It wasn't easy. Most of the performers were hesitant. With each house visited, I grew more determined. Even if it was just me up there, at least I'd done everything I could. I gave it everything.

Here I was, pimping myself out as Erik Jones, and I didn't care. This was about proving that I could let the past go. It wasn't the showcase I thought I wanted. It might make me lose all credibility, but I didn't care anymore about being taken seriously by the classical music world. If they couldn't disassociate the pop star from the composer, well, that was on them. I'd keep making music. I'd keep moving forward. Those who mattered would know. But at this point, there was one person I wanted to show that I was changed. One person I wanted to see and know the real me.

Tonight was the night. I dressed in a suit and tie. I wore dress

293

shoes for crying out loud. I came in Wes's minivan, the whole family in tow.

"It's going to be great. You'll see," my mother said.

Even Wes clapped me on the shoulder and said, "You're doing the right thing. I'm proud of you, man."

Backstage, I slid my sweaty palms down my dress pants as the hot ball of nerves ate at my gut. Andrew and Richard were on stage addressing the audience. They spoke about a bunch of things I couldn't hear. I was too wracked with nerves.

Richard said, "Without further ado, the reason you are all here. Our Maestro and composer, Devlin."

Andrew leaned forward to the mic. "You may know him better as Erik Jones."

The crowd gasped and began to clap wildly and scream.

I stepped on to the stage. The mask was gone. My face was fully on display. I had nothing to lose. The SOOK had sold out tonight's performance in minutes. Minutes.

The crowd was insane. Groups of women held up signs for Erik Jones. I flashed back in time to mall tours and morning talk show performances. How could they still care about a pop song written all those years ago?

It didn't matter. I wrote that song for Kim. I would play it for her now. Let her feel my love. I just hoped the music would find her wherever she was. I thought of how beautiful she was when she played with abandon. I pictured her laughing and playful, splashing water in my face before swimming away. I imagined the furrow of concentration on her brow when she wanted something desperately. I had been that thing and I'd let her go.

The stage was empty. The symphony hadn't come, but what had I expected with how I'd behaved? I sat down at the piano bench, wiped my sweaty palms on my dress pants again, and cleared my throat.

I spoke low into the microphone. I blocked out the hundreds of people and thought only of Kim. "This is a song I wrote for the woman I love."

The first notes of *Can't Look Back* rang out into the silent night. Soon my voice joined in. I sang the song from my heart. It was as much a part of who as I was as any classical composition I wrote for the world's best symphonies. It was all a part of the same person. A person who loved Kim Dae. As I sang, I thought of her. I poured my soul into my words.

Crushes and whispers mature into fire
Control held with a well-worn wire
Thoughts of you burn with sin
I look at you,
But you, you're looking at him.

My throat was raw from all the feelings that overwhelmed me.

I paused when emotion overtook me. The audience was silent. When I glanced up from the bright lights the whole audience listened with rapt attention. I'd forgotten there was power in all types of music. I'd forgotten this feeling.

Music wasn't about showing off talent or proving a point. It was about finding a way to make a connection to people. Like the night at the bar, or this song, music was the feeling of universal understanding.

CHAPTER 40

SHARE YOUR HEART THROUGH YOUR MUSIC.

KIM

It was a good thing I wasn't a big believer in signs. Because if I was, I might take it that the universe was flashing a big old "BAD IDEA" one at me right about now.

I ran out of gas. The car drifted to the shoulder with the telltale *click-click-sigh.* Distantly, I recalled the low gas warning icon had been flashing. But I often saw warnings and ignored them. Roddy, for example.

I was stranded all alone on the side of the road, in the middle of the Smokies. In my defense, when I took Mom's car I'd been hurrying, my nerves rattled. There were a lot of reasons I wasn't on my gas game, so to speak. The show started in less than an hour and I had no idea if I would make it in time now. I'd been practicing my butt off for days. I had a plan. Frustrated tears burned at my eyes. I took deep breaths to get my bearings. Deep, cleansing breaths. It would be alright. Someone was bound to drive by.

I gnawed on my lip and got out of the car, too anxious to sit still and wanting to wave the first person to pass. How far would the walk be to the nearest gas station? It was still a good ten-minute drive from here. Oof. In these shoes, with a cello on my back? I didn't think so.

As though from the heavens, a car came around the bend from the other direction. Anywhere else I'd have been hesitant, but this was Green Valley and the car was a white Honda Odyssey. It didn't exactly scream kidnapper. I waved my arms around like a lunatic trying to get their attention. They passed me and my shoulders slumped, defeated.

But then the car turned around! In a smooth motion, the van performed a three point turn on the narrow mountain road. As soon as it rolled to a stop behind me, I ran to the driver's window. I knocked as the driver began to lower it.

I was coming off as a total lunatic. That's okay. I was a lunatic. A lunatic in love and on a mission.

"Hi! I need help. I promise I'm—"

My jaw hit the ground.

"Kim Dae, as I live and breathe. Is that you?"

Shock. That was the only way to put it. Of all the cars, in all the world …

"Jethro Winston." I stared into the eyes of the man I'd once thought I loved.

He was still as handsome as ever. Older, for sure. But that dark hair, that beard … Maybe I did have a type.

I was transported in time. The heat of a tail pipe burned through my jeans, the vibration of a motorcycle shook my body, the smell of cloves encompassed me. The back of my knees tingled. *Oh, come on, universe.*

"Kim, what's going on? Is it your car? Need me to call Cletus?"

I shook my head back to the present.

"No. Maybe. I don't know …" I took a deep steadying breath. I could do this. "This is what I need. My car is out of gas. If you think Cletus could bring someone in time so I can leave in the next ten minutes, then maybe. But what I'd really love—"

"Daddy" a small voice called out.

Jethro—a *father*, so weird—turned in his seat to smile at the rosy-cheeked toddler in a car seat in the back. "What's up, buddy?"

Holy child, Batman.

"Water." The toddler pointed to the ground.

Jethro smiled back at me. "Hang on a sec."

As he struggled with one arm reaching behind the driver's seat, presumably to search for a missing sippy-cup, I scanned the rest of the car. The passenger seat was empty and admittedly, I was only twelve percent disappointed Sienna wasn't there. Suzie said Sienna had attended one of her classes and she was as amazing as we'd imagined her to be. I'd never seen her in person.

"She's shooting in another state," he said as though reading my thoughts. Or probably because, no offense to Jethro and his fantastic good looks, but Sienna Diaz! "Just me and the little one this week."

I cleared my throat to find my voice. I was still half bent to look in the car. The happy toddler with dark curls waved from the back seat, saying "hi" every fifteen seconds. I waved back. "Never thought I'd see you driving around in one of these."

"Never been prouder of a car." He winked and just like that my insides melted.

I made an awkward face but I was in a pickle. "This may be too much, but I don't suppose y'all could give me a ride to the performance center? I'm late."

He glanced in the rear view mirror. "Not a problem. Just so happens we're headed into Knoxville."

Hopped once excitedly. "Thank you so much! Just gotta grab my cello, hang on."

"Plenty of room," he called after as I ran to get my instrument.

Back on the road, my nerves abated a little.

"Glad to see you're back in town and playing again," Jethro said.

His voice—so many memories. This was *so* weird. If not for the fact that my mind was on a totally different man right now, I'd be having a freak out. What a place I've come to when Jethro Winston didn't turn me into a puddle on the ground. In fact, I could hardly hear what he said for my thoughts of Devlin. I just needed to get there before he finished. I just needed to show him.

"Nerves?" Jethro's voice cut through my thoughts.

I realized I was gnawing on my thumb and shaking my leg like I was making butter. "Yes. Sorry."

"Don't be. I didn't know you were playing that show tonight," he said.

"In theory. Hopefully."

"Been following your career. You've taken off lately."

"Really?" I glanced over at him.

His face was clouded over with a frown. He glanced to the rearview mirror at the kid babbling happily.

"I gotta say something real quick," he said.

My stomach dropped.

It wasn't that I had ill feelings toward Jethro. It was just that I had no feelings toward him. I had happy-ish memories of some real wild nights together, but all my big feelings, the real ones, those were all wrapped up with a man about to step on stage alone. A man I needed to get to ASAP.

"Go ahead," I said.

"I have to tell you how sorry I am for everything back then. How it all went down."

"Thank you. I know you aren't that guy anymore." We'd all talked about that in the SWS. How he'd changed. Though we would never admit it. The SWS, while formed from a place of anger, had morphed into something so much more. It was about friendship and love and support. It focused on the beauty in life and on letting the past go.

"Still. It eats me up sometimes when I think about it," he said.

"Jet, I walked into that bar looking to ruin my life. That's not on you."

"Yeah, but I was all too keen to help, wasn't I?"

How many of us are holding on to our mistakes? It made me sad, but at the same time, look where he was now. Everything had worked out just as it should.

I said, "Somebody recently told me that the mistakes in our past are not meant to be life sentences. You've moved on from that life, and so have I."

"That person sounds real wise," he said.

"He has his moments," I grumbled.

He took a deep breath and nodded once. He wasn't done. "I have to tell you something else."

His eyes scrunched up tight like he was finding courage to say the next part. "I told your parents about the drugs hidden in your cello case that night. I put them there. I'm the reason you went to rehab."

My heart jumped, skipped, then totally stalled out. "You what?"

"That night your parents confronted you, it was because I'd sent them an anonymous message. I—well, I won't go into all of the reasons why, but you were too good for that life. You know, I'd heard about you before I met you. People talked about your playing. You were so talented. You had to get out. I thought if you could get help, you could get away. I was too chickenshit to do anything more than that."

I absorbed his words. He was the reason I went to rehab. I had always thought my parents just stumbled upon it. All these years … Shouldn't I feel angry? But I didn't. Everything he'd done had turned my life around. I shuddered to think where I might still be if I hadn't gotten help. A month ago, I would have been angry. I would have felt sad at all the wasted years, but now, I didn't care. All that mattered was the future.

"Thanks for telling me, Jet. You were mixed up deep back then. I can't say I'm happy about that, but I understand."

He pulled up to the front of the performance center.

"Thanks for finding me," I said. "I don't know what I would have done if you hadn't showed up."

"It's sort of what I do." He shrugged sheepishly.

"Lucky for me." I held his gaze and smiled wide. "Bye, Jethro. Bye."

I jumped out of the seat and waved goodbye to him and the kid in the back. I grabbed my cello from the back and was about five feet from the car when the window rolled down.

"Just keep playing," he said. "No matter what happens, just keep playin'."

My heart skipped. I frowned, but he was gone before I could say anything else.

I didn't have time to replay that. I had a performance to make. I ran toward the entrance. Time to forgive my past too, and start my future.

* * *

"Where have you been?" Gretchen yelled. "I'm sweating like a sinner in church."

"I know." I had just raced up to them through the crowd of musicians gathered quietly backstage. My hair was falling loose and sweat made my skin sticky. "You will never believe what happened. I'll tell y'all later."

I peeked behind the curtain on to the stage. Devlin had already started playing. If I didn't get up there now, all those hours I'd played non-stop since returning home wouldn't mean anything. I was ready for this. I was weirdly strengthened by my interaction with Jethro. It was like running into the Ghost of Christmas Past.

Blithe, Suzie, and Gretchen circled me. The three were dressed in matching black with their hair pulled up, looking like a bunch of second-rate ninjas. When the SWS made a plan, we didn't mess around.

"Where's Roxy?" I asked, just noticing her absence.

Gretchen widened her eyes and sucked in a breath. "Girl, now that's a story for another day."

"She wanted to be here though. She told me to tell you to kick booty," Blithe said.

"She's okay though?" I asked.

Gretchen and Blithe exchanged a look. "Think so," the blonde said.

"She will be," Gretchen said. "Don't worry about that right now. You focus on getting up there."

I nodded and glanced down to check my appearance one last time. I wore a comfortable outfit of black stretchy pants and a long, see-through, flowing top that went down to the back of my knees, over a thin-strapped tank. My hair was up but not as tight as usual, with a few loose tendrils framing my face. I felt comfortable in my body.

"Is everybody here?" I asked the girls scanning the crowd around me. As far as I could tell, most of the symphony waited to go up, dressed to the nines.

Blithe nodded. "Mostly. I don't think Carla could make it."

Gretchen rolled her eyes.

I glanced toward the stage. This was it. Do or die. Only one thing stood between me and claiming my life—one teenage boy with straggly hair and a knit beanie. He was a stagehand and he currently blocked the only entrance about five feet away. Devlin's voice rang out. Chills prickled my arms. His voice would always do that to me.

"I have an idea," Gretchen said. "That guy's what? Like, eighteen tops?" Gretchen looked over my shoulder at the kid. "We're four beautiful women, or as Kim would say, 'objectively not ugly'."

"We could distract him, and Kim could run on stage," Blithe finished.

"Uh, hello?" The kid in question walked up to us. "I can hear y'all. You're actually being really loud. Can you quiet down?"

"Sorry," we all mumbled, looking at our feet and not feeling badass at all.

He looked at me and blushed. "I know Christine Day. I was here that one time with Ford's Fosters, so if you just wanna ..." He thumbed behind him.

"Are you sure?" I asked.

He shrugged. "I mean, you're not planning to mess him up, I'm guessin'."

"But we had a whole plan." Gretchen looked a little put out.

"Yeah, you're harshing our vibe, kid," Blithe said.

"I could put up a fight?" He cleared his throat before dryly saying, "No. Please. You can't go up there."

"Better. I guess," Blithe said.

I shook out my hands as dread cemented in my gut.

"Y'all, I'm gonna go up." I took a deep breath in and blew it out slowly through a pursed mouth. Suddenly, the realization settled in that not only was I playing in front of a massive crowd, I was also at great risk of total rejection.

"You got this, girlfriend." Each girl whispered words of encouragement as I gripped the neck of my cello. I couldn't focus enough on who said what, but they were all excited for me.

I made my way on to the stage. The girls ran out to pull up a chair behind the piano. He was too lost to the music to notice anything other than his performance. The audience spotted me and whispered words reached my ears between the notes of his song. I lifted my bow and began what I'd been rehearsing.

I kept my eyes closed as I played. The audience was huge, but I wasn't playing for them. I played for Devlin and nobody else. I played for him like my life depended on it. It did. My whole heart depended on it.

I could tell the moment he stopped playing the piano. His voice broke with emotion and my own tears came. He'd played for me. And now I played for him. The audience was silent. But I felt him turn to watch.

This was the power I had. This was my strength where I'd thought I had none. Here was my gift. I could give and not take. I could leave a mark on the world.

I played for him, with every fiber of my being. I imagined the night we played silent music, with his arms wrapped around me. I embodied all the emotion he was desperate to convey.

Feel my love. Feel everything, I was telling him.

CHAPTER 41

YOU TAKE MY BREATH AWAY.

DEVLIN

I noticed a shift in the audience first. I couldn't see them because of the bright lights, but I felt it. A gasp and some whispers. My song came to an end and I lowered my hands from the piano.

That's when I heard it. A soft solid note of a cello breaking through the air.

I turned on the bench.

Kim. Here. Her dark hair pinned up in a twist. A single tear tracked down her cheek. Her eyes were closed, and she played. She played my music. My song from a hundred years ago.

She played her song, picking up effortlessly where I had just stopped. Then those notes shifted to a different piece. It melted right into the first composition of my classical career. It was the first piece I'd written after my pop career went down the toilet as fast as it had begun. She morphed one into the next, one after the other. I stared, dumbfounded. In awe. My heart slamming against my chest. It took all my power not to run to her and hold her. But I was transfixed. We all were. She played like she did that night at my house. Fully into the music. Chills broke out over my skin. She played with her whole being. This was who she was meant to be.

Every single piece I'd ever written floated seamlessly from one to the other, a medley of all my pieces, until finally, she played my solo that I'd written for her.

And when she played that, the whole audience and I sat transfixed, unable to tear our eyes away.

It was perfection. She was perfection.

I sat in stunned silence listening to the last piece we'd worked together on. She had made it her own. She had made it something more powerful and beautiful than I ever did.

That was when the rest of the symphony came out. Had she coordinated all this? They all took their places, chairs appearing out of nowhere, to play my composition. They played my symphony perfectly. When I looked back to Kim, she raised her eyebrows and nodded her head to the podium.

They wanted me to conduct? I slowly moved to center stage. My eyes blurred with emotion. I hesitated. Could they really want me back? After everything?

The sound came like rolling thunder. Those who could, stomped their feet. Their smiles nudged me forward.

We performed my piece as the symphony. I couldn't keep the smile off my face. It was the proudest moment of my career.

* * *

Backstage was madness after that performance. I couldn't keep the smile off my face. I didn't try. It came so naturally now. I couldn't wait to see Kim, to know if she'd gotten my letter. To tell her everything. My heart was exploding with the need to talk to her.

The whole symphony was crammed into the small area, talking and congratulating each other. The cacophony of noise was overwhelming. Champagne flowed. But I couldn't find Kim. Every time I spotted her, a new person came up to meet or congratulate me, and when I looked up again, she'd be gone. With every new person that wasn't her, my blood pressure spiked.

"What a wonderful performance, Maestro," Andrew held out his hand.

I glared at it. His face faltered before I grinned and took his hand in return. "Thank you," I said. "The SOOK performed wonderfully."

"They did. But your piece was simply astounding." Richard shook my hand as well. "Christine was astounding."

"That she was," I agreed.

"We were thinking that maybe you could extend your stay with us? Maybe take on the fall/winter season?" Andy asked. They weren't bad guys. They were just trying to keep the SOOK afloat.

My eyes met Kim's across the room. She smiled at me, her cheeks flushed with joy.

"I would like that," I said.

My parents walked up with Wes, Kelly, and the girls as Andrew and Richard moved on. My family gave me hugs and the girls hopped up and down excitedly, replaying my performance.

"Your hands move so fast on the piano," Ellie said. She mimicked playing up and down the keys.

"That was fantastic, honey." My mom kissed my cheek. "Did I just hear what I think I heard?"

I wrapped my arm around her shoulders. "Yeah. I think I might stick around for a while."

"Damn." Wes shoved me. "Now I have to see your mug all the time."

"Deal with it. I'm the favorite." I shoved his shoulder back.

"Well, let's not be hasty," Mom said.

I faked a look of hurt. "Mom."

"When you give me grandbabies, we'll talk."

Kim chose that moment to walk up. "Grandbabies?" she asked.

"Kim," I said on a sigh. To my family I whispered, "Give me a minute alone and I'll work on it."

My mom's eyes went wide, but she quickly corralled the rest of my family away.

Kim tucked loose strands of hair behind her ear and waited for us to be alone.

"Follow me." I tugged her along the darkened corridors to the secret room. Once again, I thanked my previous self for the forethought.

The second the door was shut, Kim launched herself at me. Her arms were wrapped tight around my neck.

"I'm so sorry I left with him," she whispered as she squeezed me tight.

"You don't have anything to be sorry about. I should have told you everything." I pushed her back so I could hold her gaze, my thumbs ran over her cheeks. I'd missed her so damn much I was shaking. Looking at her again, holding her again, was a gift I would never take for granted.

She leaned back to look in my face. "Yes. You should have. Never do that again. Tell me everything."

"Everything?"

She nodded happily. "From here out until forever."

"I can do that."

I took her into my arms and held her tight. "God, I love you."

"I love you too."

"Thank you for playing my music," I said.

"You're welcome." She grinned. "It was beautiful. The piece was perfect."

"I wasn't sure that they would show up. I went to them all and groveled," I explained. "I was shocked that Carla showed up last minute."

"Carla is harmless. She's just doing her best, same as all of us." I was surprised to hear her say this. "I talked to the symphony. I might have told them about our long and tragic love story to twist some arms. Hope it's okay that I spilled the beans on your past and our shared history." She smiled mischievously.

"I don't care about anything but this right here." My head lowered to inhale her scent. I didn't care about anything else so long as she was here. "Thank you for loving me. I don't make it easy. I don't know that I'll ever feel like I deserve you."

She rolled her eyes. "That's not how it works. You've loved me from the beginning. I loved you too, but I wasn't ready. We just needed to figure a few things out. It took time, but we're here now."

"This is all that matters."

"Agreed." She kissed me. "We should probably go back out there. Your adoring fans await."

"I just need one more minute." I slid my hand up the back of her shirt and rubbed over the soft skin there.

"Just a minute?"

"You're right," I nuzzled her as I lifted her shirt off her head. "I need forever."

CHAPTER 42

YOU PLAY BEAUTIFULLY.

KIM

Devlin's hands roamed everywhere. Our mouths came together. All our love was poured into our kiss. Our hungry tongues explored each other. He held me tight, my arms wrapped around his shoulders. We kissed until we could hardly breathe. I still buzzed from the performance. It was in the greedy narrowing of his eyes. My body shook slightly. His did too. There was always that high after a show. This time it was more powerful than any drug I'd ever tried. I was on fire for this man after months of waiting and temptation and very little release.

We broke and I leaned back to take him in. His hair was ruffled from my hands. His onyx eyes glinted as they studied me. He was a sight to see in his suit.

"What are you thinking?" he asked.

I tilted my head and let my gaze drag slowly over his body. "How handsome you are. How amazing that suit looks on you."

His cheeks flushed as he cast a look down.

"I was thinking that it'll be a shame when I throw it on the floor," I finished.

When he lifted his head again, he was biting his bottom lip. "Oh, yeah?"

A thrill tickled through me. "Oh, yeah."

I reached forward to undo the button on his suit jacket. I pushed it off his shoulders. He slowly began to unbutton his shirt. He took too long. I pulled his dress shirt out from his pants and started on the bottom buttons.

We kissed clumsily while my fingers made quick work.

"The door is locked, right?" he asked as I shoved off his shirt and tossed it on the chair next to the desk. It was a small office, a little disheveled from disuse, but it would be big enough.

"Don't care."

He smiled against my mouth. "Our families are out there."

"Nobody will find us. Secret room." I kissed along his jaw, loving the way his beard burned my skin, and knowing it would leave a mark.

I bit at his earlobe and licked his neck. I was wild for this man. My hands explored his huge chest and shoulders.

He gripped my upper arms and growled. "Hang on." He took a deep breath and stepped away.

I groaned. On his way to the door he stopped and pulled a small silver packet from the drawer and set it on the desk. I bit my cheek to hide a smile.

"I'm just going to check." He locked the door and leaned back against it. Standing there shirtless and straining against his dress pants, I could hardly stand. He licked his lips. His eyes ate me up. "What am I going to do with you, Kim?"

"Anything," my voice came out as a husky whisper. "Everything."

I was leaning back against the desk, wearing entirely too much clothing. He took two steps to close the distance. He slowly pushed the see-through shirt off my shoulders. He kissed the exposed skin of my neck and collarbone. He pulled off the camisole underneath and my lace bralette with it.

With both of our tops exposed to the cool office air, we embraced again. I loved the way my soft body felt pressed against his hard chest.

His large, callused hands slid up my ribcage to cup my breasts. He lowered his head to take turns sucking on each nipple. "I love these. I haven't stopped thinking about them. About the time they bounced on top of me as you made yourself come."

"Shh. Less talking. More touching," I breathed, but only because I was already so hot. I couldn't take much more.

He grabbed a handful of my ass. "But you like the talking, too."

I sucked his bottom lip into my mouth, biting it gently before releasing it. "Good point. Both. Both is good."

He brought his mouth back to mine as he slid my pants and underwear down and off my hips. I kicked out of my heels and across the floor with the remainder of my clothes.

He stood back to look at me. He ran a hand over his mouth. "Fuck." He let out a slow breath. "I've waited so long for this."

"Me too." I leaned back against the desk, spreading my legs slightly to let him take his fill. "Your turn," I said, glancing at his bulge.

His pants and shoes quickly joined the pile of discarded clothes. When we came back together, we were sloppy and rough. Our bodies collided as our lust boiled over. No more waiting.

I loved every second of it. We kissed deeply as he explored my body, testing to see if I was ready. I was *very* ready.

"Turn around," he said in a stern voice.

Heat flooded me. I grew somehow languid and tense with antici-pation at the same time. I did as he'd commanded. He came up behind me and pulled me close. The heat of his body encompassed me. His erection nudged at my bottom. I thought I might collapse against the desk.

"That night I massaged you, we were like this, remember that?" His hands rubbed knots from my shoulders as he spoke.

"I remember a little more clothing," I whispered.

"Do you have any idea how hard," he pushed himself between my legs, not entering me, just teasing, "it was for me to not touch you like this?"

I panted and let my head fall back on his shoulder. He palmed me and pulled gently, but not too gently, at my nipples.

"You wanted it too, didn't you?"

I swallowed. "Yes."

"You drive me crazy. You know that?"

"You pushed me so hard," I groaned.

He was grinding against me, spreading my slickness around.

"Not nearly enough. Not even close. I want you so bad."

I arched my back as he continued to tease. The action caused him to slip into me without warning. We both gasped. He pumped once. Twice. Then pulled out.

"Shit, sorry," he said. "I didn't mean to do that yet."

"I don't mind." I reached down to touch myself. I was already so close.

He groaned as though in pain. He thrust one more time.

"Not like this." He grabbed my wrist and brought my fingers to his mouth to suck on them. He hummed in pleasure as he did. "Turn around. I want to see your face when I make you come."

I did as commanded. I was all about making choices in my life now. I was in command of who I was. But I'd be lying if I said being controlled by him wasn't everything. He lifted me onto the desk, rolled on a condom, and slid back into me without another word.

We moaned as he dropped his forehead to mine. Our bodies thrust, mine matching his motion for motion.

His gaze held mine. "Come for me, Kim."

"So. Close," I panted.

He shifted and grabbed my thigh to lift it higher on his hip. Something about the angle worked. He pressed right where I needed him to. I came without warning, shocking us both.

I relaxed my fingernails from digging into his shoulders. I was wrong if I'd thought I would ever get enough of this man. This was only the beginning. Even now, as he pumped toward his own release, I felt myself reaching toward another peak. There was so much to do with him, so much to try and explore. Now that Pandora's box had been opened, my curious mind was only too eager to explore the possibilities. He gripped both my knees and hefted them higher. I pressed back onto my palms to find balance. His muscles flexed and glinted with sweat as he rocked back and forth, picking up speed. He looked magnificent and took me over the edge a second time.

"Kim," he called my name as he came. His head was thrown back, the tendons in his neck strained. Now that was an image I wanted rendered in marble.

It took a minute before he seemed to return to his body. His breaths eventually evened out as he lowered my legs gently and brought my upper body back to him. When he did, he cupped my face to drag a thumb over my bottom lip.

"That was amazing," he said before kissing me deeply.

We broke the kiss but only to catch our breath.

His forehead was against mine. He seemed to like the connection it brought, and I liked looking into his eyes. I didn't mind the sweat; if anything, it reminded me how freaking naughty this all was. He was still inside me and hard.

"You're so sexy. I knew it'd be like this with you," he said.

"You did?" I asked, clearly fishing.

"Yes. You've always been so full of curiosity and passion. It was all locked down inside you, but I knew it was there."

"You've freed me," I said holding his gaze and pouring all my love into it.

He kissed me so deeply that an aftershock shuttered through me. I clenched on him and he groaned. He broke the kiss and started to pull out. His gaze focused on where our bodies connected. I watched amazement come over his face, the high color in his cheeks, the sweat on his brow. This man was beautiful. Inside and out.

I gasped when he pushed back into me.

"Sorry. I just—"

He pumped two more times. Controlled but strained.

"Again?" I asked breathless.

His pace picked up. "I've waited so long."

This time it was faster, dirtier, sweatier. I was slick. Our bodies were so slippery, I had to hold on tight as he used me and I used him in return. We both came again in seconds. This time when he finished, he pulled out right away.

"If I don't get out now, I may never leave." He threw the condom in the trash and grabbed a towel near a punching bag in the corner. I may have watched his amazing ass the whole time.

"There're worse things in life." I smiled at him.

"It makes walking tricky."

"We'd figure it out." I shrugged.

He came back to me and handed me the towel. "God, I love you."

"I love you too."

After we'd cleaned up and started putting on our clothes, I gestured to the large punching bag. "Hey, what's with that?"

He followed my gaze as he did up the last button of his shirt. "Anger issues. I've been working on them for a while. Only recently I realized I was never really angry."

"You were scared." I finished for him.

He stepped back to me and grabbed my hands. "I was. I was always afraid to lose everything. But then I had a taste of what it really was to lose everything. When I pushed you out of my life— like I'd pushed away everything else of importance—my worst fears were realized. I was alone. I had nothing. You were with someone else."

"I'm so sorry," I said. "I was so scared too."

He nodded sadly. "It's all the past now. The only thing that matters is this moment."

"You're right." I grabbed his hands in mine. "Now that we both truly understand that, we won't go back to a place where the past has so much power over us."

"Thank you for coming back to me."

"Thanks for risking your career to show me your love." I put my head on his chest. His heart beat loudly against my ear.

"Not being with you almost killed me."

I nodded against him. Then looked up into his eyes. "You brought Kim Dae back to life."

CHAPTER 43

THE NEXT APRIL

KIM

"What are you doing?" Devlin asked from the doorway.

"Just going through some of these boxes. Deciding what to keep." I sat back on my heels, where I'd been kneeling.

"Why do you sound sad?" He was at my side, pulling the shoebox out of my hand. He brushed back my hair to kiss my temple.

"I'm not sad. Sentimental, I guess. It's my curse." I sighed dramatically.

"I can't believe you kept all these." He flipped through the old notes with tender care.

"I couldn't quite bring myself to get rid of them."

"I like that about you. It makes me happy that they meant so much to you." He held my gaze, a small furrow between his brows. "Want to hear a joke?"

"Always."

"What did one musician say to the other?" he asked.

"What?"

"Nothing. He left a note."

I snorted a laugh. "Terrible. I love it."

He gently turned my face back to his. "Tell me why you're sad."

"I'm not sad." I nestled into his hand. "I'm happier than I have ever been. It's just hard not to think about the what-ifs. What if I'd sought out who sent the notes? What if you'd told me? Imagine if we'd met before I ever even met Roddy?"

His face hardened before relaxing into a sad smile. "It wasn't our time."

"I can't believe he lied to me about sending them, and for so long. I can't believe I trusted him."

"Why would you have any reason not to trust him? There's nothing wrong with trusting people you care about. It's not your fault he turned out to be…"

"Just the worst." I shuddered.

He scowled. "I never trusted him. Even back then."

"Well, you were right." I sat back on my palms when my legs started going numb.

"Speaking of—apparently, his parents are in some financial trouble. That was why he pushed so hard for the tour. He was living beyond his means. His business is screwed. Markus Savagno and Caroline Tetch have both dropped him."

"Really? I was wondering why the check I got came from his parents." I wasn't surprised. Not really—you could only be two-faced for so long until people caught on. "He all but told me he was the reason Carla missed that performance. The one that got me my first solo."

"Scumbag," he grumbled.

"I was so willfully blind to it …"

"Hey, stop. If these notes are going to upset you, you shouldn't read through them."

"I just think about all the time wasted."

He grabbed me and pulled me into his arms. "You know we can't think that way. Everything that led us to this moment was worth it. If I had to stay away a hundred years just for five minutes of your time, I'd take whatever I could get."

My heart fluttered in my chest. "Thankfully, we have all the time in the world now."

"I love you."

"I love you, too. Thanks for cheering me up."

"Always." He grinned. He lowered his head to kiss the area behind my ear that was quickly becoming my favorite spot. "Then I get to do this."

"Hmm. I also like this." We kissed deeper.

Our hands roamed each other's bodies greedily. Soon we were on the floor, mostly naked. He slid into me and I gasped. We panted and ground against each other. Every time was better than the last.

"Why can we never make it to a bed?" I asked a few minutes later, now dressed and under control.

"Beds are overrated."

He helped me to stand and we looked at all the boxes still stacked in his foyer.

"We better get going. Or we will be very late. We can finish unpacking your stuff later."

"Screw unpacking, I want to do that again."

"I could handle that."

His eyes drifted to the box of notes, half spilled from our fooling around.

"What's this?" he asked handing me one of the notes.

"That's the note you sent while I was in rehab."

"I didn't send you a note in rehab. I was already on tour and I didn't know about all that until later."

I blinked at him in surprise. "Really?"

"Really," he said.

We bent our heads to read the note, now seeing noticeably different handwriting. "Just keep playing."

"I'd just assumed it was you. Well, the author of the notes."

He shook his head.

"Huh." I shoved the notes away. "Not important. Let's get going. We need to tell Andy-Dick about our plans."

"I regret telling you I called them that," he said.

"It's hilarious. They're all right though. At least they love our idea for a Christine Day/Erik Jones concert."

"Of course they do—it'll sell out in minutes." He squeezed my hand. "I had an idea. What if we donate all of our portion of the proceeds to help teens who have gotten addicted to drugs? Help them get on a better path."

My heart swelled in my chest. Just when I didn't think I could possibly love him more. "Genius. I know Ford has a lot of connections for just that sort of thing. I'll text Suzie tonight. My rehab changed my life, but not everybody can afford that level of personalized help."

He kissed my forehead.

"It'll be so weird to perform as them now," I said.

"People love a good love story. Plus, they're just our stage names. Not who we are. It helps to keep it separate. Being on stage with you is all that counts."

"Ditto." I held his face and looked deep into his eyes. "You know, none of that mattered to me. Your big tough guy act, the pop star background. Everything I love about you, is you."

"Once I understood that, none of the other stuff mattered to me either. Thank you for loving me."

I hugged him before he slid into his leather coat. "Mmm. You smell good," I said.

"The weather is perfect." He glanced out an open window.

"Let's take the bike then." I grabbed my own jacket as I tugged him along.

"Really?" He let me pull him outside and into the garage.

"Yes. I miss it."

He gave me a look before handing me a helmet. "Let's go, beautiful." He winked at me and I felt sixteen again. But in the good way.

I straddled the back of the bike and wrapped my arms tightly around him. It vibrated to life with a roar.

"Ready?" He turned to yell at me.

"I'm so ready."

He squeezed my thigh. We headed down the driveway and soon

were on the mountain roads. The wind whipped my skin and the sun warmed me. I was fully alive. I rested my head on his back and smiled.

My life was just beginning.

THE END

ACKNOWLEDGMENTS

I saw "The Phantom of the Opera" at the tender age of seven when my Aunt took me to see it in downtown Chicago. I was transformed. It single-handedly launched my love of musicals and misunderstood, brooding men. "The Treble With Men" was one of those books that I always dreamed of writing. The pressure to write a book that played homage to such a work of art was immense but I'm incredibly proud of this story and my own growth as I wrote it.

To all the readers who endeavor to one day write your own story, please remember, when things get hard, put on good music and just keep writing. Write for yourself. And above all you MUST believe in yourself. Also, having an amazing support system is oh, so necessary. So here is mine that I must thank for this book's existence.

J.R., so many people talk the talk but few walk the walk. You, my love, walk the walk and how. Thank you for always believing without an ounce of doubt that I could finish this book. Thank you for politely and lovingly refusing to let me quit on that chilly October walk. Thank you for entertaining the kiddo so I could write even though you were just as exhausted. Thank you for losing sleep so I could maintain sanity. Thank you for the thousand other little sacrifices that go into unconditionally loving and believing in someone but that never get proper recognition. You are the reason I write love stories.

Tracy, for some reason you still believe in me too – surely you must be getting tired of me. Thank you for the middle of the night words of encouragement when insomnia struck. Thank you for coming to my side, grabbing my hand, and pulling me from the darkness by sheer determination when I couldn't find the strength to even stand. Thank you for always pushing me to be the best possible version of myself. This book owes so much to you.

Pipe's Peeps – though we be but small, we are fierce. YOU are my people and I'm so thankful for each and every one of you.

To the Sharks of Awesome, who are totally Penny's people, but who I found when I needed them the most and where I met so many strong, amazing, and hilarious role models.

Rebecca and Michelle – you took this book and made it shine. I'm sorry I will never really understand how commas work.

To the Smartypants Romance authors, including Brooke and Fiona. Can you even believe we are here again? It goes without saying that I would not be here without you all. You make me laugh when I need it the most. [Piper] You offer words of wisdom and encouragement as only those deep in the trenches can.

Kelly, Layla, and Shannon – I hope you know what you mean to me. What is life?!

And, of course, to Penny. We are all here because of you. Your love and kindness knows no bounds. I intend to spend the rest of my life paying forward everything you've done for us all. You are a gift to the world.

ABOUT THE AUTHOR

Piper Sheldon writes Contemporary Romance and Magical Realism books that hope to be NYT bestsellers when they grow up. For now, she works as a technical writer during the day and writes about love the rest of the time. Of course she also makes room for her husband, toddler, and two needy dogs at home in the Desert Southwest.

* * *

Find her online:
Website: http://pipersheldon.com/
Facebook: http://www.facebook.com/195485244722745
Goodreads: https://www.goodreads.com/PiperSheldon
Twitter: @piper_sheldon
Instagram: @pipersheldonauthor

Find Smartypants Romance online:
Website: www.smartypantsromance.com
Facebook: http://www.facebook.com/smartypantsromance/
Goodreads: www.goodreads.com/smartypantsromance
Twitter: @smartypantsrom
Instagram: @smartypantsromance

Read on for:
1. Piper's Booklist
2. Smartypants Romance's Booklist

<u>**The Higher Learning Series**</u>

Upsy Daisy by Chelsie Edwards

<u>**Seduction in the City**</u>

<u>**Cipher Security Series**</u>

Code of Conduct by April White (#1)

Code of Honor by April White (#2)

<u>**Cipher Office Series**</u>

Weight Expectations by M.E. Carter (#1)

Sticking to the Script by Stella Weaver (#2)

Cutie and the Beast by M.E. Carter (#3)